## KELLAN

I wasn't supposed to fall for my older brother's best friend. Unfortunately, that ship sailed when I was a teenager, even though Chase Hawthorne always treated me like nothing more than a younger sibling. Things were worse after my parents died. Chase was sweet and supportive, which only strengthened my feelings for him. But then he'd act like I couldn't take care of myself, and that part didn't go over well with me. Yeah, I had a habit of screwing up. I'd always been the weird boy in our small town, but just like my big brother, he took overprotective to a new level. Until one night when I was eighteen and Chase and I hooked up. It was a ding to the ego that he left town right afterward. Ridiculously, I'm still not over him.

## CHASE

I betrayed my best friend, Griffin, the night I messed around with Kellan. So I ran—first to the Marines, then into law enforcement. Ten years later, I'm back home, this time as a patrol officer rather than a troublemaker's son. Oh, and unable to keep my hands off Kellan Caine. There's always been something about him…the way he stands strong in who he is, even when he's standing alone. I'm trapped between someone I want more than anything and Griff, the guy who's like family to me. Yet the more time I spend with Kellan, the harder it becomes to deny there's something real between us.

With my dad stirring up trouble, and me going behind my best friend's back, everything's a mess. The more tangled the web gets, the more I realize I need Kellan. And that there might be something in the Hawthorne family history that'll make me lose both Kellan and Griffin for good.

# GIVING CHASE

## (Havenwood Book One)

by
**RILEY HART**

Cover Design by Sleepy Fox Studio
Cover Photography by LUKEography
Edited by Keren Reed Editing
Proofread by Judy's Proofreading and Lyrical Lines Proofreading

*Special thanks to Riley's Rebels 2.0 member Melinda for helping me name Havenwood.*

# PROLOGUE

## *Kellan*

"THANKS FOR COMING over to stay with him, man." My brother gave Chase this dude-bro fist bump that made me roll my eyes.

"No biggie. I'll watch some movies with the twerp or something," Chase replied, and obviously that was a bit of a ding to the ego. It sucked being secretly in love with your older brother's best friend…especially when he was very straight and thought of you as a twerpy little bro. Go me.

"I hope you realize how annoying it is that you talk about me like I'm not standing right here. Also, I graduated high school last weekend. I'm old enough to spend a weekend by myself. Hell, I could *live* by myself if I wanted to." If I had money, or a job, but that was beside the point. What mattered was I didn't need Chase Hawthorne *babysitting* me like I was a kid.

"Uh-oh. Is my baby brother mad?" Griffin taunted.

"He sounds mad to me. Poor Kellan," Chase added.

I hated them. I hated them *both*. And by hate I meant love—Griff in the brotherly way, and Chase in the *marry me* one. He was so sexy. I loved his blond hair and how he kept it cut short. His brown eyes that were full of kindness, and those thick lashes and how they fell across his cheeks when he closed his eyes. And he was a nice guy, at least when he wasn't teasing me with my brother.

"I despise both of you." I crossed my arms, pouting. Yep, I was pouting, and I didn't give a shit.

"Nah, you love us. Don't smile, or you'll ruin it. If you smile, Twerp, we'll be able to tell you don't really hate us," Chase joked, so I flipped him off, stormed to my bedroom, and slammed the door. I could hear them laughing through the walls.

I plucked my headphones from the nightstand, slipped them on, and found one of my sad, sappy playlists. I quietly seethed over the fact that my brother had made Chase stay the weekend with me, while at the same time, I was glad I got to spend time with Chase. I was a bit of a mess; maybe always had been.

Griffin was overprotective. He'd been like that constantly, threatening bullies who gave me shit, taking the blame when I broke Mom's favorite vase while trying to dance, when I *so* wasn't a dancer. That was just how Griffin was. It was sewn into his DNA.

Then, when I was fourteen and Griffin nineteen, our parents died in a mugging gone bad—something that never happened in Havenwood—and it made things a million times worse. Griffin thought I was going to be hurt or attacked everywhere I went, or obviously at home too, if he or Chase weren't there to protect me.

Yet not a day went by that I didn't realize how lucky I was. Griffin had dropped everything for me. He'd quit college and come back home to Havenwood to raise a fourteen-year-old kid. He'd never once complained. Logically, I knew there wasn't anything Griffin wouldn't do for me, but fuck, he was stifling sometimes. He never let me fight my own battles. He protected me even when I didn't need it. He kept me on a leash like I was a damn dog, afraid I'd die like our parents had, or, I don't know, a fucking meteor would fall from the sky and crush me.

Sometimes I felt like I couldn't breathe.

Like I couldn't *be*.

I couldn't imagine what would happen when I told him I was gay. If someone looked at me wrong, Griffin would be all up in their shit. Chase too, but I didn't mind that as much because it was sexy thinking of him defending my honor.

It was Chase Hawthorne who helped me realize I was gay. All it took was a shirtless hug from him when he was wearing a pair of swimming trunks. My dick took notice, and a whole lot of shit suddenly made sense.

Chase and my brother had been best friends for what felt like forever, even though Chase was a year younger. Chase had practically lived at our house when we were kids. Anytime his dad got drunk—and his dad got drunk a whole hell of a lot—Chase would show up at our place. Our parents had accepted Chase like he was their own, and when they died, he'd been Griffin's second line of defense in taking care of me. Sometimes I wondered if something could be going on between them, but that made me want to curl in a ball and cry, so I pretended I never had those thoughts.

I was *so* stuck in little-brother zone, it wasn't even funny. Even if Chase did like men, he would never like *me*.

So I pouted for an hour or so before my bedroom door was pushed open. Tugging off my headphones, I scowled at Chase. "You could at least knock. What if I was jacking it?"

Ugh. Why had I said that?

"Aw! Our little boy is growing up! Did Griff have the birds and bees talk with you yet?" He laughed, and I again gave him the bird, which only made Chase laugh harder.

"You do realize I'm eighteen, right? I haven't needed that talk in a long time. Hell, for all you know, I might not even be a virgin."

Chase playfully plugged his ears and started chanting, "Lalalala."

And *I* was supposed to be the kid? Sometimes you could forget he was twenty-two.

"Can you leave me alone?"

Like I said, Chase had been a fixture in my life for as long as I could remember. Even when Griff went off to school, Chase had stayed in Havenwood. He'd been apprenticing at an automotive shop, and had likely reported my activities back to Griff every day.

"Come on, Twerp. I ordered pizza, and I figured we could watch some horror flicks."

"No, thanks. I'm not hungry." My traitorous stomach growled.

"It's all veggie, just how you like it. I even got that apple-cinnamon dessert you devour."

Why did he have to be so *nice*? Chase liked all-meat pizza, and he'd gotten veggie for me. "Fine, but only because I'm hungry." Trying to pretend I wasn't as interested in spending time with him as I was, I got off

5

the bed and ignored Chase as I made my way into the kitchen.

As far as weekends went, it could have been a lot worse. We spent Friday night eating crappy food and watching movies. On Saturday I ran errands with him, he took me out to lunch, and then we explored some walking trails.

It was Saturday night that everything started to go to shit. One could say it was mostly my fault. The day had been so awesome, so perfect. I hadn't felt like a favor to Griff, or Chase's friend's kid brother, or even his little bro. It made my insides start feeling things they shouldn't.

We were watching movies again that night, when I got a text from my best friend, Natalie, asking me if I wanted to go over. Chase, nosy as ever, looked over and read it.

"You can go if you want. You don't have to hang out here with me. I'm pretty sure Griff knows Natalie's house is safe," he teased, and this panic clung to me.

"No, no! I don't want to go." It was stupid, and a little pathetic, but I wanted to spend more time with him. I'd been so angry that Griff made him stay, but then it had been awesome too.

"It's not good to keep your girl waiting." He waggled

his eyebrows.

"Huh? She's not my girlfriend. She's my best friend." Come on. He had to know that. Nat was really the only friend I had. There weren't many boys like me in Havenwood.

"I was kidding with you. Do you have one? A girl-friend?" Chase asked, and damned if my heart didn't take a nosedive to my gut.

"No."

He was quiet...watching me. I wouldn't look at him, but I could feel his penetrating stare trying to see through me to steal all my secrets.

"Boyfriend?" he asked after a few moments, and I thought I was going to throw up. Nausea twisted my gut, and my vision went a little blurry.

"What! No! Why would you ask that? I can't believe you just asked that."

Chase held up his hands and chuckled. "It's okay, Twerp. I didn't mean anything by it. I thought I'd put it out there, if that was something you were worried about, and let you know it was okay. That Griff would be okay."

He knew. Oh God, he knew. Both Chase and Griffin knew my secret. That was exactly what he was saying. Chase wanted me to know that Griff had guessed and he was okay with it. Until that second, I hadn't realized how much I'd needed to hear those words. That they made this calm feeling wrap around me. Griff was my family. He was all I had. Even though logically I knew it wasn't a real possibility, the fear of losing him had been overwhelming.

"I'm going to tell you a secret, one that no one knows, not even Griff."

I nodded, unable to look at him.

"I'm bisexual."

My whole body froze, my brain basically exploding. Chase was bi? Chase liked men?

"There's absolutely nothing wrong with it—being gay, bi, or anything else. I haven't told anyone close to me yet, but that's not because I'm ashamed. It's just...fuck, I wasn't ready, I guess, and if you're gay or bi, I won't tell anyone about you either. It's your truth to tell, whenever you want. You don't even have to answer the question now."

It took me a moment to realize I was crying. It wasn't until Chase wrapped an arm around me and pulled me close, murmuring, "Shh, it's okay, Twerp," that I felt the wetness running down my face. Somehow I knew my tears were confirmation, and Chase did too because he added, "You know we love you. This doesn't change anything."

He loved me. God, why couldn't he love me the way I wanted him to?

"I'm gay," I whispered because I'd never said the words out loud before, only in my own head. "I'm gay," I said again, and God, it felt *good*, like this weight was suddenly lifted from my chest. I was gay, and it was okay. I liked men, and I loved Chase, and the two most important people in my life, Griff and Chase, would be okay with it. Well, minus the loving-Chase part.

I cried until I fell asleep, right there on Chase's shoulder. He smelled so good, a light tinge of sweat mixed with cologne and this woodsy scent that was all Chase. I needed more of him, so I rooted my nose around in his neck and inhaled. Still, it wasn't enough. I wanted to taste him, so I sneaked my tongue out and licked at his flesh.

"Shh, it's okay, Twerp," Chase whispered again, and sure, I could have gone without the twerp part, but one couldn't control their dreams. On some level, I knew I was dreaming, so I kept going, kissing my way up Chase's flesh, like I'd done so many times before in my fantasies. Only this time, it felt more real.

"Chase, I've wanted this for so long."

"Umm…Kell…"

My body went so tense, I thought it might break apart. Oh God. I wasn't dreaming. Not fully. I was kissing Chase, licking his neck and inhaling him.

I was going to *die*.

But then…then I looked down and saw Chase's hand squeezing the couch pillow, saw the bulge between his legs. He was hard. Chase Hawthorne was hard from what I was doing to him.

*"I'm bisexual."*

Chase was *bi*, and he had an erection from me kissing him.

If there was a gay Jesus, he gave me strength right then. I didn't know where it came from, but I suddenly knew this was my chance. That if I stopped, I'd regret it for the rest of my life, so I kissed his neck again.

"Please, Chase," I begged, and he growled, this throaty, sexy, needy growl that made an earthquake go off inside me.

I straddled his lap and wrapped my arms around him, and we were kissing for real then. I felt his stubble against my face, and his tongue in my mouth, and holy motherfucking shit, nothing in the world tasted as good as Chase Hawthorne—the first person I ever kissed.

"We can't," Chase said as I kissed his throat again. "Griff will kill me." He didn't say he didn't want me, only that Griff would be upset.

"Griff doesn't have to know. I'm an adult, Chase. He's not my keeper."

Then Chase was kissing me again, and his arms wrapped around me, squeezing me tight. It was all my favorite things in life, every good memory combined in this one moment in time.

I moved on his lap and felt his erection against me. His hands slid down, and he grabbed my waist, squeezing my hips, his fingers digging in. He growled again, and I swallowed it and moved more, and it was everything but still not enough. This was my one chance with Chase, and I wanted it all.

I climbed off him, lay on the couch, and went for his shorts.

He grabbed my wrist. "Hey, Twerp. Kissing is one thing. I think that's a little much."

"Please." I leaned down and rubbed my face against his length. He thrust against me, and his hand fell away. He was breathing heavily, and then I had his dick out, and holy fuck, Chase had a huge cock. It was thick and long and he smelled so damn good. When I had him in my mouth, it was like the fucking angels sang.

His hand was in my hair, and he was whispering my name over and over. I was making Chase feel that way.

*Me.* I was pleasuring him and causing those hoarse sounds to pull from the back of his throat.

"I'm gonna come, Kell. Fuck, I'm gonna come."

But I didn't pull off, and he shot in my mouth. Not gonna say it tasted good. In fact, I gagged a little, but still. I swallowed every drop, my orgasm slamming into me, making me dizzy and like I was flying as I came in my shorts.

"I…uh…should return the favor," Chase said.

*The favor.* Those words made me feel so cold, but what did I expect? That he was suddenly going to tell me he loved me? That he'd dreamed of this moment with me? Yeah, right. This was a favor. An orgasm. That was it.

"Whatever. It's fine. I finished already."

"Fuck," Chase gritted out, his head dropping back against the couch. "I can't believe I did that."

He couldn't believe he did that? Couldn't believe he enjoyed me? Dizziness made my brain swim, and my hands tightened into fists. "Fuck you!" I shouted, pushing away from him.

"I didn't mean it like that, Twerp. Nothing against you. Jesus, you're Griff's little brother. I've known you most of your life. Your brother is going to kick my fucking ass."

"I won't tell him if you don't." I shoved to my feet. "I hate you." I was fully aware I was acting like the child I'd told him I wasn't, but I couldn't seem to stop myself.

"Twerp…"

"You just came in my mouth. You can at least use my name."

He closed his eyes again, and I knew, fucking knew, he regretted it. That he regretted *me*. It was my fault, but my heart shattered into a thousand pieces.

I walked away and locked myself in my room.

Chase didn't come after me.

He didn't say goodbye when Griff got home the next morning.

I didn't see him the whole week, and then the next weekend he was gone. He'd joined the Marines, Griff said.

And all I could think was he'd left to get away from me and hadn't said goodbye.

After that, Chase Hawthorne didn't return to Havenwood, though he talked to Griff often. My brother would tell me stories about where Chase was and what he was doing, about all the girls he was hooking up with—and Griff would shake his head at that, because hooking up wasn't Griff's thing.

I hated Chase Hawthorne.

I still loved him too.

# CHAPTER ONE

## *Kellan*

*Ten years later*

"**B**E CAREFUL NOT to press too hard," I told Annabella, one of the little girls taking my pottery class. "We use gentle fingers. Remember when we talked about gentle fingers versus firm ones?"

She nodded, getting back to work, her tongue sticking out cutely as she concentrated. She was one of the kids I could tell truly loved art, loved to create, and I got that, as I felt the same about it. Art was my constant in a lot of ways. It was the one thing I'd always been good at. No one had to fix it for me, or tell me how to do it, or what I was doing wrong. Art was mine.

I finished up the class full of eight- to-ten-year-olds, and then signed them all out as their parents came to pick them up.

"Annabella did great today," I told her mom, Tracey. "She's really talented."

Annabella blushed, but I could see how much the compliment meant to her. She was shy, quiet, didn't seem to have a lot of friends. I'd been there. I'd never totally been the quiet type. Most of the time I didn't know when to shut up, but I hadn't had a lot of friends growing up.

"Thanks, Kellan. She loves your classes. They've been good for her," Tracey replied.

It was my last class of the day, so once the building was empty, I turned the sign to CLOSED, locked the door, and cleaned up. My buddy Josh would be there in a few minutes. He was my best friend outside of Natalie. Josh had moved to Havenwood a few years back, when his grandmother got sick. He used to visit her during the summer when he was a kid, but I never knew him. When she passed, she left him her house and some money, and he'd never left. Josh owned a local gym, and we'd met when I started working out there. Josh was hot—thick arms, brown hair, and a Marilyn Monroe beauty mark. I'd noticed him right away, and he'd noticed me, and then guess who I found on Grindr not long later?

We'd met up, and I'd blown him, because I was quite fond of giving head and good at it, thank you very much. Then we went out for ice cream, and he'd been my best friend ever since. Josh was a bit more *dude bro* than me, but somehow we fit, so that was that. It was sad really, that I couldn't see Josh *that way*, because he was one of the few people in my life who didn't spend their time telling me what to do, or thinking they had to take care of me, but life had never been quite fair, had it?

Just as I finished, Josh knocked on the glass door of Safe Haven, my art studio.

I grabbed my shit, set the alarm, locked up, and saw that he'd met up with Nat somewhere along the way. "Oh, look, my posse is here," I teased. Josh rolled his eyes as Nat kissed me on the cheek. "I need a drink. Please tell me there are drinks in our future."

"When aren't there drinks in our lives?" Natalie asked, and the three of us laughed.

Unfortunately, there wasn't a gay bar in Havenwood, and we nixed the idea of driving into Richmond because we were lazy-asses, which meant I knew what they were going to bring up next.

"So, Griff's?" Josh asked, and I groaned, because of course Griff's bar was the next best option. It always was. And yes, he was my brother and I loved him like crazy, but he still forgot sometimes that I was twenty-eight years old.

Ever since I'd come out after *the night that shall not be named*, Griff had designated himself my bodyguard, the way I knew he would, protecting his queer brother with his super straight-guy abilities. But he was also Mr. PFLAG brother, who would do anything for me and had a pride flag hung up in his straight bar, in a small city where being LGBTQ+ wasn't perceived to be as fabulous as it actually was, so I couldn't complain.

Still…it would help if he didn't treat me like he thought I was weak, naive, and helpless.

I shoved those thoughts out of my head as the three of us made our way down the street. It was about a mile and a half from my shop to Griff's bar, but I knew we would walk. We always did, as we laughed and talked and Josh and I rambled about our latest Grindr tricks and Nat said she was jelly. I felt so bad for the straights sometimes. They didn't have nearly as much fun as us.

The bar was a lone building with a brick front. When we stepped inside Griff's, it was fairly busy for being early in the evening. My brother was behind the bar as always, because he was a workaholic, didn't know how to have fun, and in his thirty-three years on this planet—I wouldn't say since birth because I wasn't sure Griff was human—he'd never been serious about anything other than his work, his friends, and me.

Griff needed a life.

Griff needed a woman.

I'd tried to hook him up with Nat a few years back, but he wasn't interested. And Griffin never dated.

"Hey, Kell, Josh, Nat," Griff said as we approached him. The long bar was along the left of the building, with tables throughout the middle, billiards and darts on the right side, and a small stage along the back wall. Perched on chairs at the end of the bar were Lawson and Knox, who had taken Chase's place as Griff's friends over the years. They were hotties—Law with these blond curls that were to die for, and Knox in this daddy sort of way, with his dark hair, smoldering eyes, and the beard he always kept. Knox had been married, but was now divorced with a couple of kids, who lived with their mom. He had a local hardware store. He was a Havenwood transplant, whereas Law grew up here. Law's parents were basically Havenwood royalty—the small population of town that had more money than they knew how to deal with and likely thought the rest of us below them. Law wasn't like that, though. He owned a little café and spent his free time at Griff's.

"What's up, brother of mine. We've come to grace you with our presence."

Griff rolled his eyes at me. He did that a lot. "You're here because I give you guys half-priced drinks."

"Lies!" I replied, but obviously, it was partly true.

Who passed up cheap drinks? "Hey, Knox. Hey, Law," I said to my brother's friends. They were good guys and good friends to Griff, but they weren't Chase. No one was Chase, and ugh, *stop, stop, stop*. It was long overdue that I stopped obsessing over Chase Hawthorne.

"Hey," Law and Knox replied simultaneously.

Without having to ask what we wanted, Griff made three margaritas. We were simple people.

"For the three musketeers," Griff said, which was what he called us.

"Thanks, big bro."

We clinked our glasses together and drank.

Griff went about his business, and the three of us went about ours. We didn't talk with Knox and Law much, but every once in a while, they'd say something to us or we to them. There was this clear separation between my friends and Griff's. It had been like that ever since I started having friends. I was definitely glad things had changed a bit in Havenwood over the years. There were more out gay people, and I had Josh.

One margarita became two, and then we ordered fries because who didn't need salt and grease with their alcohol?

It was after handing us our third drink that Griff had a lull in customers. "Oh, I meant to tell you something.

Guess who I heard from?"

That quickly, my heart dropped to my stomach. He didn't have to tell me who he was talking about. I *knew*. Still, I teased, "Santa Claus?"

Griff rolled his eyes. "Chase, you smartass. He's coming back. He's going to be the new patrol officer, since Tom finally retired. Can you believe that? Chase Hawthorne, a police officer in Havenwood."

The rest of his words were a blur. Natalie's hand immediately went to my arm, and it was a good thing, because otherwise I might have fallen off the barstool. She was the only person I'd ever told what happened with Chase. The only one who knew how I'd always felt about him.

I didn't have to look at Josh to know his brows would be pulled together, that he'd have questions, because nothing got past Josh when it came to me. He just got me.

"Wow…that's great," I forced myself to say.

"I'm tired. Are you guys ready to go? I'm working urgent care tomorrow," Nat said, and I wanted to kiss her. She was a nurse; the best nurse. I was so lucky to have this amazing woman in my life.

"Yeah," I replied. "I am too. It's been a long day."

Griff frowned but didn't say anything.

"It's my turn, right, babe?" Josh said as he took money out and paid. God, I had the best friends in the world.

We went to Nat's apartment, which wasn't far from the bar.

"Who's Chase?" Josh asked as soon as we walked in.

I buried my face in my hands. It was stupid, this obsession I had with him. God, I didn't know why I let him get to me the way he did.

"The guy Kellan's been in love with since he was fourteen years old," she answered for me.

*I COULDN'T BREATHE. God, I was going to die too. Why couldn't I breathe?*

*"It's okay. I go'chu, Twerp." Chase's strong arms went around me, holding me so I didn't fall. He helped me down easily until we were both sitting on the floor, his grip on me so tight, I thought he was keeping my pieces together so I didn't shatter and fall apart.*

*My parents were dead. Dead. Gone in one night, taken from this world.*

*Hot tears streamed down my face, and Chase wiped them away. I didn't even have it in me to be embarrassed. I ached too much. Was too broken. How could we go on without Mom and Dad?*

*"Griff'll be here soon. He's doing the best he can," Chase told me.*

*Griff had a three-hour drive ahead of him, three hours where he would rush here, to get to me. Three hours knowing our parents were dead. "Oh God. He shouldn't drive. What if something happens? What if he wrecks?" I lost it even more then, crying loudly as snot ran down my face. I couldn't lose Griff too. What if I somehow lost Griff?*

*"Hey, he'll be fine. There's no one in this damn world who's stronger than your brother. He'll keep it together because that's what Griff does."*

*Suddenly another wave of sadness sucked me under. This one wasn't for the loss of our parents, but for my brother. He'd left Havenwood. He was off at college, following his dreams and not taking care of his baby brother anymore. What would happen now?*

*Griff would come back, that's what would happen. He would have to come back to take care of me. "What about school? I don't want Griff to have to leave school. He needs to stay. It's his dream." As soon as the words left my mouth, I felt guilty for them. Was it okay to also worry about my brother when I'd just been told my parents had died? "I don't want him to come home, but then, what will I do?" I asked, as if Chase had all the answers. It was stupid, but it* always felt like Chase knew everything, like there wasn't anything he couldn't do.

"You and me both know there's nothing that can stop Griff from being here for you, but I get it. I know you want him happy and…hell, Twerp. I'll help take care of you. Come on, you know that."

Chase was right. He was that kind of guy. If there were no Griff, Chase would take care of me like his own. He would work his ass off to try and raise me, to give me more than he'd ever had. He'd be a better surrogate family than his real family was with him. There was nothing in the world that would make me think differently. Chase took care of his own, and because Griff was his best friend, I was Chase's too, and that made something unfamiliar flutter in my belly.

As soon as the feeling came, it was washed away by sadness. My parents were gone. I started crying all over again.

"I'm so sorry, Kell, so damn sorry." Chase hugged me, speaking like he would do anything to fix this.

"What are we going to do?" What if they wouldn't let Griff keep me? How would we survive?

"We'll figure it out, okay? Don't worry about that right now. Me and Griff'll figure it all out."

And when Chase said it, somehow, I believed him.

# CHAPTER TWO

## *Chase*

I COULDN'T BELIEVE I was back in Havenwood. What in the hell had I been thinking?

The place didn't hold the best memories for me.

Alcoholic dad: check.

Struggles to make ends meet: check.

Verbal and sometimes physical abuse from dear old dad: double check.

Judgment from almost everyone in town outside of the Caines: check, check, check.

Havenwood hadn't been the easiest place to grow up in. Locals didn't tend to like people who weren't as good as them, and when your dad was the town drunk, you definitely weren't good enough. Been there, done that, had the battle scars to show for it.

All that had changed when Griffin Caine became my best friend. When his family taught me what it meant to have people there for you, and I would owe Griff for that for the rest of my life. He'd become the brother I never had. His parents were the parents I never had.

And Kellan...fuck, I wasn't ready to go there yet. The kid had been like a little brother to me. I'd taken him under my wing like Griff did...until that one night when I fucked up, made the biggest mistake of my life by giving in to this desire for him I hadn't even known I'd felt until he'd kissed me. And in the process, I'd betrayed my best friend in the world.

Griff would never forgive me if he knew what I'd done. And I'd never forgive myself for hurting Kellan.

Again, what the hell had I been thinking, coming back here?

And to be a local patrol officer, no less. My dad was going to love that, wasn't he?

But the longer I'd been gone, the more I realized I'd missed it...fuck, how I'd missed Havenwood...well, at least some of the people here. It was crazy how you could miss something that held so many bad memories, but the truth was, it held good ones too. I'd wanted comfort and familiarity, and there was only one place I'd ever felt that—with Griffin Caine and his family, which really meant Griff and Kellan.

I sighed as I looked up at the sign for Griff's. A bar. Shit, I was proud of my friend. No matter what life threw at him, Griff always pushed through, he always came out on top, and he did it while being the best guy around. The world needed more Griffin Caines.

I got out of my truck and went for the door. It was late, almost closing time, which possibly made me a coward. I wasn't sure why I was so damn nervous to see my best friend, the only real family I ever had, but when you considered I'd let his eighteen-year-old brother blow me, then bailed…left for ten years…I guess it made sense.

The moment I walked through the door, Griff's eyes snapped to me, as if he'd sensed me. He looked a little older, a little more weathered, but otherwise the same, with his messy dark hair, tall, bulky frame, and kind smile.

"Holy motherfucking shit. Chase Hawthorne. It's good to see you, man."

He walked around the counter, and we were moving toward each other, meeting in the middle, wrapping each other in a strong hug. Fuck, it felt good to see him again. I'd known I missed him, but I wasn't sure I'd realized how much until that moment. "It's good to see you too, brother."

"What do you want to drink?" Griff asked as we made our way to the bar. "You remember Lawson Grant, right? And this is Knox Wheeler."

I did remember Lawson. He had a wealthy family in town. They owned Grant's, a grocery store chain. The first one was in Havenwood, and now they had them throughout three states. His mom had been old money, on top of his dad's stores, but I couldn't remember her family history. Lawson and I had never been close, but this was Havenwood, so obviously I knew some things about him. I knew he'd left after his high school graduation, but never knew much about him from there. "Hey, man. Good to see you," I told Lawson as we shook hands.

"You too," he replied.

I shook with Knox next. "Nice to meet you," he said, his voice deep and raspy.

"Can I get a Corona?" I asked Griff as I took a seat. He got me a drink, and the four of us chatted for a few minutes before Knox and Lawson paid and were on their way. I had a feeling they were giving me time with Griff.

He closed the bar after that, locking the door, and then it was just the two of us. Griff smiled and crossed his arms as he took me in. "Christ, man. It's good to have you home. I missed my brother."

Guilt and happiness created a tornado inside me, wreaking havoc. Being friends with Griff had always meant something. He cared about his family fiercely, in ways I wasn't even sure were normal. There weren't many people like Griffin Caine in the world, and when he'd taken me in as his family, my life had been better for it. Hell, I wasn't even sure I would have had the balls to try and become anything more than my old man was if not for Griff's friendship and his family. Which triggered the guilt again. Logically, I knew it had been ten years. That it had been one blowjob, not the end of the world, but it felt like I'd betrayed Griff.

"I missed my brother too," I told him.

We shared a beer and talked about life. I told him about my four years in the Marines in more detail than I'd done in our phone calls over the years. I'd ended up in San Diego, then went to the police academy. We'd only seen one another a handful of times since I left—Griff always coming out to see me, of course, but we talked on the phone regularly.

"What in the hell are you doing back here?" Griff asked with a laugh.

"Family." I shrugged. We both knew I wasn't talking about my father.

"Yeah, I get it. At least you got out for a while. I sure as shit never will, not that I mind. Havenwood is home. Plus, you know how my overprotective ass is. I couldn't leave Kell, even though he wants to kill me for it most of the time."

I took a long swallow of my beer and shifted uncomfortably on the barstool. "Yeah...yeah, I get it. But he is twenty-eight now."

"And he still has a habit of getting himself into trouble. The latest was a catfishing situation. He didn't send the guy money or anything, but he wasn't who he said he was, and Kellan was devastated."

My muscles tightened at that. I hated the thought of Kellan getting hurt as much as Griffin did. "Shit, man. I'm sorry."

Griff waved it off. "Nah, don't worry. He makes me crazy, but I'm proud as hell of him. He owns a little shop in town. Sells his art and teaches all levels of classes. He's good, real good. Just don't tell him I said that. He's got this buddy too—Josh. He's newish to town, owns the gym. He's a good guy."

"They dating?" I asked, curious, even though I shouldn't be.

"No, not that I know of. He might be someone I'd actually approve of, though." Griff chuckled. "I think Josh helps him feel more comfortable here. Like I said, Kell's doing great, but he still doesn't always fit in, ya know? A little too wild and different for a lot of the folks around here, and they don't always refrain from showing it. The problem is, I like Josh, and that scares me because if he ever hurt Kellan, I'd have to hate him." Griffin laughed.

There was nothing about what he said that surprised me. Griff had always made it his responsibility to run Kellan's life. "Not sure it's your decision to make."

"Probably not, but that doesn't mean I won't try. Kellan doesn't always make the best decisions."

That made me frown. Sure, he'd always been a little quirky and impulsive—I mean, the kid had kissed and blown me—but it sounded like he was doing well, outside of the catfishing thing. I couldn't imagine the Kellan I remembered doing anything too drastic, and I sure as shit knew he wouldn't appreciate Griff still treating him like a kid.

"What about you?" I asked him. "Anyone in your life?"

"Nah, not really. Got my bar, got my family, go out on a few dates from time to time. Nothing serious. That's all I need. What about you?"

My skin suddenly felt itchy and almost like it was too tight, which pissed me off. I'd made peace with who I was a long time ago. My bisexuality wasn't something I hid anymore, and I'd made sure the station knew before

I came back to town. Still, the thought of telling someone I cared about was scary as fuck, and considering there wasn't really anyone I cared about more than Griff, I was sweating bullets. But again, I wouldn't hide it either.

"Same, really. You know how I roll, not looking to get serious." My parents had been too volatile, and the way mom had left...fuck, I wasn't putting myself in the position to get left. Ever. Not that my father hadn't deserved it, because he had. Just wished she hadn't left me in the process. "There have been a few women...and men over the years. Get laid when I need to, but that's all I want."

Griff smiled, didn't miss a beat, and I could tell he didn't give a shit. Not that I was surprised. He'd never considered not accepting Kellan. Worry about him? Yeah. Care that he was gay? Fuck no.

"Bi, huh?"

"Yep."

"Keep your dick away from Kellan. I'm pretty sure he used to have a crush on you," he said on a laugh, then playfully shoved my arm. "I'm giving you shit, Chase. He's like a kid brother to you. I know you'd never touch him."

But I had touched him, hadn't I? Then I'd left town

and never spoken to him again.

"GET ME ANOTHER *drink, will ya?" Dad said, his eyes drooping, his words slurred. My hands fisted. I hated him. I hated him so much—for drinking all the time, for being mean. For yelling at Mom and calling her names until she couldn't take it anymore and left. Then taking it out on me, calling me all the names and making me watch him drink himself stupid every night.*

*"Chase. You stupid or what? I said get me another drink."*

*I didn't know what came over me, what made me shove off the couch and look him in the eyes without trying to hide my hate of him. "No."*

*"What did you say to me, boy?" he asked through gritted teeth.*

*"I said no!"*

*Before I realized what was happening, he was on his feet. His arm swung through the air, and I stumbled backward when his hand connected with my face. It had been open-handed, and I was lucky for that. Still, pain shot through me, and fear took over. He came at me again, and I ran, through the living room and out the door.*

I heard him call after me, but I didn't stop, just kept running along the path through the woods surrounding our house on the outskirts of town.

When I was far enough away that I knew he wouldn't still be coming after me, I fell into the leaves and cried.

God, I couldn't wait to get out of there. Couldn't wait to leave Havenwood and never come back. I'd find my mom...maybe she went to that lake house in North Carolina. We went there one summer, the three of us. Dad hadn't been drinking at the time, and it was the best few weeks we ever had. I could find her, and we'd be happy, a family, without him.

I didn't know how long I sat there before I heard the crunch of leaves. My eyes darted up and landed on this kid—Griffin, I thought his name was. We were in the same grade, but Griffin had been held back in kindergarten, so he was a year older.

"Hey...you okay?"

Shame washed over me. God, I was sitting there crying in the middle of the woods. He would tell everyone. They'd all make fun of me.

"I'm fine," I bit out, turning away from him.

"You're, um...under your eye. It's bruising and swelling some. What happened?" When I didn't reply, he added, "Did someone hit you?"

"I'm fine," I snapped again. That was all I needed, him to try and save me. I hated my dad, but I sure as shit didn't want to get taken away from him either. Where the hell would I go? "I...fell." Lamest excuse ever.

"Oh. You should be careful," Griffin said softly. "You might fall harder next time, ya know? And if you keep falling, I'm going to have to get you some help."

Anger shot through me, but there was something else there too. Appreciation. It was stupid. He didn't know me. It wasn't like Griffin could care, but it almost seemed like he did. No one paid much attention to my dad or me. Who gave a shit about George Hawthorne or his son?

"Hey, I got an idea," Griffin said. "You wanna come to my house? We can put ice on your face and play video games. I bet Mom will let you stay the night. Maybe we can even order pizza."

My eyes went wide, held his. Why would he try and be friends with me? I didn't get why he'd care.

"Your parents won't mind?" I asked with too much hope in my voice. I wanted to eat pizza and play video games and stay the night at Griffin's house. I wanted to be his friend...to be like everyone else.

"Nope."

This time, my eyes darted toward the ground, unable to stay on him. "What about my face? Will your mom ask *about my…fall?"*

*"Probably. That's how moms are, ya know?"*

*No…no, I didn't know. My mom had left.*

*"We'll tell her we were running and you tripped over a log, but like I said…if you keep falling, I'll have to say something. You promise you'll tell me?"*

*"Yeah…yeah, I promise." I would have promised him anything to get to go to his place.*

*"Okay, let's go."*

*We got to his house, and his mom had baked chocolate-chip cookies. She fussed over my eye and then gave us each a cookie and said I could stay over. We had dinner together, and they asked about our day, and all I could think was…so this was what it was like to have a family? And I wanted it, wanted it more than anything.*

*After dinner, Griff's dad, who was a therapist, they said, took me aside and asked about my eye. He wanted to make sure I was okay, and that if I wasn't, I needed to tell him and he would take care of it, which I knew meant turning Dad in, which meant I'd get taken away, and now that I had Griff and his family, I wasn't going anywhere.*

*"I'm fine," I told him. "I just fell." He let it go that time, but I didn't think he would again.*

I WAS BEST friends with Griffin Caine from that day forward. His family became my family. He always stuck by me, and there was nothing I wouldn't do for him.

And the next time my dad hit me, I told him, and brave-ass Griffin went to him, all of thirteen years old, and told him if he touched me again, he'd tell his dad.

My father, coward that he was, never hit me again, but his words became as painful as his fists, maybe more so. Those, however, were easier to hide from Griff.

# CHAPTER THREE

## *Kellan*

I'D MANAGED TO make it a little over a week without seeing Chase Hawthorne, and by *managed*, I meant worked my ass off, became a ninja, and avoided him at all costs. It was ridiculous, really. I was aware of that, but a man had to have his pride.

Okay…maybe that was a bad example, because hiding didn't seem real prideful, but when you had an uncontrollable response to someone—that even you couldn't understand—I blamed chemistry—avoidance was the best way to keep a little bit of your dignity. Especially when your attraction to said person made them run away from home for ten years. It wasn't an ego boost, that was for sure.

I should have known it wouldn't last. Part of me did and was angry as I peeked out my living-room blinds and saw him standing on my porch, but the other part was irritated it had taken so long. He'd walked away after I'd practically begged to blow him, and he didn't even have the decency to talk to me for ten years? And as soon as he came home, he went straight to Griff, ignoring me completely. It shouldn't have surprised me. Somewhere deep inside I still feared Chase was in love with my brother, which would basically kill me.

For a minute I considered not answering the door…or maybe opening the blinds, flipping him off, and then ignoring him, but I knew I wouldn't. So I straightened my spine, held my head high, walked over, and opened the door to the home I grew up in, the one I still shared with Griff.

"Is there a problem, Officer?" I asked, and fuck, why did he have to look so good? Uniforms were hot. I'd always thought so, but seeing Chase in his dark-blue Havenwood police uniform was a whole different thing.

He looked older, obviously, but the years had been good to him. There was scruff on his strong jawline, and his dark-blond hair was still short, buzzed along the sides and the back, the top a little longer and pushed forward on his forehead to almost reach his brow.

And his body…fuck, the way his arms stretched the short sleeves of his shirt made my head spin. Chase had always been too sexy for his own good. Mine too.

"Holy shit, Kell, look at you." He rubbed a hand

over his chest as he stared at me, and my stupid pulse sped up.

"Do I know you?" I was being petty, but I didn't care. Chase had hurt me, probably more than he realized.

"Come on, Twerp. Don't be like that."

Twerp? Would he never stop seeing me as Griff's little brother? "Don't call me that, Chase. I'm not a kid. You've had your dick in my mouth, remember? The least you can do is show me some respect." I turned and walked inside, leaving the door open. We might as well get this over with. It had to happen at some point.

Chase muttered a quiet, "Fuck," behind me, and then I heard the door close. "You look good," he said, and I whipped around to look at him, probably with fire in my eyes. I felt like I was blazing.

"Flattery will get you nowhere, Chase Hawthorne. I can't believe you just said that to me. Unless...oh, did you come for a round two? Thought you'd get me on my knees before you left for another ten years?" Part of me felt I wasn't being fair to him. We'd basically been kids, and I'd started it. I'd kissed him, straddled him, gone down on him, but he still *left*. And he kept in touch with Griff, but not me. He didn't talk to me for ten years.

"That's not why I'm here, and you know it."

"Oh... *Oh.*" Everything began to click into place. "I

get it now. You're here to make sure I don't tell Griff, which, *duh*. If I were going to, I already would have. You likely also want to make sure I know you're straight now because you were just horny and it was only a blowjob, right?" How many "straight" guys had I heard *that* from over the years? God, what did I ever see in him?

"Did you make that up on the fly, because it doesn't make a damn bit of sense. I assure you, I'm very bi. You can ask your brother."

I stumbled backward. Oh God. No. Chase and Griff? It was something I'd thought about, but hearing it? Hearing it was like a knife to the heart.

"What? No, not like that. Christ, Twerp—I mean, Kellan. I meant I told him. We didn't…" He shook his head. "Griff is my best friend. My brother."

And I'd been nothing more than head from his other brother, apparently.

"I told him I'm bi when I came back. I thought he should know, and do you want to know the first thing he said to me?"

No, no I didn't. "Nah, I'm good. Thanks."

Chase shook his head as though he didn't know what to do with me, and spoke anyway. "He said to keep my dick away from you. Do you know what it would do to him if he found out about our slip-up?"

Slip-up? *Slip-up?* I picked up a couch pillow and chucked it at him, which Chase easily caught.

"Still impulsive, I see."

"Still an asshole, I see. You don't get to come here and judge me. You don't know me anymore. You came in my mouth and then bailed. A lot can change in ten years."

His jaw tightened, and I could have sworn I heard his teeth grinding. Chase was pissed, and good for him, because I was fucking pissed too.

"I know you're still getting yourself into messes Griff has to fix." The moment the words came out of his mouth, I flinched, and he quietly cursed, dropping his head back. "Shit. I shouldn't have said that."

"He told you?" I spit out. My whole world was spinning. My knees were weak, and I was surprised I could still hold myself up. I couldn't believe Griff had told him.

"Kell…I'm sorry. I shouldn't have—"

"No, it's my turn, Chase. I've waited ten years. I think I should get to speak first."

I was surprised when he simply nodded.

"I don't ask Griff to fix anything for me. Am I perfect? No. But I don't ask for anything from him. And that was a long time ago. I might have been a stupid, brokenhearted kid after you left, and I ended up in a bad situation, but that was *ten fucking years ago* and *fuck you* for throwing it in my face."

"Wait. What are—"

"I'm not done yet. Who the fuck *are* you? The Chase Hawthorne I knew never would have used that night against me. I might have been young and stupid, but I was assaulted, and it wasn't my fault." I'd blamed myself for years after that night, and I sure as hell wasn't going to let anyone else blame me now.

"Assaulted? What the fuck are you talking about?" Chase's face was red, his hands fisted, his pupils blown wide.

Oops. I might have misjudged the situation. "You said..." He'd said Griff told him.

"Griff told me about the catfishing. He never said anything about... Fuck, Kell. What happened to you?"

Chase rubbed a hand over his face, and it was shaking, fuck, the thing was shaking. He sat on the couch, his leg bouncing up and down, and I knew he was torturing himself, that his thoughts were worse than what I would have to tell him, and as much as I wanted to force him to leave, I couldn't put him through that either.

"I mean, you don't have to tell me. You have that right, but..." He looked up at me like a wounded dog, looked at me the way he used to look at everyone before Griff took him in—broken and scared.

"I, um, fucked up." I sat down on the couch beside him. "No, it wasn't me. I didn't do anything wrong, but after you left, I was angry and hurt. I didn't want to be a kid, ya know? I didn't want to be that little brother Griff had to protect or the one who sent you running. I wanted to prove I could do what I wanted and didn't need either of you."

The room was so quiet, I didn't think Chase was breathing.

I took a few steadying breaths myself and continued. "I went into Richmond and met this guy. He bought me alcohol and brought me back to his place. It was stupid. I thought he liked me. How could he like me when he didn't even know me? But when he started kissing me, it felt good. I felt desired, so I let it keep going." It'd been so foreign to me—being wanted. Chase hadn't wanted me. I hadn't had many friends. God, I'd been so dumb. "He had more in mind than I did. I got scared, told him no. He kept pushing, trying to force me. I nearly ripped his dick off, and he hit me, and I ran. I went to Griff. We reported it. The guy got in trouble, and that was the end of it." Well, mostly. It took longer to work through mentally than I wanted Chase to know about.

"Why didn't he tell me?" Chase's whole body was rigid. His hands were fisted so tightly, I knew his nails had to be digging into his palms.

"Because I told him not to. It was none of your business," I said frankly.

"It was my fault."

I rolled my eyes. What was with both Chase and my brother to think the whole world rested on their shoulders? "Don't think so highly of yourself. I might have been hurt when you left, but I was also a horny, eighteen-year-old boy who had just given his first BJ and wanted to know what it felt like to be on the other side of it."

Chase didn't speak, didn't move, and damned if I didn't feel bad.

"I didn't want him to tell you because I knew you'd blame yourself and come back. This wasn't where you wanted to be. I wasn't who you wanted. You ran away from me, but you also have a loyal streak a hundred miles wide. I knew you, Chase, and I knew you'd come back, just like Griff did when our parents died. I wasn't going to be the reason you came back somewhere you didn't want to be. It wasn't your fault. It wasn't my fault. It was his, and that's all there is to it."

The silence stretched on so long, I wasn't sure what

to think. Finally, Chase looked over at me, his eyes watery. The sight hit me in the chest. I'd never seen Chase Hawthorne cry. Not when his dad showed up drunk to his high school graduation and made a scene, or when he got arrested for drunk driving, or when Griff left, or my parents died.

"I was scared," he admitted softly. "Scared because the minute you kissed me, I realized I wanted it, and I felt…fuck, I felt like a dick because you were a kid, just eighteen, and Griff's brother, and he was like my brother, which twisted my head all up. Then I thought about Griff, who was my fucking family, Kell. I only had family because of him. You and your parents, you'd only loved me because Griff had loved me, and it felt like I was stabbing him in the back. Kissing you meant losing him, my family, and I didn't know how to do that."

So he'd chosen Griff over me. That shouldn't surprise me. Griff was everything to Chase. I was the little brother. Of course he would choose Griff over me, but it still hurt. Because if Chase had been serious about me, if he'd really cared about me, Griff would have understood. Being scared that kissing me would result in losing Griff meant it hadn't been nearly as real to Chase as it had to me.

Griff had always been better than me. He'd always

been the one to do the right thing. Everyone loved him, and I had always just been Kellan—the weird one, the loud one, the gay one, the one no one liked. At least not as much as Griff. "That's not true," I finally managed to say. "We loved you because you're you, not because of Griff."

Chase ignored me. "I'm sorry. I am so fucking sorry for letting all that shit happen. I should have stopped you. I shouldn't have let it go as far as it did. I was older than you, so I should have been able to keep my head on straight. And I shouldn't have left the way I did. You deserved better than that."

"Yeah. I did."

Then, just like he'd done ten years ago, Chase Hawthorne wrapped an arm around me. Hugged me. Kissed the top of my head. And it felt so good…so *right*. I'd been with my fair share of men over the years, but none of them felt the way Chase did. None of them had their own little home right inside my chest.

I was still in love with him, but I'd never have him, and I didn't know how I was going to deal with that.

# CHAPTER FOUR

## *Chase*

I COULDN'T STOP thinking about Kellan, about what he'd told me, what had happened to him when I wasn't there. It could have been worse; fuck, it could have been a whole lot worse, but that didn't change the fact that it had been bad, that he'd been hurting after how I treated him, and I hadn't known.

That twisted up my insides in this way that was a constant discomfort no matter what I did. It had been four days since I left him sitting on the couch, yet he hadn't left my mind. Kellan could have gotten hurt, and I'd never forgive myself for what happened.

If there was one thing my friendship with Griff had taught me, it was that you took care of the people you loved. That's what I'd been doing when I left, because Griff would have lost his fucking mind if he'd found out what happened. Griff was the first person who ever loved me, and I loved him—him and Kellan both. That made this an even bigger clusterfuck than I'd imagined because before Kell had told me what happened, when he'd first opened the door, all I'd thought was, *Damn, he looks good.*

He wasn't that same impulsive, bratty, insecure eighteen-year-old he'd been when I left. Well, he was still impulsive, but he was also stronger, more confident, and yeah, the years had been good to him. His beautiful chocolate-brown hair hung into his eyes, making him keep pushing it back. He had sharp cheekbones, almost like they'd been chiseled, but in a strangely soft way. It all complemented those green eyes of his that always looked like they held secrets inside of them.

He had long, sinewy muscles, a swimmer's body, but as far as I knew, Kellan wasn't a swimmer. Hell, he'd hated any and all sports when he was younger, but that didn't mean he still did. He was...fuck, he was sexy as hell, and yeah, I had to nix those thoughts the fuck out of my head and quickly.

"Hey, Chase? We need you to go out to the Chapmans' place on Mills Pond Road. You remember where it is, or do you need an address?" Daphne asked. She worked dispatch in our small station that consisted of a whopping six officers. This hadn't been what I'd had in mind when I'd gone into law enforcement, but then I figured it made sense—being back here, coupled with why I became an officer in the first place.

"I remember it. They still fight like they used to?" I pushed out of my chair.

"Always. Don't know why the two of them are still together after all these years, though I guess they're perfect for each other." Daphne chuckled.

"I'll take care of it." I went straight out to the cruiser. It only took eight minutes to get out to the Chapmans' place. They lived on an acre of land, which meant there was no one around to hear whatever squabble they were into this time. It was always one of them who called the station on the other. It had been that way for as long as I could remember. When we were kids, sometimes we'd play games where we dared each other to provoke them into an argument over something. Not something I was proud of, but that's the way it was.

As soon as I parked in front of their small, white farmhouse, Mrs. Chapman came running out. "Finally! Took you long enough. He let Tootsie out, and she's gone! He did it on purpose. He's always hated my dog."

"Ah, hell, woman. You called the police. They have more important things to worry about than your crazy dog," Mr. Chapman replied.

"See! See what I mean! He hates her, and she's gone.

He put her out without making sure the back gate was closed, and I was busy making her dinner."

"Her dinner, not mine, of course. She cooks that dog a three-course meal and feeds her at the table! What kind of dog eats at the table?"

"One who loves me more than you do!" Mrs. Chapman threw back at him.

"Okay, I'm gonna need you both to calm down for a minute, okay?" Christ, I was already frustrated.

Two pair of eyes trained my way, as if they really paid attention to me for the first time. "Chase Hawthorne, is that you? I heard you were back in town. Look at you! All grown up."

"Thank you, ma'am."

"Now, if you'll do me a favor and arrest my husband so I can look for Tootsie, I'd appreciate it."

I bit back a laugh, but before I could ask what I was supposed to arrest Mr. Chapman for, he did it himself. "What is he arresting me for? Letting the dog out to pee?"

"You did it on purpose!" The two of them started yelling at each other again.

"That's enough," I interrupted. "Did Mr. Chapman do anything to hurt you?" They'd never laid a hand on each other, at least not as of ten years ago, but I had to be sure.

"What? No, why would he do that?" Mrs. Chapman asked.

I ignored her and turned to him. "Did Mrs. Chapman do anything to hurt you?"

"Other than love that dog more than me?"

"I'm sure that's not true. She loves you very much."

"You think I love Tootsie more than you?" Mrs. Chapman asked.

Her husband's eyes darted toward the ground, his cheeks going pink. "Sometimes…but I didn't know the gate was open. Come on, honey, you know me better than that."

"It sounds like an accident to me, and like maybe the two of you need to talk a little bit. Maybe do something special just the two of you, without Tootsie." Christ on a cracker, I couldn't believe I was telling a grown-ass couple they needed a night out without their dog.

"I…I'd like that," Mrs. Chapman told him.

"I'd like that too," he replied.

Just then a Yorkie came running at me, barking like crazy and nipping at my ankles.

"Tootsie! You're home!" She swooped the dog into her arms, and then the two of them were hugging and baby-talking to the dog, before they went inside like I wasn't even there.

All in a day's work in Havenwood.

I finished my shift, then headed to Get Pumped. It was the new gym in town, which I remembered Griff telling me was owned by Kellan's friend Josh. That obviously wasn't *why* I went. It was the only gym in town, and I needed to join somewhere anyway, but I had to admit, I was curious about Josh.

There was a woman behind the counter when I got there, someone I didn't recognize, even though she was around my age. She grinned at me, her eyes making their way up and down my body, and mine did the same to her. I'd always loved women, men too. I loved people and sex—not relationships, because I didn't believe in those for myself, but the rest of it, yeah, I fucking liked that.

"Well, hello there." She smiled at me, and I gave her one right back.

"Ma'am."

"Oh, no. My mom is ma'am. I'm too young for that. Officer…"

"Hawthorne. Chase Hawthorne."

"You're obviously the new one I've been hearing about. Small-town boy makes good? Moved away, then came back to take care of the hometown that raised you?"

Yeah, she was definitely new here. She didn't know who my father was, that much was clear. "Something like that."

I told her I was interested in joining, and she started going over prices and classes with me. She flirted the whole time, and I'd be lying if I said I didn't flirt back, but I still found my eyes making their way around the room, trying to figure out who Josh might be. I didn't know why in the fuck I was so interested in the kid, but I was.

It didn't take long to get me all signed up—and for Jasmine to slip me her phone number. From there I went to the locker room, changed, and headed back out into the gym.

I was there for ten minutes tops when I heard Kellan laugh and looked over to see him walking in with a guy with dark-brown hair sticking out from under a baseball cap. Kellan playfully pushed the guy, who laughed and wrapped his arm around Kell, kissing the top of his head, the way I'd done a few nights ago.

My gut tightened, and I frowned as I watched them walk up to the counter. They were telling Jasmine something, Kellan animated and talking with his hands the way he did. Josh—I assumed—stood behind him with his hands on Kell's shoulders, shaking his head at Jasmine where Kellan couldn't see him.

They were close...fuck, they were close, and it was so fucking weird because I'd never seen Kellan with anyone that way. Of course I hadn't. But if Griff hadn't already told me they were only friends, I would have assumed they were a couple.

My pulse kicked up a notch, and I wanted to punch myself, because why in the fuck did it matter if Kellan and that guy were close?

Jasmine began talking, and I noticed her nod toward my area. Just as she did, both Kellan and Josh turned my way. Without giving it a thought, I turned quickly, as though it hadn't been clear I was watching them. I fumbled the kettlebell weight I'd been ridiculously holding on to.

Fuck...*fuck*.

Because that hadn't been awkward. Not at all.

Before I made a bigger fool of myself, I put the weight away, just as he and his buddy approached me.

"Oh, hey. Decided to join the gym?" Kellan asked.

"Yeah." I shrugged, then looked over at his friend.

"Josh Westbrook." He held out his hand, and I shook it, his grip tight on my hand. Ah, so that's how it was. Evidently, he knew I was an asshole who'd hurt

Kellan.

"Chase Hawthorne." I didn't let go, and Josh didn't either.

"Oh, hi. I'm Kellan Caine. Did you two forget I'm here?" He shook his bangs out of his face, and Josh and I finally let go.

"You know I could never walk away and forget you," Josh replied, and my temper immediately spiked.

"Hey, listen—"

"*Josh,*" Kellan cut me off.

"Sorry. My bad." Josh held his hands up in surrender, but he'd already done what he'd set out to do—remind me I was an asshole, that I'd bailed on Kellan, and that Kellan had him. "I'm going to get to work. You want to grab some dinner tonight, babe?"

Kellan's expression didn't change at all at Josh's term of endearment, which meant he was used to hearing it, and damned if I didn't feel a slight twitch in my gut.

"I don't know. I haven't decided if I'm pissed at you yet."

Josh chuckled and kissed Kellan's temple. "Call me later." His eyes found me. "You know I'll always be around." And then he walked away.

"Your friend is an asshole," I told Kellan.

"I can see why it might look that way, but no, he's

not. I am a little pissed at him, though, because usually he's the only person in my life who doesn't treat me with kid gloves, like I'm helpless or something."

I frowned. Shit. Did he really feel that way? I mean, Griffin did, obviously, but not everyone. "I don't treat you like you're helpless."

"Oh, yeah, okay. That must be the other Chase Hawthorne who's best friends with my brother. My mistake."

Did I treat Kellan like he was helpless? I never thought I did. Hell, I hadn't seen him in so long that I hadn't treated him like anything in years, but I hadn't ever meant to treat him like I didn't think he could take care of himself.

Before I could say any of that, Kellan added, "So…Jasmine thinks you're hot."

"She's not wrong," I teased, and Kellan laughed. Fuck, I'd missed the sound of his laughter. The kid had never had it easy, but he'd never stopped laughing.

"Well, you're cockier than you used to be."

"I'm a lot of things I didn't use to be." I winked…then groaned because I was fucking *flirting* with Kellan, which I had no business doing. "Were you here to work out or just so your friend could paw you all over?"

"*Tsk, tsk.* If you're not careful, someone might think you're jealous. I mean, I obviously know that's not true, as I'm simply Griff's little brother, but not everyone knows you only see me that way."

For the second time in less than a minute, I groaned. I had a feeling Kellan would make me do that a lot. There were so many things to unpack in what he said, but it wasn't smart, and honestly, I planned to ignore the ways I wanted to take apart what he said, tell him he wasn't only Griff's little brother. It was a whole lot easier to let it slide. "You want to work out with me?"

Kellan's brows pulled together as though he hadn't expected that, which made two of us. He was good at making me do and say things I knew I shouldn't do or say.

"Yeah, sure," he replied.

We spent the next hour exercising. The whole time I tried to ignore the way Kellan's muscles moved when he did, muscles he didn't have ten years ago.

Kellan never stopped talking or laughing, and I realized I'd missed that. He'd been good at making me forget other shit, even when we were kids, and he apparently was still good at it.

When we finished, he was wiping the sweat off his face, and my mouth opened and words tumbled out.

"You still like horror movies?"

"Yes." He crossed his arms and cocked a brow at me.

"If you don't have plans with your bodyguard, you're welcome to come over tonight. I can grill some dinner, and we can watch a movie. I figure I owe you one since the last one ended the way it did."

Bringing up the blowjob probably wasn't the smartest thing to do, but hell, neither was asking Kellan over. I'd never been the smartest guy around, and I did owe him after how our last movie night had ended.

"Why?" Kellan asked, studying me, and I shrugged.

"Not sure." It might have been a non-answer, but it was the truth.

"Yeah...okay." He pulled his phone out of the pocket of his shorts. "What's your number? I can text you so you'll have mine, and you can send me your address."

We did exactly what Kell said, and then I watched him walk away...right over to Josh, who stood behind the counter, watching me.

What the fuck was I doing? Kellan Caine screwed with my head.

# CHAPTER FIVE

## *Kellan*

"WHAT WAS THAT?" I asked Josh when Chase left and we went into his office together. I crossed my arms and tapped my foot for emphasis.

"First, you look ridiculous, and second, I don't know what that was. I guess I was defending your honor."

A sharp laugh jumped out of my mouth. "Defending my honor? Have you lost your fucking mind? I don't need you to defend me in anything. That's not how we work. Unlike my brother and Chase Hawthorne, you actually see me as the grown-ass man I am."

"Why do you call him by his full name?"

"I don't know…to put some distance between us? And that doesn't matter. What does matter is I love you and appreciate you, but please don't become someone else in my life who thinks I can't take care of myself." It didn't matter if it came from love or not. I couldn't deal with that shit. It made me feel like they saw me as weak, and that was the last thing I was or wanted to be.

"I'm sorry, babe. You're right." Josh wrapped his arms around me and kissed the top of my head, and for the millionth time I wished I could see him as more than a friend and that he saw me that way too. "I get what you see in him. He's fucking gorgeous."

"Right?" I pulled away and sat in his desk chair. "He always has been, but it's more than that. I can't even put my finger on exactly what it is, but Chase has always been different to me. He's always been *more*. He lived with a shitty, alcoholic dad, and his mom left him, which made Chase fiercely loyal and protective of those he cared about. He's the only one who can ever talk sense into Griff, and he tried for me more than once. I'd pull something crazy, and Griff would freak out, and Chase would simply tell me he'd take care of it and did." Somehow Chase always made me feel like I was someone better than I was, but I couldn't share that with Josh.

"You got it bad. Even after all this time?"

"I don't really know him anymore, so I guess I can't really be in love with him, can I? And I was a kid before, so I'm sure it was a ridiculous crush." I didn't really believe any of the things I was telling Josh. "He invited me over tonight, so I'll probably realize he's awful and picks his nose or something, and the magic will be gone."

Josh sighed. "Just be careful, okay? I've never seen you like this, and no matter what, remember this is the guy who let you blow him and then bailed on you, without a word for ten years. Oh, while he happened to continue talking to your brother. Do you think he's into Griff?"

My heart stopped beating—just curled the fuck up and died. "I've wondered... Oh my God, do you think he's in love with my brother?" Jesus, I couldn't imagine it. I mean, I was almost a hundred percent sure Griff identified as straight, but then, who the fuck really knew? He'd always cared about Chase in ways he didn't with others.

"I don't know. You know the guy, not me. Seemed like a bit of an asshole to me."

"Maybe that's because you were being one to him?" I cocked a brow at Josh.

"Eh, he should have known he had it coming. I'm not going to let him hurt my boy."

He meant boy in the dude-bro way, not the sexy one.

I rolled my eyes and chatted with him for a while longer before telling him I had to go. Chase texted me his address, and I told him I'd be there around seven. I went home first and douched and showered because you never could be too prepared. Maybe this time I'd be the one to walk away from Chase instead of the other way around. I put on my lucky underwear, favorite jeans with the hole in the knee, and a sky-blue V-neck.

Chase lived on the outskirts of Havenwood, in a cabin down a long driveway and secluded from the world. It reminded me of his house growing up, except without all the broken-down cars and old shit in the yard that his dad collected; well, and the house was in much better shape too. It looked like it had a large deck out back, which didn't surprise me. Chase had always been an outdoorsy guy, hiking and all that shit.

Fuck, I couldn't believe I was nervous. There was a part of me that wanted to drive away, that didn't want to give Chase the time of day. I couldn't believe he'd invited me in the first place. What would Griff say if he knew we were hanging out without him? I assumed he'd be relieved because I obviously couldn't get into trouble if Chase was on babysitting duty.

The door opened. Chase came out and leaned against the railing, crossing his arms. I'd be lying if I didn't admit I whimpered. He'd showered too—his hair was wet—and he wore a tank that was tight across the muscles of his chest. His arms...fuck, his arms were nice. I'd always had a thing for those, especially forearms, which I thought came from Chase arm porn as a kid.

But I wasn't that kid anymore, was I? Which was why I took a deep breath, told myself I was stronger than this—that I wouldn't revert back to that boy who thought Chase Hawthorne hung the moon—and got out of the car.

"Got excited waiting for me?" I teased.

"If you say so." He gave me a simple nod, but I noticed the right side of his mouth curled up slightly. He was trying to hold back a grin.

"I do. Though one might wonder...what would Griffin do? Or think? I usually wear my bracelet to remind myself, but I forgot it at home."

Chase didn't seem to think that was funny and frowned.

"Relax. We're watching a movie and eating food. Griff would approve. I checked."

"You *asked* your brother before you came over?"

"Oh God, no. It was a joke. You know, funny, ha-ha. You really don't know me at all anymore. Are you going to show me your place or what?"

Chase shook his head as if he wasn't sure what to do or think, then pushed off the railing, opened the door, and stepped aside.

"Such a gentleman." I played it off as a joke, but Chase was and always had been that kind of guy. He would have been the troubled kid in an after-school special, who helped the elderly across the street and got kittens out of trees, but then secretly let his best friend's brother blow him.

I walked into what was basically the definition of *man cave*. All dark colors, brown leather furniture, and reclining chairs on each end of the couch. His coffee table looked to be one of those where the top pulled up so you could conveniently eat and watch a game at it. The television was the centerpiece, a big-ass flat-screen on the wall, which of course had ESPN on in the background.

"I believe this is the most Chase Hawthorne room I've ever walked into. Though it doesn't smell as strongly of gym socks as Griff's room used to when the two of you were in it."

"You better be careful, or I'll give you the Kellan Special like we used to."

Ugh. They used to always torture me. One of them would hold me down, and they would give me noogies until I told them both they were like, kings of the universe or something stupid like that. It had been annoying as shit, but now I knew how to make Chase squirm, so I winked and said, "You better be careful, or I'll hold you to that promise. I like it a little kinky."

He crossed his arms again and shook his head, but he couldn't hide that twist of the right side of his mouth. It gave Chase away every time he wanted to smile. "Don't smile, or you'll ruin it. Then I'll know you aren't really mad at me." How many times had he said that to me over the years? It was fun to be on the other side of it now.

Chase groaned, that sexy, throaty sound that made my dick hard. "I'm beginning to feel like this was a mistake."

"I'm wondering what took you so long to figure that out," I replied, making my way toward the kitchen. "What's for dinner? And do you have a beer? I could use a drink."

"You and me both, Twerp."

For now, I let the *twerp* go. I had a feeling Chase had no idea what to do with me.

# CHAPTER SIX

## *Chase*

THERE HAD ALWAYS been something special about Kellan. Griff saw it too. We'd talked about it more than once as Kell got older. He brought out something in people, whether he made you feel good, or made you laugh, or made you want to throttle him because he drove you batshit crazy. He had the ability to do it all. There had been moments I'd wanted to protect the kid from the world, and others when I'd wanted to strangle him. It was usually a toss-up between the two, sometimes going back and forth minute by minute.

But he'd also always made me feel comfortable. I didn't know what it was about him. Even that night when I told him I was bisexual. Yeah, one could say it was because we'd wondered if he was gay and wanted to make sure he knew he wasn't alone, but a part of me had wanted to get it out for years, to be open about that aspect of myself, but I hadn't had the balls to share it with anyone other than Kellan. It wasn't something I could explain, but something that simply *was*.

As much as Griff meant to me, there had always been that insecure side of me that believed he felt sorry for me, like he knew I needed him. And yeah, I *did* need his friendship. It had always been one of the most important things in my life, but I sure as shit didn't want to feel like Griff thought he had to take care of me.

*The way Kellan likely feels about both of us…*

Well, shit. Why had I never seen it that way before? It made perfect sense after he told me, and I hated my role in it.

I pulled two bottles of beer from the fridge and handed them over to Kellan, then grabbed the foil-wrapped packages of potatoes and the steak, and we made our way out to the back deck.

"I did the potatoes like your mom used to—sliced up with the onions and peppers."

"Dad loved them that way." Kellan raised the beer to his mouth and took a swallow. There was a wistful sadness to his voice. "I forget those little things about them sometimes."

"Yeah. I do too. Not that it's the same. They were your parents, not mine, but—"

"They loved you like a son, Chase. Come on, you

gotta know that. And they'd be so proud of you. The Marines, and now you're a cop. Have to admit, I never saw either of those things coming."

"I…" My words lodged in my throat. I wasn't good at shit like this. Kellan must have known it because he nodded, letting me off the hook, which only made me want to continue. He sat down, and I turned my back to him as I checked the charcoal because fuck that gas-grill shit. "Thank you. That means a lot to me. They were the only parents I really knew." I'd never called them Mom and Dad or anything like that, but I'd always known I'd had the Caines in my corner.

"I know. I want to make sure you know they loved you too. I might have been younger, but even I could see that. You have the right to grieve for them as much as Griff and I do."

I didn't know what made me want to do it. Maybe it went back to what I'd been thinking earlier, about Kellan being different and having the ability to pull secrets out of me without trying, but as I set the foil packages on the grill, I found myself asking, "Can I tell you something?"

"Yeah. Of course."

"I knew I was going into the Marines before we…"

"Fucked around. You can say it, Chase. As far as I know, Griff isn't waiting in the woods to pounce."

But I didn't really feel like we'd fucked around. I felt like I'd taken advantage of him, and that was something I wasn't sure I could ever forgive myself for. That piece of information I kept to myself, though. "I'd already known I was going into the Marines before we fucked around. I didn't tell you because..." Why hadn't I told him? Griff had known. It wasn't a secret, but I hadn't told Kellan.

"Because you knew I'd be devastated. Come on, Chase, we both know that's why. You had to have known I had the world's biggest crush on you. And I was dramatic, so obviously I would have thought my world was ending."

That made me turn around to look at him. Fuck, Kellan was brave. Did he know how courageous he was? We'd always made it our job to try and protect him, but sometimes I wondered if Kellan was the strongest of us all. He hadn't wanted Griff to come home for him, and he wouldn't have wanted me to try and take care of him either. He'd been brave as shit when he'd kissed me, and what he dealt with from that guy in Richmond. Yeah, Kell didn't need any of us to take care of him.

And honestly, as I stood there looking at him, I knew why I hadn't told him about the Marines. Because I had known it would hurt him, that he would have been sad. I knew that if I had seen it, Kellan's pain over me leaving, I likely wouldn't have gone. He just…got to me that way, and seeing his sorrow always made me go into fixer mode. I'd always wanted to make it better.

What I said, though, was, "You might have been a little dramatic." I cocked a grin, trying to keep things light.

"Dude, you were the star player in my jack-off fantasies. Most kids grow up and dream about marrying their favorite movie star. I was going to score Chase Hawthorne. The dramatics were very well called for."

And, holy fuck. There went my dick. The thought of Kellan jerking it while thinking of me made all sorts of wires cross—not young Kellan, of course, but this one. It was crazy really, that he had looked at me back then and seen something special. I sure as shit had never felt it.

"Be good," I told him, and then I fucking winked. I was playing a dangerous game, but I couldn't find it in myself to stop.

"I'm always good, baby," he said with this sexy, flirtatious confidence in his voice, and fuck, my cock was really in the game now, swelled and aching.

"We're getting offtrack here." I fought to keep my thoughts off how good Kellan would be and on the topic at hand. "You want to know why I wanted to be a cop?"

He set his beer on the patio table and leaned forward, a little wrinkle between his brows as he concentrated on me. "Yeah."

"Because of your parents. What happened to them that night, and the fact that it was never solved. I couldn't fucking deal with that shit, ya know? I want to protect people the way your parents should have been protected."

Kellan stood there for a moment, looking at me, those eyes of his studying me and penetrating all my defenses. "Holy shit, Chase. That's…" Then he walked over to me, and I held my breath like a scared virgin, as if I hadn't shared my bed with countless men and women over the years. This wasn't the same, though, and it wasn't about sex, despite my dick being hard enough to pound nails. I was horny, but there was emotion behind it, because Kellan had always meant something to me. And that was new for me.

He put his hands on my hips and dropped his forehead against mine. "Thank you for telling me that. I know you're not good with stuff like that, and…wow, Chase. You really went into law enforcement for my parents?"

"Yeah," I admitted, my voice rough.

"You forget about yourself too…to protect people

like you should have been protected."

I knew he meant my dad, and I sure as shit didn't want to go there. Things sucked with him, but they could have been worse. "Nah, I was fine."

"You shouldn't have had to be fine. You should have been happy."

"I was happy when I was with you guys."

We were looking at each other then, Kellan's sea-green eyes firmly on mine. And he was close, so fucking close. His fingers started to move on my hips, pushed under my shirt so he was touching me, skin to skin. My brain had no say in the matter, and then my hands were lifting and I was cupping his face, brushing my thumbs against his cheekbones.

Fuck…what in the hell were we doing?

Kellan answered my silent question by leaning in and brushing his lips against mine. Just that quickly, my mouth was open and I was dipping my tongue inside his, tasting him and swallowing his groans. He pushed against me, his cock along mine, rubbing, and fuck, it went to my head and I was kissing him harder, tangling my hands in his hair until he pulled back and tried to go to his knees. "Kell…"

"It's okay. I love sucking guys off. I'm a lot better than I was at eighteen."

It was that last part that woke me up, and my dick was going to hate me because when he tried to lower himself again, I stopped him. "We can't."

"Why not? You obviously want it." His eyes darted toward my bulge.

"You know why."

"Griff? Jesus fucking Christ, grow a pair already, Chase. He's my brother, not my fucking owner. If I want to blow someone, I'll blow them. If we want to hook up, we can hook up."

"It's not that easy for me. You and Griff are the only family I have. I can't lose that, and you know we would. What would happen when Griff found out? When shit went sideways? I don't really do the relationship thing." Because I sure as shit wasn't ever going to open myself up to losing someone I cared about, and definitely not when it was Kellan or Griff.

"Um…what about me trying to blow you on your back deck made you think I was looking for a relationship? I just wanted to suck cock."

"Oh God." I rubbed my hands over my face. "I can't get used to you saying shit like that."

"Now *that* is a good reason for us not to do this. If you can't handle me talking about liking dick, you still see me as a little brother."

In some ways I did…but in others I sure as fuck didn't. Because I wanted him. Wanted him so damn bad, I could hardly breathe. I felt the same thing at twenty-two. The same way when I'd thought about him over the years.

"Let's just…sit down. I want to finish having this meal with you, and then we're going to watch *Nightmare on Elm Street* because that was your favorite as a kid."

Kellan frowned. "You remember that?"

"Yeah, because it was weird. Even back then it was an old-ass movie. It's basically ancient now."

"Older scary movies are the best. You have so much to learn."

"Sit down." I rolled my eyes at him playfully.

"No, I don't think I will. You cook. I'm going into your bathroom to rub one out real quick, since someone can't finish me."

"Oh, I could make you come so hard, your brain melted," fell out of my mouth.

"But you won't, so I'm going to do it myself."

"Are you serious?"

"As a heart attack." With that, Kellan went inside, and I was left standing there dumbfounded. Holy fuck. Kellan was going to my bathroom to jerk off, and all I could think was what a fucking idiot I was for not going with him, or doing it for him, or getting on my knees for him.

Grumbling, I continued cooking, and he came back a few minutes later, his bulge gone and a smile on his face again. Fucking Kellan Caine would be the death of me. I had lost my mind and passed up a really good opportunity.

We talked about random shit as I made our dinner—places I'd been, things I'd done, and Kellan told me more about his shop and his art.

We were sitting down and eating together when he cleared his throat and asked, "Have you seen your dad yet?"

"No." I shook my head, feeling my gut twist up. I wasn't looking forward to being reunited with him. "Being a cop here...it's ironic. He's going to lose his shit."

"He doesn't deserve to even speak to you, Chase. He never has. I hope you don't forget it."

"No," I said quietly, watching him. "I won't."

And like always, I felt better. The Caine family had a way of doing that for me. Kellan maybe more so than the rest, even though I'd never let myself admit it until that moment.

# CHAPTER SEVEN

## *Kellan*

I COULDN'T BELIEVE how quickly I'd fallen into the trap of Chase Hawthorne again. Okay, maybe I could believe it because he was hot as hell and I'd known I wasn't over him, but still. And how could I not want him when he was so vulnerable? I wasn't sure most people saw that side of Chase, but I always had. Whether it was him comforting me after my parents' death, or sticking up for me with bullies, or admitting to me he was bi because he knew it would help me come to terms with my own sexuality. It had always been those things that endeared Chase to me, and yes, it didn't hurt that he was gorgeous.

But going into law enforcement for my parents? God, he wrapped me up. Did shit to me I didn't think he could ever understand. He hadn't done it because he was an abused child with an alcoholic parent. He'd done it for Griff and me. And it was *so* Chase that I couldn't even be surprised.

So I'd had to kiss him and try to blow him again, because apparently I was crazy. No wonder they thought they had to keep tabs on me. I was a bit of a loose cannon.

It had been a few days since what I referred to in my head as *the incident*. I hadn't told Nat or Josh about it because…well, because it was embarrassing, if I was being honest. At some point I needed to realize that Chase didn't want me the way I wanted him, at least not enough to go for it. There were other men who did, though, and they sure as shit didn't turn me down.

"How's this, Kellan?" Ava, one of my students, asked.

"Oh, wow. That's beautiful. Add a little more water to your hands, though. That'll help." And clearly, I needed to stop thinking about Chase, especially when I was teaching a class.

Pushing thoughts of Chase out of my head, I went around the room, checking with each of the children and giving them pointers. Before I knew it, class was over. Everyone's parents had picked them up, except Ava's, which meant her dad was coming. When her mom picked her up, she was always on time, but on the weekends her dad got her, he was late. Honestly, I was surprised he let her take classes with me when he took her for the weekend—me being queer and all. Buck was that kind of guy.

"Do you have any plans this weekend?" I asked Ava, trying to make conversation.

"My brother has a game this afternoon. He doesn't wanna play, but Dad makes him. He asked if he could come here instead, but Dad said it would make him soft like you." Ava smiled, having no idea what she'd just said. I didn't give a shit about me. Her dad could think whatever the fuck he wanted about me, and he did. He'd been a senior when I first got into high school, and he'd been one of the first to call me a fag, but it broke my heart when I thought about his son. That he was being forced to play sports he didn't love and had an interest in art that his asshole of a father would stifle.

It was times like this I wanted as far away from Havenwood as I could get, but I wasn't sure I could ever truly leave. As much as I complained about Griffin, I couldn't imagine not living close to him and seeing him all the time.

"I'm sorry to hear that," I said to Ava, and made a mental note to talk to her mom. Bridget was a great woman with an asshole of an ex, and I didn't think she would be okay with the way he was treating her son.

Hell, I'd let him take classes for free if she would allow it.

Just then the door opened, and Ava's dad, Buck, came in with his father, Jimmy. "Let's go," he told her, nodding toward the door without so much as a word to me. Jimmy's eyes snagged on me, a hateful glare I could feel. I hated people like them, and I sure as shit wasn't going to let them win.

So I smiled and pretended I didn't notice. "Ava did great today. She's really talented." I had to bite my tongue to be nice to him, but the last thing I wanted was to make it more difficult for either of his kids to take my class.

Buck grunted. His father shook his head, and then the three of them walked out, which sadly, again, was nothing new. Buck worked out at Josh's gym and would never treat Josh the way he did me. It wasn't a phrase I liked to use, but Josh could pass for straight, so that made him "better" to some people. I was too *soft*, too feminine for someone like Buck.

That made the rest of my day shitty. I had a few more classes, but Ava's brother—damn it, I didn't even know the kid's name—never left my thoughts. I'd been lucky. I'd had great parents and Griff, who would have supported me in whatever the hell I wanted to do. I might have had to deal with assholes like Buck sometimes, but I had a support system, and not everyone had that.

At the end of the day, I closed up shop and headed to the house. My favorite thing to do after a shitty day was take a bath, so I filled the tub, added bubbles, and sank in.

As much as I tried to clear my head, all I could do was think about Chase…about his dad…about Griff…Griff and Chase, and me and Chase, and stupid fucking Chase Hawthorne. "Get out of my head!" I grumbled into the empty bathroom.

Which he did, for the moment at least, but then I was obsessing about Ava's brother and Buck and his asshole dad. Maybe it would be better for me to get out of Havenwood. I could always come back.

Realizing nothing was going to happen besides me sitting there obsessing about things, I let the water out, dried off, and got dressed.

It was early in the day, but I went over to Nat's because talking with her always helped. "Hey, you," she said when I went inside.

"Hi. I'm miserable." I plopped down on her couch. "And don't call me dramatic."

Natalie laughed. "I wouldn't think of it." She curled up beside me and set her head on my shoulder. "Chase

Hawthorne?"

"Yeah. I tried to blow him again." It wasn't something I'd planned to admit, but obviously that shit had needed to come out.

"Oh my God. Are you serious?"

"Ugh! Yes. I know it was stupid, but it's not just him. I really do love sucking dick."

"Nope. You're right. It has nothing to do with this being Chase."

"I think I need to get him out of my system somehow, ya know? He was this unachievable goal, and then I had him once and he bailed, so maybe I need him again and to be the one to walk away…or the one to show I don't need him. I'm sure that makes no sense."

"No," Natalie replied. "In a strange way it does, but I still think there's more to it than that, and I believe it's a bad idea."

She was right. Of course she was right.

"Maybe you and Josh should go to Richmond tonight?"

"But then we'd have to leave you, and I can't bear to be away from you."

She laughed, seeing my reply for exactly what it was—a lie because I didn't want another guy; I wanted Chase. Maybe I really did need to prove that I could have him and walk away.

Her phone buzzed on the coffee table, and she leaned forward and grabbed it. "It's Josh. He wants to know what we're doing."

"Tell him to come over. We can get started drinking a little early tonight, before the three musketeers go take over Griff's stupid straight bar."

"Hey, I might need that straight bar if I'm ever going to find a man myself."

I kissed her cheek. No one deserved to be happy more than Natalie. "You're not the kind of girl to meet the love of her life from a random hookup at a bar."

"Hey! I could be. You don't know." She sighed. "But you're probably right. Do you know where I'll meet him, though? I'm ready."

"You're the best, Nat. Boys are dumb."

"That they are…besides you and Josh, of course. Straight ones, bi guys, gay guys. They all suck."

"I mean, we do that too."

Natalie laughed, and I laughed too, which I really needed. It wasn't long before Josh showed up, and the three of us had a couple drinks to get ready for our night out. With them there with me, Chase Hawthorne didn't matter so much. I had my best friends who loved me, and I'd made more of a life for myself than I'd ever really thought I would. That was enough. If Chase didn't see how fucking fabulous I was, it was his loss.

# CHAPTER EIGHT

## *Chase*

GRIFF'S WAS BUSY as shit, which I guess shouldn't surprise me as it was a Friday night. It wasn't as if there were a lot of other things to do.

My friend was working his ass off behind the counter, along with another bartender—a woman named Kerry—and a waitress working the floor. His friends Knox and Lawson sat at the far end. It was where they had been the last time I'd seen them, almost as if Griff reserved it as their spot. A stool was set behind the bar, and I wondered if Griff had held it back there for me.

It was strange seeing new people in Havenwood. There were many faces I didn't recognize. It felt like the town had stayed the same the whole time I grew up, with all the same people, and now there were people like Knox, whose past I didn't know and who had no idea about mine, unless someone ran their mouth. Law grew up around here, but we hadn't been friends. Still, I knew who he was.

"Hey, man. What's up?" Knox said when I approached. He had this black, shaggy hair that he continuously pushed behind his ears so it didn't fall into his face. He was a big guy, tall and muscular, reminding me of a lumberjack. Gorgeous as fuck, though not my usual type.

"Hey," I replied.

Law turned and nodded at me. He was muscular too, though more sinewy than Knox, his body more slender, but equally gorgeous with those blond curls of his.

"How was your day fighting crime in Havenwood?" Law asked, and we all laughed as I stood beside him.

"This is for you." Knox grabbed the stool I'd seen and slid it over to me.

"Thanks. And to answer your question, someone stole a garden gnome out of Old Lady Benson's yard, and she doesn't want me to rest until I find it. Curtis Webb called to make sure the rumors were true and I really was a police officer in Havenwood. And I got a call about someone drunk in Cherry Hill Park." Thank fuck it hadn't been my father. I'd been worried it was. We hadn't crossed paths yet, and I didn't look forward to when we did, especially if I had to go out on a call and it was him.

Lawson laughed. "Sounds like you could use a beer."

"You can say that again."

Griff made his way down to us and brought a bottle of Corona with him, which was what I typically drank. "Hey, man. Glad you could make it down." He handed it over.

"Feels good to be out." Good to be out in Havenwood. "This place is great." This was the first time I'd been to Griff's on a weekend. He'd made a good life for himself. I watched a couple of people come up to him to chat, and it was obvious everyone still loved him.

It had always been that way for Griff, but not for Kellan, which pissed me off. People could be such assholes sometimes. But then, what did I know? I was comparing eighteen-year-old Kell to the twenty-eight-year-old he was now.

As soon as they left, Griff turned to reply to me but was caught up with someone else who wanted his advice. People respected the hell out of Griff, they listened to him, valued his opinion, which I understood because I was the same way with him.

"Sorry, what were we saying?" he asked when he had a moment, and I waved him off. He took an order and began mixing a drink but looked at me. "You happy being back home?"

"Still getting used to shit, but yeah." What I didn't mention was the fact that I'd had Kellan over for dinner and stuck my tongue down his throat. Griff wouldn't want to hear about that.

"Jesus fuck, who is that?" Law said.

"Jesus fuck?" Knox laughed and playfully shoved him.

Still, all our eyes went toward the door as a leggy blonde with a huge rack walked in. She definitely wasn't from around here. I hadn't been home long, but I sure as shit would have known if she was a local.

"Dibs!" Law called, and I rolled my eyes.

"You can't call dibs on her, asshole. She's a person." But I'd be lying if I didn't admit to being attracted to her too. She walked with this sultry sort of swagger and had a smile that could knock you on your ass.

"You're jealous I said it before you."

I shrugged because he was right, which made a small twinge of guilt pinch at me. There was no reason I should feel guilt over thinking someone was beautiful, but damned if a pair of expressive green eyes didn't pop into my head.

*Imaginary Kellan Caine...go away. I don't want you!*

How long would I have to tell myself that before I believed it?

Behind blondie, another woman came in who was just as gorgeous, but her, *her* I recognized. "Becca's still here?" I said even though she was obviously standing across the room from me.

"You mean, people other than you and me leave Havenwood?" Law asked, and Griff chuckled.

"Yeah. Did I forget to mention that?" Griff waggled his eyebrows at me.

I'd never been serious about anyone in my life, but there was a time when I'd wondered if I could have been with Becca. I'd lost my virginity to her, and we'd fucked on and off through high school. Griff took her best friend to prom, and I'd taken Becca. She wanted something serious then, but I turned her down, and she started dating…fuck, I couldn't even remember who. It lasted a couple of years, but when they broke up, she and I became fuck buddies again.

"I always said if Chase ever settled down, it would be with Becca, but then I remembered I was talking about Chase and there was no way that asshole was settling down," Griff joked.

I flipped my friend off playfully as Knox and Law laughed with him.

"Says the group of equally single guys?" I threw back at them. I wasn't in this shit alone. Hell, Law had called dibs on the woman.

"Hey, I've been married before," Knox replied. "Sure as shit not going there again."

"You can say that again, brother." Law clanked his beer with Knox's. "Though I haven't been married, but I don't plan on it."

Griff added, "This fucker got laid everywhere we went. I swear to Christ it was like he had some magic formula or something." As if Griff couldn't have done the same. He never did because he'd chosen not to.

"Viagra?" Knox teased.

"Aw, does Knoxy struggle to get it up?" Law tossed back at him.

"Fuck you. I can assure you that's not a problem." Knox grabbed his cock for good measure.

"This one time…" Griff launched into stories about our adventures when we were younger and precarious situations he'd caught me in. I couldn't say he was lying. It hadn't stopped after I left Havenwood either, except I added men to the mix now. While I sure as shit never planned on giving my heart away, I didn't have the same qualms about getting my dick wet.

We went back and forth between the four of us, Griff going off to make drinks and making his way back to us when he could. It became a discussion of sex and sports because both went well with beer.

Knox and Law were great. I liked them and felt like I would get along well with both of them. As far as I knew they were both straight, but every once in a while I caught Lawson giving me a look that made me wonder…and one that probably wasn't recognizable to anyone who wasn't looking for it.

"Holy shit!" a female voice said behind me, and I knew without looking that it was Becca. "Chase Hawthorne, is that really you?"

I turned around just as Griff said, "Aw, come on, Bec. Don't pretend you didn't know he was back. This is Havenwood."

"Stop ruining my game, Caine." She flipped him off, and I smiled because she was still the Becca I knew.

"Hey. It's good to see you." I pushed off the stool and gave her a hug. She wrapped her arms around me tightly. I'd missed her. Bec had always been a fun girl to hang around.

"It's so good to see you, Chase. You look *good*."

"Thanks, Bec. You too."

We pulled back, and she signaled to the blonde with her. "This is my cousin Cynthia. She moved from Baltimore to stay with me for a while. Cynthia, this is Chase, Lawson, Knox, and Griff."

Cynthia's eyes lingered on Griff longer than the rest of us. Griff noticed she wanted him, but he rarely hooked up. Griffin was the guy who took people he cared about seriously, and I couldn't ever see him having meaningless relationships.

I offered Becca my seat, and both Knox and Law scrambled off theirs for Cynthia, who turned them both down, which meant they continued to stand because they sure as shit weren't sitting while a woman was standing. I did the same.

"I can't believe you're back," Becca said. "What have you been up to?"

I told her a little about the past ten years of my life, and Becca did the same. Griff gave everyone a drink, then another, but I'd said no. Becca touched me more and more as we spoke, and I had to admit, I liked her hands on me. She was gorgeous, always had been, and we were both single, so why not?

Her hand found a spot at the back of my neck, and she danced her fingers through the hair at my nape. Fuck, I'd always loved that. Felt like a dog, and any minute I'd be shaking my leg, it felt so good. Becca looked over at me and winked because she knew I liked it.

There was a noise behind me, coming from the door.

When I looked over, Kellan was walking in with Natalie and Josh, who had his arm around him. Our eyes locked immediately, like they were drawn together and he knew I would be exactly where I was, looking back at him. I shifted suddenly, the weight of Becca's hand on my neck too heavy, but then Kellan looked away from me. Josh kissed the top of his head, and the three of them went to the other side of the bar, toward the pool tables.

"Chase?" Becca said, and from the sound of it, I could tell it wasn't the first time she'd said my name.

I pulled my attention away from Kellan and his friends. "Sorry, what did you say?"

"Do you want another beer?"

"Nah, I'm good, thanks. Gotta drive tonight. How's everyone getting home?" I asked, because I had to.

"I don't drink. I'm at work," Griff said.

"Cynthia's my DD," Becca added.

Both Law and Knox said something about a car service, and then they gave me shit, calling me *sir* and asking if I was going to arrest them.

"What's up?" I heard from the other side of me, Josh's voice rubbing me the wrong way. I didn't get this guy and his friendship with Kellan. Was it more than we thought? But then, would Kellan have tried to hook up with me?

"Hey, man. You guys want your usual?" Griff asked him. "And Kell can't even come say hi to me? He sends you?"

"Kellan has already had a few too many, and he's getting demanding. You know how he is, and when Kellan wants something, he gets it."

I didn't have to look to know Josh's eyes darted to me when he said that. I couldn't stop myself from wondering if Kellan had ever wanted Josh and if he'd had him.

"Better you than me, brother. He's spoiled as shit is what he is," Griff replied as he made drinks.

"Eh, what are friends for? I know a good thing when I see it, and I know how to appreciate it."

Oh, fuck him. I hated Kellan's friend. The guy obviously wasn't going to stop busting my balls.

"What's wrong with Kell?" Griff asked, and as soon as he said it, I knew something must be. If Griff said it, it was true. Those two could read each other like no one's business.

"Some guy was an asshole at the shop. He's fine. Kellan is a big boy, and he can take care of himself," Josh challenged, and I had to admit, the kid had balls because no one challenged Griff when it came to Kellan. I was surprised when Griff simply nodded.

"What happened?" I couldn't stop myself from asking. "Is someone harassing him?"

Josh shrugged. "Not my place to say, Officer." He took their drinks and walked away.

Did I mention I really fucking hated Josh? Because I really did.

The conversation continued around me. Becca still played with my hair, but it didn't feel as good anymore. My eyes kept finding their way back to Kellan and his friends. They were playing pool, and he was laughing that contagious fucking laugh of his. He sat on Josh's lap at one point, the other guy's muscular arms around Kellan's waist, and this stab of jealousy pierced through my chest.

Fuck, what was wrong with me? I needed to evict this shit with Kellan out of me. I had no business wanting to fuck my best friend's little brother…but I did. I'd wanted to fuck him for ten years, and that shit didn't seem to be going away.

# CHAPTER NINE

## *Kellan*

"**I**'M FEELING VERY used right now," Josh said into my ear.

"You're poking my ass with your hard cock. I think you're getting something out of this too." I shifted to tease him. Griff's was the only straight bar in the world I would feel comfortable doing this, and it was less because of Havenwood and more because it was Griff's and everyone knew there was no bigotry here.

"Eh, what do you expect when I have a pretty boy on my lap? I'm only so strong."

I looked back at him over my shoulder and rolled my eyes.

"It's a good thing you're my best friend and I don't see you like that," Josh added.

"Your dick doesn't seem to agree."

He shrugged. "My dick doesn't get us."

No…no, it didn't. "I love you." I kissed him quickly

on the lips. I really did love him. The day Josh had come into my life, my whole world had changed. He was the one person in my world who cared about me and had no connection to my past or my brother. It was all about me for Josh, and that felt good. Even with Nat, I loved her like crazy, but she wanted to bone my brother. That wasn't why we were friends, but it was still a fact.

"Your man is seething over there. I thought he was going to punch me," Josh said.

"He's not my man."

"What did I miss?" Nat asked as she came back from the bathroom. "Is Chase still shooting daggers out of his eyes at Josh?"

The three of us laughed, and I knew Chase was watching. I looked over and cocked a brow at him, and then Becca—*the* Becca—who I was pretty sure Chase would end up with again, said something to him.

Damned if he didn't turn around and look at me again, this sadness there I didn't really understand. It twisted me up and snatched my breath, making me wiggle and get off Josh's lap.

"What's wrong?" Josh asked.

"Nothing. I…need to go take a leak." Which was a lie. Still, I made my way to the bathroom. There was a guy at one of the urinals. I went to the sink and washed my hands, then splashed some water on my face. It was ridiculous, the way Chase affected me. It made me feel weak, and honestly, sort of pathetic. I *hated* that, but I didn't know how to fix it.

The guy pissing finished, washed his hands, and walked out. When I didn't hear the sound of the door closing, I looked up and saw Chase standing in the doorway, watching me. He stepped inside, and the sound of the door shutting echoed through the room.

"Do you fuck Josh?"

Oh…well, this was interesting. "Why do you want to know? Jealous?"

"Shit," Chase gritted out, running his hands through his hair, then fisting them in it, tugging on the strands.

That was new. Chase had never had this reaction to me before. He was pacing the bathroom like he didn't know what to do, like he couldn't stay still, and watching him, I felt a tightness in my chest. "Chase?"

As soon as his name left my mouth, he was on me. I didn't know how he even got to me so quickly, but suddenly his mouth was crushing mine and we were stumbling backward toward one of the stalls.

My back slammed against the wall.

"Shit. I'm sorry," Chase said as his mouth made its way down my neck.

"Don't be. I like it a little rough."

He growled against my skin, and then he was kissing me again and we were in the stall and shoving the door closed in the bathroom of my very protective brother's *straight* bar.

But it was Chase, and *he* was kissing *me*. I was always the one who kissed him first, but now it was his hand knotted in my shirt and his other hand grabbing my ass as he bit at my lip and let his tongue taste every millimeter of my mouth.

"Fuck…why do we keep ending up this way?" he asked, then bit into my shoulder, making a tremble rock through me.

"I want you." I grabbed his cock through his jeans, pressing the palm of my hand against his thick rod. "God, I want this stretching me out."

And then…then he wasn't kissing and he wasn't holding me. His hands fell away, and he closed his eyes, dropping his head against the wall. I knew…fucking *knew* he was going to put a stop to this again.

"Fuck you, Chase," I gritted out.

"Not here," he replied, which was definitely not what I was expecting. When he opened his eyes, those big brown irises trained on me, I saw what he was saying.

Still, I asked, "Excuse me?"

"Not here. We can't do this here. Fuck, Griff would kill me. I can't believe I'm in the bathroom stall with you. But I just…"

He didn't finish, and somehow I knew he wouldn't. It killed me. I so wanted to know what in the fuck he was going to say. He just…what? Couldn't help how much he wanted me? Needed his hands on me? There were so many possibilities, and not all of them were good. But then, I figured we were destined to end up this way. It would happen, and then I'd walk away. "Just once," I finally replied. "That's all we need." It was the biggest lie I'd ever told because I knew to the marrow of my bones that once with Chase Hawthorne would never be enough for me.

"Yeah, okay. Just once. And then we'll know, and the novelty will wear off. It's not like either of us is looking for anything serious."

He wasn't wrong. I wasn't looking for anything serious and never had been, but that didn't stop him from being serious to me. Fucking Chase Hawthorne and the way my stupid heart bled for him. "We'll get it out of our systems, and then I'll go back to being Griff's annoying but sexy little brother who you don't want to fuck."

He smiled, but it looked a little broken, like there

was pain behind it. "I, um...I'll go first. You hang out in the bar another ten minutes or so, and then come around the back. I have my truck there. You can come home with me. Will Griff wonder where you are?"

"I'm twenty-eight, Chase. Jesus, I don't have to ask my brother's permission to stay out all night. I don't come home plenty." I really needed to get my own place, but for now, staying in our childhood home worked. We both loved it there, and it wasn't as if I was raking in the big bucks teaching pottery and art to kids.

"Okay, let's do this." He nodded, didn't look at me, and walked out.

I waited a couple of minutes and then went back into the bar, but made myself not look over at Chase.

"You have whisker burn on your neck," Natalie said.

"I don't know what you're talking about."

"Holy shit, Kell. What happened in there?" she asked, but I shook my head, and she hugged me.

"I'm going to leave in about ten minutes."

"I'll go too," Nat replied, and I kissed the top of her head in a quiet thanks. That would help. If it seemed like I was leaving with Nat, it would appear more natural. It was shitty that I had to hide this, that I had to sneak around to fuck someone I wanted. Usually, it was something I refused to hide, but this was Chase, and he loved my brother more than anything in the world. I would never forgive myself if I came between them.

*Then why do you keep finding yourself in Chase's arms?*

Shit. Consciences were annoying.

"He just left," Josh said, then held my chin and turned my head so I faced him. "Are you sure you know what you're doing? This isn't only fucking for you."

I tried to swallow the boulder in my throat, but it wouldn't go down. Josh was right. This would be more than fucking for me, but that wasn't going to stop me from doing it, from having him. Having Chase once was better than not having him at all, even if it did end up breaking me. "Yeah, I'm good. It'll be fine."

"I question your taste in men. What is it about that guy?" Josh asked. "I kind of hate him."

"You don't know him like I do. He's a good guy, J." Chase was the kid who had been looking for love and acceptance and found it in my family. The guy who would do anything for someone who was important to him, even though the world hadn't been kind to him. "He doesn't want to hurt me. It's not his fault I'm in love with him, and it's not like he knows." If he knew, he sure as shit wouldn't be taking me home tonight.

Josh nodded but didn't look convinced. "Be careful, babe," he said, then, "You two head out."

Josh stood and went to the bar as Nat and I went for the door. "I'll order a car for you," I told her, and she shook me off.

"I'm a big girl. I can do it."

Still, I waited for it to arrive and then saw her inside safely. Chase would understand why I was late. When the vehicle pulled away, I walked around the west side of the building and to the back, where I saw Chase sitting in his truck by the side of the road.

I stumbled, caught myself, took a deep breath. We were really doing this. I was going to hook up with Chase Hawthorne, even though I knew it was the biggest mistake I would ever make.

# CHAPTER TEN

## *Chase*

THERE WAS NO question in my mind that this was a mistake, but I was going to do it anyway, because fuck, I wanted him. He was gorgeous, obviously, but that wasn't even what this was about. There was just something about Kellan, and I couldn't get it out of my system. It had been ten fucking years, and it was still there, as if his kiss had unlocked something inside me that I hadn't been able to close since.

"Did Becca expect to go home with you?" he asked as I drove out to my place. It was the first time either of us had spoken since Kellan got into my truck.

"Don't know, but she gave me her phone number," I replied, wanting to be honest. Kellan and I were just hooking up, we weren't committed, and hell, I didn't know if anything would happen with Becca in the future or if I wanted it to, but I also wasn't going to lie about her to Kell.

We were quiet the rest of the way back to my place. The motion detector light came on when we pulled in. Kellan put his hand on the door, and mine went to his arm. "You sure you're okay with this?"

"Don't treat me like I'm a kid. It's fucking. Why wouldn't I be okay with it?"

When he put it like that, it made sense. I opened my mouth to say so, but Kellan spoke first. "I love that you ask, though. Typical Chase."

I cocked a brow at him. "What does that mean?"

"Nothing. And can we use your handcuffs? That's always been a fantasy of mine."

Damned if my dick didn't twitch at the thought of locking Kellan's hands behind his back, fucking his throat…

"Ooh, someone likes that. You groaned."

"Get your ass in the house. I hope you're ready for a long night." If I was only going to have him tonight, I planned on having him more than once, in every position that I could.

"Yes, Officer." Kellan winked, and I knew right then and there that I was fucked. There was no turning back from this, and it would change things, maybe in ways I didn't even understand yet.

We scrambled out of my truck and were both running for my front door like a couple of horny teenagers about to get laid for the first time.

My hands were shaking as I tried to unlock the door.

"Hurry!" Kellan said, pushing my arm. The keys fumbled from my grasp and to the porch.

We both bent to pick them up at the same time, and our heads smacked together. We stopped, looked at each other, and laughed.

Christ, I had fun with him. He could always make me laugh. I wondered if he knew that. He had this electric personality that made me feel…light. "You stand, I'll bend." He nodded, and I knelt for the keys. I could see the bulge in his tight pants, so I palmed it, rubbed him through his jeans. It was as if my hand was drawn to him. Even if I'd wanted to, I couldn't have held back from touching him. And I definitely didn't want to hold back. "You're fucking dying for it, aren't you?"

"Oh shit." Kellan leaned back against the door and grabbed on to my hair. "I felt your dick earlier. You are too." I could tell he was trying not to sound as hungry for me as he was, and that made me smile. It felt good that Kellan wanted me as desperately as I wanted him.

"Never said I wasn't. I can't wait to take you apart." I leaned in, nipped at his erection through his pants. Kellan whimpered, and I shoved to my feet.

"You're a mean, mean man, Chase Hawthorne."

This time, it was me who winked at him. "I'll be real good to you, Kell. I promise."

Finally, I managed to get the door unlocked, and we stumbled inside together, kissing. He tasted so fucking good. I kicked the door closed, dropped the keys, and wrapped my arms around him as he moaned into my mouth.

I lifted him, still fucking kissing, and his legs went around my waist as I made my way to my room. God, I wanted to make him come undone, put him back together, and then take him apart again and again. He went straight to my head, made me dizzy. Made my goddamned cock ache.

The second I got to my room and turned on the light, I dropped him on the bed. Kellan kicked out of his shoes, rolled right off, and went to his knees, deftly working the button and zipper on my jeans.

"I'm going to blow your mind."

I laughed. "Blow my mind while you blow my cock? Somehow, I don't doubt that."

"Aww, that might be the sweetest thing you've ever said to me." And then he was shoving my pants down to my knees and sucking on me through my boxer briefs. "Fuck, you smell good." He inhaled.

"Christ, you're gonna kill me before we even get started."

"I can't help it. I love sucking dick." Kellan mouthed me through my underwear. There was a wet spot. I was aching and already dying to come.

"Take me out. I want in your mouth."

"Yes, Officer," he replied, and my bones melted.

I tilted his head up and looked at him. "We playing that game?"

"Could be fun."

There was no *could* about it.

He pulled my underwear and pants down my legs. I stepped out of them, along with my shoes, and ran my hand through Kellan's hair. I had a moment of panic about being there with him, but pushed it away. We were adults. We wanted each other. We would have each other and then move on.

"I didn't get to properly admire this last time. You have a great dick, Chase." Kellan stroked my erection. "It's really fucking thick."

"Get your mouth around it," I rushed out. I needed him. We had one night, and I planned to take advantage of it.

"My pleasure." Kellan took me deep, all the way to the back of his throat, swallowed me down, his nose buried in my pubes.

"Jesus fucking Christ, Kell, you're good at that." I was about to embarrass myself and end this before we had time to get started. Not that he would struggle to get me hard again, but I wanted it to last, so I pulled out, grabbed the base of my shaft, and traced his lips before pushing the head inside. "Tease me a bit, unless you're ready for a mouthful of come."

"You won't hear me complain about that."

My knees went weak, almost gave out on me, and Kellan laughed, then said, "You lead the way."

So I did. I took control, and he let me, fucking into his mouth in slow, short strokes. He wrapped his arms around me, holding on to my ass, and my hand was still in his hair, and holy fuck, Kell looked good on his knees for me.

I got myself under control a bit and took it deeper, thrusting into his mouth. My balls were heavy and tight, and my skin felt sensitive, so I pulled out and tugged him to his feet. "Take your clothes off. I didn't get to suck you last time."

"I definitely like the sound of that, Officer Hawthorne."

Kellan made quick work of his clothes as I pulled my shirt off. Then he was standing naked in front of me, and we were both breathing heavily. He was shorter and thinner than I was, but had tight, firm muscles. His dick stood tall, the tip leaking. He was long and veiny with shortly trimmed pubes I wanted my nose buried in. And was that… "You have a tattoo?"

"Kind of. I mean, obviously, but it's only a heart on my hip bone." Surprisingly, he looked shy as he said it, this light pink flush to his cheeks.

"It's sexy as hell. Get on the bed so I can taste it."

Kellan laughed and fell onto the mattress. I knelt between his legs and pushed him back so he lay down, then licked his tattoo.

"Oh fuck, why is that so hot?"

I licked it again. His skin tasted sweaty and salty, and I fucking loved it, so I went to his other hip bone, then the inside of his thighs, but kept away from his cock and balls.

"Chase Hawthorne is a tease. Why am I not surprised?"

"I'm not a tease…just getting started."

He spread his legs and wrapped a hand around his cock. I swatted it away. Kellan obeyed and didn't touch himself. I nipped at the skin of his inner thighs, savoring the taste of him and the little whimpers that pulled from the back of his throat.

"Chase…get your mouth on my dick!" he called out, and I chuckled into the crease at his groin.

"That's Officer Hawthorne to you," I teased. "And you're not the boss of me."

"Oh God. I'm having flashbacks. How many times have I said that to you?"

"But I think you really wanted me to be the boss of you, Kell. Now shut up so I can suck your dick." I swallowed him down. I'd be lying if I said I took him as deep as he did me. That I could work my throat around his cock the way he did, but from the way he basically thrashed and pulled my hair, I didn't think he minded.

I inhaled the scent of him, musk and something sweet. That was Kellan, though. He'd always been sweet beneath the surface. He just didn't let that show.

I pulled off and stroked him as I went to suck his smooth, tight balls.

He pulled my hair, gasped, and thrust up into my mouth, making me gag. "Sorry," he groaned. "Fuck, you feel good. I can't believe Chase Hawthorne is blowing me."

"Believe it," I told him, then tried to go deep on him again. His body jolted, and I tasted precome on my tongue before he pushed me off.

"That feels too fucking good. You're going to make

me come, and I want to do that with your dick in my ass. Please fuck me, Chase."

Glancing up at him from between his legs, I grinned. Goose bumps spread across my oversensitive body. I liked pleasuring Kellan. Maybe I liked it too much. "Since you asked so nicely...I guess I'll give you my cock."

"Oh, fuck you." He playfully pushed away from me. I grabbed him and held him in place.

"On the contrary, I'm going to fuck *you*."

He swallowed and looked up at me with something in his eyes I couldn't describe...but I felt it. Felt it like a touch, a caress against my skin. Just as soon as the look came across his face, it was gone.

"Then get your ass going with it. I'm getting bored."

A laugh tumbled out of my mouth. I should have known fucking Kellan would be fun.

# CHAPTER ELEVEN

## *Kellan*

I HAD TO admit, I was pretty proud of the fact that I was in bed with Chase and not freaking the fuck out about it. Cool, confident, and detached was the theme I was going for, when the whole time there was a voice in my head saying, *I love you. Why do I love you?*

Stupid, stupid heart, and stupid, stupid Chase, and *oh…* My body jolted off the bed when he rubbed his finger over my hole.

"You like that?"

"Since it's one step closer to getting fucked, yes." See? I could do this. I could be cool, calm, and collected.

Chase chuckled and shook his head. "What am I going to do with you?"

"I can think of a lot of things." *Love me. You can love me.* Ugh. I was ridiculous. I really needed to get over this, over him. Somehow, I wasn't sure sex was the best way to go about that, but I sure as shit didn't plan on stopping.

Chase grabbed a condom and a bottle of lube from his bedside table. I noticed a bottle of PrEP there, and I didn't know why that surprised me. I was on it too.

Chase knelt behind me, and I pushed my ass higher in the air for him, arching my back prettily so he knew how good I was at this.

"Fuck, you're sexy," he whispered as he danced his fingers down my spine.

"I could say the same to you, Officer Hawthorne."

"Then you should."

"*Fuck*, you're sexy."

Chase grinned, and my pulse sped up. Before I did or said something I shouldn't, I leaned farther down so my face was in the pillow and my ass in the air where he needed it.

A wet finger rubbed against my rim, and I practically fucking purred.

"Christ, this is a pretty hole. You want me inside it?"

"Nah, I'm good," I teased, making him laugh.

"Ask me," Chase said. "Ask me to fuck you."

Oh Lord, he was going to make me come before he even got inside me. I liked this bossy, sexy Chase. "Fuck me, Chase."

He pushed his finger inside, perfectly tormenting me

with it. "You didn't say please."

"You're pushing your luck," I replied, but really, I was pushing my ass back against his fingers and silently begging for more.

Another finger pressed in, stretching me so good, I trembled.

"I'm waiting," he added.

Goddamn, son of a bitch, motherfucking asshole. "Please," I moaned. "Please fuck me, Chase." Even his fingers nearly sent me over the edge, and he was being careful about avoiding my prostate.

"Let me stretch you a little more."

I shook my head. My whole body was vibrating like I was going to burst out of my skin. "I don't need that. I like it when it stings a little more. Just get your cock inside me before I use my fingers on myself instead."

"So impatient." But then he was ripping open the condom and rolling it down his thick rod. He lubed himself up, and then he was there, pressing against my rim, opening me up with the head of his cock and making my eyes roll back in my head.

God, I couldn't believe this was him. That Chase's cock was pressing inside me.

"So good...fuck, you feel good, Kell."

I pushed back on him, giving us both what we needed. We cried out at the same time, and then Chase's hands were tight on my hips and he was fucking into me like his life depended on how hard he could nail me to the mattress. He was so big inside me, stretching my hole, digging his nails into me. Telling me how good I was, and how tight I was, and…

"Fuck…I thought about this… too much."

Chase had thought about fucking me? "Like…for how long?"

He didn't answer, just kept pumping his hips. And it felt good, obviously really fucking good, but I also wanted to know how long he'd been thinking about fucking me.

Suddenly Chase grabbed me and pulled me up so I knelt. He wrapped his arms around me, kissed the back of my neck, and slowed his thrusts, fucking into me with long, measured strides. "Your ass feels so good on my dick. Tell me you want it, Kell."

"I want it…more than anything."

He bit into the spot where my shoulder and neck met, then licked the sting away. He pulled back slightly then, still holding on to my hips. "This is so hot. You should see my cock slide in and out of your ass. Every time I pull out, you're sucking me in again."

"I want to see too," I whined. I mean, if this was

going to be the only time and all…

"Want me to record you?" he said, still dicking me down nice and slow.

"Fuck yesss…" I hissed out, and Chase froze.

"Are you serious?"

"You weren't?" Was I supposed to be embarrassed about that? Because I wasn't. It was hot as hell, if you asked me. "I like to see myself with someone. It's hot. I haven't done it often, but—you haven't?"

"Kellan, do you know how dangerous that is? A video of you could easily get into the wrong hands!"

"Could you not lecture me with your dick in my ass? And that doesn't mean take your dick out. It means shut up and keep fucking me."

Chase growled in response, and then he was railing me hard and fast, dirty and raw. His hips pistoned, slapping against mine, sweat slicking our bodies.

"Christ…need to lock you away, is what I need to do. Keep you handcuffed to my bed so you don't go getting yourself into any trouble."

Like more trouble than fucking my brother's best friend? I didn't mention that part because I didn't want Chase to stop.

"You jealous? Sounds like you're jealous," I teased, and he growled again, which went straight to my dick. I spit in my hand, wrapped it around myself, and stroked as Chase grabbed my face and turned it so he could kiss me. His tongue shoved into my mouth as his dick slammed into my ass. I was pretty sure I disintegrated, went up into ash as I shot my load, mumbling in some make-believe language, because it certainly couldn't be real words I rambled off as I had the most powerful orgasm of my life.

Chase kept fucking into me, holding me against him as his cock spasmed in my hole and he shot his load into the condom. He fell on top of me, and we breathed heavily, a mountain of limbs, sweat, and come.

It was uncomfortable when he pulled out and got off me, and it took everything in me not to ask him to stay.

Chase got rid of the condom and then fell beside me again. "Do you really record yourself having sex?"

"I have once. And I'm a grown-up, so shut up. I don't want to hear it."

He smoothed his hand over my ass, and I whimpered, damn it, pushing it closer toward him.

"That was really good," Chase said.

"Yeah, it was."

"Stupid, but good."

I could have gone without the stupid part.

"Your brother would kill me."

"Can we not talk about Griff when I'm naked, in your bed, and my ass is sore from your cock? Jesus, Chase. Talk about a buzzkill."

"Shit, you're right. I just don't want this to fuck anything up."

With Griff. He didn't want this to fuck anything up with Griffin. Not me. "It won't. We got off. The novelty is gone. It won't happen again. I sure as shit won't tell anyone. I assume you won't either."

I was surprised when I felt his lips against my shoulder, then his tongue slide down my spine. "You taste so fucking good, Kell."

"I'm sweating."

"Maybe I like your sweat."

"Gross." But really, it was hot as fuck. I dug shit like that. I'd lick every drop of sweat off him. "Are you with men often?" I asked, and immediately regretted it.

"Sort of? I mean, I enjoy sex. I'm with women more, I would say."

I didn't know why, but that made me deflate some. He was bisexual, so obviously he enjoyed sex with women. I was sure Chase would end up married to a woman one day, if he ever got serious about anyone.

"Do you ever bottom?" I found myself asking.

"I have a couple of times. It wasn't my favorite." He

kissed his way up my spine, then rolled me over. He leaned on his elbow as I lay on my back looking up at him. "Why do you ask?"

"Dunno. Just curious." I wanted to know everything about him. If he still ate meat pizza and how he took his coffee in the morning. What his favorite color was and if he snored or liked to cuddle.

"Are you usually a top?" Chase asked.

"No." I shook my head. "I'm vers, I guess, but I mostly like to bottom. I love being fucked. I was just being nosy."

I almost died when he dipped his finger in the come on my stomach and sucked it into his mouth. "I'm bummed. This is a one-time thing, and we didn't get to the handcuffs," he said around a grin that settled in my chest. "Though like I said, I can have you more tonight."

One-time thing.

Only tonight.

God, this had been stupid. So fucking stupid. What had I been thinking?

"Yeah, sorry. There's a DO NOT ENTER sign on me for the rest of the night. You plowed me good."

"Are you okay?" His brows pulled together, and I rolled my eyes.

"Yes, Dad. I'm fine."

"That's Officer Dad to you." He winked.

"I should go," I told him and tried to get up, but Chase didn't let me.

"Stay. It's late, and I can suck you again later. Plus, I'd have to take you back to town anyway. I need to be up early, so I can drive you then."

Oh God, oh God, oh God. Chase Hawthorne was asking me to spend the night. In his bed. Maybe in his arms. I was so fucked. This was going to kill me. Still, I replied, "Okay."

"I'll go get something to clean you up."

"No." I shook my head. "Sex is supposed to be messy. Just turn out the light and get back into bed."

He nodded and did as I asked. I figured we would simply lie there, but Chase pulled me close, wrapped his arm around me, and held me. He felt so good...so right. I wasn't surprised when a single tear leaked out and rolled down my cheek.

"I had a good time with you, Kell."

"I had fun too."

He kissed the back of my head and went to sleep. I stayed up most of the night, then sneaked out of bed, got dressed, and got the hell out of there.

I jogged down the driveway, waiting until I got to the road to call Josh.

"Where are you?" he asked, without me having to tell him I needed him to come and get me.

I told him where Chase lived.

"Shit, Kell. I knew this would happen. I'll be right there."

# CHAPTER TWELVE

## *Chase*

I'D BEEN PISSED when I'd woken up to find Kellan gone. With most of my hookups, we never spent the night. When overnights did happen, I'd been the one gone in the morning, or they'd been gone in the morning, and I'd been glad. There had also been hookups where I wished one of us had been gone by morning, but I'd never been angry to wake up alone.

This time I was annoyed as shit.

This was Kellan, and he was important to me, and that made this...different.

It hadn't taken me long to realize there was more than anger there as well—there was disappointment. I had been hoping for a round two. I'd wanted to take Kellan in too many ways to count. We hadn't gotten to use the cuffs, and I really wanted him to come in my mouth the way I'd done to him all those years ago.

But honestly, that wasn't all that had my head spinning. I enjoyed spending time with Kell. He made me feel good, and even though I didn't show it, there wasn't much in my life that made me feel really good.

He was one thing.

Griff was the other.

And didn't that make shit difficult?

So I'd spent the day grumbling at work and basically being an asshole. It was near the end of my shift when dispatch called. "Chase, there's a drunk-and-disorderly call at Grant's. You're the closest, and Roger is out on another call."

The hesitation in her voice told me she knew it was my dad. She obviously didn't want to send me out on this call, but we'd all known this could happen at some point. This was my job, and he was nothing to me, so I cleared my throat and said, "On my way now."

"I'll send Roger over as soon as I can, just in case."

I was only about a minute and a half from Grant's. There was an annoying twist in my stomach as I parked, radioed that I was on scene, and went inside. The moment I did, I heard my dad's voice, and for a second I was that wounded fucking kid again, the one who was scared and alone and whom he'd tortured.

"You can't kick me out of the store! I didn't do anything wrong!"

"Mr. Hawthorne, please lower your voice," one of the employees told him. I walked around the corner in time to see my dad stumble, which was a familiar sight. He had on a pair of cut-off shorts, with no shirt or shoes, his beer belly having grown over the years. He looked…old; fuck, he looked old and belligerent, and the familiar hate I felt for him began to bubble over. Christ, I detested this man.

My eyes scanned the area to see if anyone was with him and also because I was curious if Lawson's dad or brother were there. I hated the thought of a friend's family seeing my father this way. Luckily, they weren't. "Excuse me, what's the problem here?" I asked as I approached.

My dad tensed up and looked at me. "You gotta be fuckin' kiddin' me." He slurred his words.

"He was making a scene because we wouldn't allow him to buy beer. He became angry and was yelling and cursing out one of our cashiers. We also have a dress code, which he isn't adhering to either," the employee answered.

"Fuck you," my father said to him before turning his anger on me. "I heard you were back. Aren't you too much of a pussy to be a police officer? Oh, no, actually, fuck cops. You *are* a pussy, which is why you became one. You couldn't man up to me before. I don't know what makes you think you can do it now."

Bile and hate burned my throat. There was so much I wanted to do, so much I wanted to say. People were beginning to watch, stopping what they were doing to see how I would react to what my dad said. There was nothing I wanted more than to take him down a notch, to show him what it felt like to be bullied or hit by someone bigger than him, because I sure as shit wasn't scared of him anymore, but I knew I couldn't do that. "You need to come with me, Mr. Hawthorne."

"Fuck you!" He spit toward my feet, then stumbled, almost fell and knocked down a cardboard display.

Everything inside me shut down then. I was completely cut off from my emotions, because he was so fucking *sad*. I pulled out my cuffs, and he struggled to get away from me. He was too drunk to do much, so I was able to read him his rights, get his hands behind his back, and lead him outside.

Roger pulled up and gave me a pitying frown. "Sorry, Chase. I woulda taken care of this if I could have gotten here in time."

"It's fine. He's nothing to me," I replied as my dad began to yell, calling me a pussy, a pig, weak.

"Want me to take him in?" Roger asked.

"No, I got this. Could you go inside and take a report, though?"

"No problem," he replied as we parted ways.

I was detached from the moment, from him, as he yelled and cursed while I put him in the back of the cruiser. He was fighting to get free, still yelling and cussing at me as I drove to the station.

"Fuck you for thinking you're better than me," he slurred.

"I am." It wasn't professional, but I couldn't hold it back.

"Nah, you're my piece-of-shit son who always thought he was better than me, but you weren't then and you aren't now. You hide behind that badge just like you hid behind the Caines. Couldn't fight your own battles then, and you can't now."

"I was a kid. That doesn't make you strong."

He lost it then, and I managed to tune him out. *He's not worth it, he's not worth it, he's not worth it.*

It didn't take much time to get him booked at the station. He was passed out less than five minutes in, and I knew he would be right back at it when he got out. They wouldn't be able to hold him long, and he'd be doing the same thing on a different day. Some things never changed.

When my shift ended, I drove out to my place in silence. After locking my gun away, I went straight for the shower, stripping out of my clothes and hoping the hot water would help wash away my thoughts—about my dad, my hatred for him, and the part of me I liked to pretend wasn't there, that still felt inadequate because of him.

Then…then my thoughts shifted to a certain guy with a contagious smile and expressive eyes, who looked at me like I was something. Kellan had always looked at me as if I was important, as if I mattered, in ways no one else ever did. Not Griffin, not other friends I'd had over the years or people I fucked. He looked at me like he could see me, like there was nothing I could hide from him, and damn if I didn't like that.

And it scared the shit out of me.

I turned off the water and got out of the shower. I wrapped a towel around my waist, looked into my room, and remembered him staring up at me from his knees…the way he'd tasted, the way he'd felt, how much I wanted to do it again.

I had his number. I could call him, even if it was only to talk, because I liked talking with Kell.

I groaned, shoving that thought right the fuck out of my head. He'd left my place that morning, and that was supposed to be it between us. I had no business wanting to call Kellan Caine. No business at all.

Too bad that didn't stop me from wanting it something fierce.

# CHAPTER THIRTEEN

## *Kellan*

I T HAD BEEN a little less than a week since I sneaked out of Chase's cabin with my tail between my legs. It wasn't something I was proud of, but I still supported my decision. Well, the one about leaving, not the one about fucking. Okay, so I still supported the sleeping-with-Chase choice too because he fucked me so good and I deserved that, but now it was time to move on.

That's what Josh said last night when I got sloppy-drunk and told him all about Chase's cock. He wasn't impressed, but in Chase's defense, that was only because Josh didn't actually see said cock and he had my best interests at heart.

So today I'd slept half the day, nursing my hangover. I was off, one of the other younger local artists was teaching classes, and it was a good thing. I did not need to be around children at the moment.

Groaning at the pounding of my head, I made my

way into the kitchen.

"You look like you were run over by a truck," Griff said.

"Shhh… Too loud."

"I'm speaking in a normal voice."

"Speak in a normal voice minus a few levels."

Griff rolled his eyes. "I'll make you coffee and breakfast."

"Thank you. You're the best brother in the world." And he was, even if he did make me crazy.

I sat down and rested my head on my arms on the table. I remembered drinks, Josh bringing me home and putting me to bed, but I had no idea what time that had been.

A few minutes later, something was set on the table beside me. Coffee, water, Tylenol. "Oh my God, I love you."

"You better," Griff replied.

I took the pills, a drink of the coffee, and holy fucking shit, at the moment, that was better than an orgasm.

Griff put a bowl in front of me filled with scrambled eggs, peppers, and ham. Surprisingly, it made my stomach growl when I'd expected it to make me nauseous.

"What's going on with you lately?" Griff took the

seat across from me.

"What do you mean?" Obviously, I knew what he meant. I'd been on edge since Chase had come home, and it was hard for me to get things like that past Griffin.

"I don't know. You're just…off. The last week especially."

*I'm in love with your best friend. I've always been in love with him. I slept with him, and I soooo want to do it again.* "Nothing's off." Ugh. I was such a liar.

"Kell, you know you can talk to me, right? About anything? I might freak out at first, but I come around."

I couldn't stop my eyes from finding his then. There was nothing but concern on his face. There were times I felt judged by Griff. There were times I knew he judged me, and he often freaked out and went off the deep end, but he was right—he always came around, and I knew it all came from his heart. He had this hero complex he couldn't ignore, which was amped up when it came to me. I felt lucky to have him, but also frustrated that he had appointed himself my keeper.

I also couldn't help but think that maybe it would be okay. If I told him how I felt about Chase, maybe Griff wouldn't care. Or he might lose it, worried about me getting hurt, but then he'd be supportive.

I opened my mouth. What I was going to say, I

didn't know, but then reality shoved its way in, reminding me that Chase didn't feel the same. He wanted to fuck me, yeah, and he liked me, but he didn't love me the way I loved him, and when he didn't want to be with me anymore, it would cause issues with Griff. That was the last thing I wanted.

"You're imagining things. I'm fine, bro. No worries, okay?" And I *was* fine. I always made sure of that. I'd been in love with Chase for most of my life, and I hadn't let it break me. I didn't plan to start now.

Griff and I chatted while I finished my breakfast, which okay, yes, was technically lunch. Afterward, I went to shower. Then, since we were running out of groceries, I went to the store to do all that boring adulting shit I wasn't real fond of.

I parked my car, and as I was making my way into Grant's, I saw Chase loading bags into the cab of his truck. Because *of course* I would run into Chase. My karma sucked ass.

The heavy gray clouds hanging in the sky matched my mood. I knew it wouldn't be long before the sky opened up and we got hit with a storm. Still, I squared my shoulders and walked over to him because I wasn't going to ignore him. I was stronger than that.

"Hey, you."

Chase turned, and holy crap, the right side of his mouth kicked up in that way I loved. "Hey. Fancy seeing you here."

"Not really. We live in a small town. Odds are we'd run into each other," I teased.

Chase tossed the last bag into the truck and closed the door. He'd parked by the carousel, so he slipped his cart inside. "One would think. I was beginning to wonder if you were avoiding me, which, oh hey, you were, starting with you sneaking out of my house in the middle of the night."

"I didn't *sneak out*. I left."

Chase cocked a brow at me.

Of course he had to be right and know me so well. "Okay, fine, I sneaked out. Whatever."

He crossed his arms against his chest and leaned on the truck. There was something different in his stance, like he was…fuck, like he was unsure, which didn't make sense to me at all.

"Why'd you leave, Kell? You should have let me take you home, at least."

Because obviously that was what it would be about. He was worried about me getting home or thought it was his responsibility to get me there. "Ugh. Fuck you."

He frowned. "Why are you pissed at me? What did I

132

do now? I feel like I don't know which way is up, like I'm always making you mad or saying the wrong thing." There wasn't anger in his voice, just this quiet curiosity that told me he really wanted to know.

On cue, the sky opened up, fat raindrops falling down on us. "Shit. Get in the truck." Chase opened the door and signaled for me to go in, but I simply stood there stupidly for a moment. "We gonna stand here all day getting wet?"

The question snapped me out of it, and I jumped into the driver side of the truck, then crawled over to the passenger seat. Stupid Chase Hawthorne and his gentlemanly streak.

He got in behind me and slammed the door. We were both soaked already, his hair plastered to his head, his shirt tight against the body I wanted to explore even more.

"That came quick," he said. "I forget how fast that happens here. Now, are you going to tell me why you're pissed at me?"

"I'm not pissed at you." But really, I was pissed at him. And myself. And the whole situation.

Chase rolled his eyes. "You can't lie to me, and you know it."

There were some things I needed to consider,

though. He made it sound like his biggest worry was how I got home. I was so fucking tired of that shit. "You know I'm capable of getting home on my own, right?" At that, the bastard started to laugh. It was throaty and sexy, and the fact that I thought it was hot pissed me off even more. "You're an asshole. Drive me to my car."

That shut him up. He looked at me and shook his head. "No. Why are you mad at me because I wanted to take you home after fucking you?" He flinched, and that annoyed me too. It made it seem like he felt guilty for sleeping with me.

*Because it means more to me than it does to you. Because I didn't want to go. Because you still see me as a responsibility.*

"You can say it, Chase. That's what we did. We fucked. We fucked, and then I left because there was no reason to stay. I called Josh, and as you can see, I'm fine. I didn't get lost along the way or anything."

He groaned, dropping his head back against the seat. "Of course you called him."

"What the fuck does that mean?"

"It means you can call him, but you can't ask me. You don't mind him being there for you, but I'm a prick if I want to? Excuse me if I think it makes me a nice guy to bring someone home—someone who doesn't have a car with them, I might add—after I sleep with them."

Oh, this was rich. How did he not get it? I felt like I was on a merry-go-round. "Because Josh is there for me for completely different reasons than you are! He's my *friend*. It's a give and take. He doesn't think I'm helpless or someone he has to look after. Get a clue, Chase. He *wants* me around."

I was breathing heavily, half regretting what I said but half proud as well, as we sat there staring at each other. It seemed like hours passed, but it likely wasn't even a minute.

His eyes darkened. His jaw was tight, a tick in the right side of it, before he opened his mouth and said, "I want you around, Kell. If you haven't noticed, I want you too much."

He wanted me too much? That definitely wasn't possible. My brain short-circuited, unable to process the words. I mean, I was a good fuck, but this sounded...different, like he wasn't just talking about being inside me. His words had slid across my skin like a caress, and I could still feel them there, lingering, pleasuring.

And then...then Chase Hawthorne grabbed me, pulled me toward him, and crushed our mouths together.

# CHAPTER FOURTEEN

## *Chase*

I WAS PRETTY sure Kellan Caine fried my brain. I couldn't be around him without making stupid decisions, but when we touched, it was easier to forget all the reasons we shouldn't. I pushed my tongue into his mouth, and he moaned before sucking on it. His hand tightened in my hair as he pulled me closer yet somehow crawled over and onto my lap at the same time. It was a tight fit because of the steering wheel, but I didn't care. It made me closer to him, and damned if I didn't want that. Maybe even needed it.

Our clothes were wet and uncomfortable, made worse when my cock swelled beneath him, but he was rocking on me and kissing me like his life depended on it, and yeah, everything else went haywire, my synapses misfiring, and all I could think was *Kellan, Kellan, Kellan*. My hand roamed down his chest, around his body, as I tried to sneak it down the back of his wet jeans.

A roll of thunder rocked across the sky, and suddenly it was as if that had woken us both up. Kellan jerked his mouth away, and I cursed because what the fuck was I doing? I was mauling the guy in my truck, in the parking lot of the store I'd arrested my father in.

"Realization hit that you're kissing your best friend's brother again?" Kellan asked with what sounded like bitterness in his voice.

"No, actually. Griff was the furthest thing from my mind, which I'll remind you, makes me an asshole. I remembered the fact that I'm an officer of the law, and that I was about ready to strip you bare and fuck you in the parking lot of Grant's Grocery."

"You want to fuck me again?" Kellan asked, and I shook my head. Damned if I could keep myself from smiling too.

"*That's* what you focus on?"

"It's a good thing to focus on."

I grabbed his hand and made him cup my hard cock. "Feel like I'm going to die if I don't get inside you," I admitted. See? *Stupid, stupid, stupid.* I couldn't seem to help myself where he was concerned, and I was tired of trying.

Kellan sighed, then climbed off my lap and back into

his seat. "I want you again too," he said softly.

"Then why'd you leave?" I hated the vulnerability in my voice. It had no business being there. Having sex was supposed to make this craving for him go away.

"I told you why I left."

"Bullshit. I don't see you as a responsibility. I thought we were friends, and the fact that I hated waking up to an empty bed means I still want you. I wanted you that morning, and I want you now, and I'm not sure what in the fuck to do about it."

Kellan gasped. I wasn't sure if it was because he hadn't expected me to admit it or because he didn't believe it was true. How he couldn't see I wanted him was beyond me.

"I still want you too," he said again, without looking at me.

"Fuck." I rubbed a hand over my face and ignored the voice in my head. "Why do we keep ending up here?"

"Pretty sure we just answered that. The want, re-member?" he replied, and I couldn't help but smile. Kellan was good at making me do that.

I wasn't sure what made me do it—well, other than the fact that I wanted to, and like I said, Kellan fucked with my brain—but I reached over, grabbed his hand,

and twined our fingers together, brushing my thumb over his rain-slicked skin. "I was disappointed when I woke up alone. That's never happened to me before, Kell. Usually I want to get off and be done, but not this time. Then later, when shit went down with my dad… Fuck, he was a mess, drunk and belligerent, calling me names. I had to arrest him, and when it was over, I wanted to call you and talk to you about it. I don't know what it is about you that just sort of calms me."

He inhaled a sharp breath, his chin shaking a bit. "Jesus, Chase. I'm so fucking sorry about your dad. You could have, ya know? Called me. You can always call me. You're fam—" His word cut off, and I turned, cocking a brow at him.

"I'm family, that's what you were going to say. That's what makes things difficult. You and Griff are the only real family I have. I'm the only family you guys have left. I know you both have your friends, and you have Josh, but—"

"It's different, Chase, and you know it. Josh and me is different from you and me."

Kellan lifted my hand and kissed it. I wasn't sure anyone had ever kissed my hand before. It was a strange thing to realize. That, and how much I enjoyed the simple contact.

"We keep this up, and what happens when things go sideways?" I asked him. "I'm not good at letting my feelings get involved. I'm not looking for anything serious. My parents…they loved each other once, but they ended up hating each other, and they were so volatile together. Love hard and fight harder." I wasn't risking that shit, especially not with Kellan. Not that he wasn't worth it, because he was, but what we chanced losing.

"I don't want to come between you and Griffin."

And we both knew it would. If Griff knew I was fucking around with Kellan, he'd lose his shit.

"Yeah, I know you don't. But that doesn't help us, because I don't want to lose you either, and we keep finding ourselves here. One time wasn't enough with you, Kell. Don't quite know what that means or how to come to terms with it."

"One time wasn't enough with you either." He kissed my hand again, and again. It was so fucking simple, so innocent, but felt intimate too. "We're friends, right? You said so a few minutes ago."

"Of course we are." Did he really think I only cared about him because of Griffin? There wasn't anything I wouldn't do for Kellan. Never had been.

"And we're both adults. We both want each other.

Neither of us wants anything serious. Why don't we just enjoy ourselves? We can keep it between us—no strings, fuck around when we want. We're allowed to hang out. No one would question that if they saw us together, not even Griff. We keep the benefits part to ourselves."

I turned to look at him, and he gave me a small smile. "Is that what you want? Friends with benefits?" I was leaving this up to Kellan.

He nodded slowly, and I almost asked him if he was sure, but then a cocky grin kicked at his mouth. "Sugar, I've wanted to fuck you since I was eighteen. Obviously, I'm down with it. I haven't even shown you all my tricks yet."

My stomach tightened. Fuck, Kellan Caine tied me in all sorts of knots.

"Yeah, yeah, okay. Only not in the Grant's parking lot." We laughed. I untwined our fingers and reached out, fingering a lock of his chocolate-colored hair. "Fuck, you are so goddamned sexy."

Kellan trembled, pink dotting his smooth cheeks. I wanted to fucking devour him, to wreck him in all the best ways. To lose myself in him until I could sate this desire that only seemed to get stronger and stronger.

"You be careful what you say to me, Chase Hawthorne, or I might not be able to stop myself from blowing you in the Grant's Grocery parking lot."

That easily, my dick began to chub up again. Kellan had some kind of effect on me that I obviously couldn't control. "I think you might kill me, you know that? I'm not sure I'm gonna survive this. Impulsive, naughty, stubborn Kellan was hard enough to deny, and now I have gorgeous, confident, sexy Kellan to deal with? I don't stand a chance."

Something unfamiliar washed over his face then. I couldn't read it, and just as I was about to ask if he was okay, the look changed. "Baby, you ain't seen nothing yet." Kellan winked.

A growl started in my chest and made its way past my lips. "What are you doing today?"

"Grocery shopping. *Duh.*"

I rolled my eyes. "What are you doing afterward?"

"I'm hanging out at Josh's place tonight."

Well, shit. That hadn't been the answer I was hoping to hear. The unfamiliar burn of jealousy lit inside me again.

"We'll plan something soon, okay? Call me. And if you need to talk, about your dad or anything else, you can always call me for that too." Then he pressed a quick kiss to my lips, jumped out of the truck, and ran in the rain toward Grant's.

I was left there trying to figure out what just happened and wanting him back already.

# CHAPTER FIFTEEN

## *Kellan*

I HAD TO get out of the truck before I said or did something I'd regret. *I* was going to kill *him*? *He* didn't stand a chance? It was definitely the other way around, and it had been on the tip of my tongue to tell him right then and there that I'd been in love with him all my life and this might literally kill me. But if I had, I knew I wouldn't be able to have him, and I wanted him so much, I was willing to risk getting my heart trampled on.

It was moments like these that I understood why Griff thought I made dumb decisions. I knew what I was doing would hurt me, but I didn't have it in me to stop. I wanted Chase. If he wanted me, I was going to have him.

But for now…for now I had to try and go back to that adulting thing. I didn't really have plans with Josh tonight, but I would make them now. See? I was attempting to make smart decisions. How easy would it have been to jump right into bed with Chase today? I could have not given myself time to think and prepare, but I wasn't doing that. I was giving us a little bit of space to make sure we didn't change our minds. Maybe I *could* handle this.

I was wet, miserable, half-hard, and uncomfortable, but I still did my grocery shopping. Back in the car, I texted Josh to invite myself over later that evening. Luckily for me, he loved me and was fine with it, then said he'd call Natalie over too.

Once I was back at home, I put the groceries away, then took my second shower of the day. I had my face mask on, when there was a knock on my bedroom door.

"I don't know why you put that goop on your face," Griff said when he came in.

"So I don't ever look old like you?" I teased, and he flipped me off. "Don't get mad at me because I know how to take care of my skin. I can give you some pointers. It might not be too late for you." Griff was all rugged gruff—oh, hey, Griff the Gruff. That was cute.

"You're a funny guy," Griff replied, only I wasn't joking. Still, I let it go because I was pretty sure my brother was a lost cause. "You seem happier than you were this morning."

*Because I kissed your best friend and we're going to start a friends-with-benefits relationship even though I love him and it might kill me. Don't hate us, 'kay?*

Of course, I didn't let loose the truth running around inside my brain. Instead, I said, "It was the hangover. I feel better now."

"Are you going out tonight?"

"Is it any of your business?"

I could see he realized he overstepped. It wasn't that it mattered if Griff knew when I was going out—well, minus the Chase thing—but I knew his dad voice when I heard it, and that's exactly what he'd used to speak to me.

"You're right. Fine. I'm going to go hang out with Chase for a bit, take advantage of a day off."

Automatically I turned away, pretending it was to check my mask, which was already cracking because I couldn't shut my mouth. "Good for you. You deserve to go have fun with your friend."

"Yeah, it's good to have him back. He's more like a brother to me than a friend, which obviously you know since he's like one to you too. I missed the dumbass."

If by *brother*, he meant *dude I wanted to fuck*, then yes, that was what Chase was to me, but I didn't think Griff meant that, and *ew*, on thoughts of fucking and

145

brothers in the same sentence. "I know you did." I wet a washcloth and began taking off the mask, without letting myself look at Griffin.

Guilt tumbled around in my chest. I hated lying to Griff. A lie by omission was still a lie, but Chase and I were grown-ass men. We were allowed to fuck around if we wanted to, but Griffin would never understand it. He would worry about me and get angry with Chase. It would come between them, which I'd known, but thinking it made the guilt turn thicker and heavier. This was a bad idea. Why did this have to be such a bad idea?

"I'm going to Josh's. Me, him, and Nat are going to hang out," I finally said. It didn't help me feel better that I conceded and told him what I was doing that night.

"Have fun. Be good. Don't get yourself into any trouble."

"With Josh and Natalie? What do you think I'm going to do? And I'm allowed to be bad, Griff. I do it quite often." Now I was pissed at him again. What twenty-eight-year-old wanted their brother to tell them to *be good*?

"Someone's touchy. I didn't mean anything by it."

He never did, did he? Griffin was being…himself, the person who loved me most in the world. That didn't change the outcome. "It's fine. Whatever. Have fun with

Chase." Who I was pretty sure had called Griff to hang out because he felt guilty about me. Not that that was the only reason he wanted to hang out with my brother, but I knew it was part of it. That was how Chase Hawthorne worked. "I probably won't be home tonight."

"Okay. You have fun too," Griff replied, then walked out.

I finished getting ready and packed a bag for Josh's. He had an extra room at his place that I often crashed in. He'd offered for me to move in and be his roommate, but I said no. Maybe I would take him up on that offer. It would be good for me to get out of the house I shared with my brother. We probably needed space from each other. We would probably both benefit from it.

Josh had a little blue house on one acre, which was still in town, but down a longish driveway and set back from the road. When I got there, I opened the door without knocking because that's how Josh and I were. Natalie was already there. They were both leaning over the table, looking at what I knew was a model car, because Josh was a weird-ass and dug building toy cars.

I dropped my bag. They both turned around and looked at me. "I'm going to start a secret friends-with-benefits relationship with Chase," tumbled out of my mouth. It was dumb, and I should have tried to stop it, but this was Nat and Josh. I didn't keep things from them. I couldn't even if I wanted to.

"Ah, hell," Josh groaned.

"Are you sure that's a good idea?" Nat asked.

"Gee, thanks. I already regret telling you both. What about a response like, *Hey, Kell. That's awesome. You deserve to have as much sex as you want with your childhood crush!*"

"Except it's not a childhood crush because you're twenty-eight," Josh replied.

"And you're in love with him," Natalie added.

"And the last time you fucked him, you sneaked out of his house and I had to pick you up."

"Sorry you had to get out of bed and come get me." I crossed my arms.

He rolled his eyes. "Stop being dramatic. You know I don't give a shit about that. I'd do anything for you, and you know it."

Natalie walked over and wrapped her arms around my waist. "We just don't want you to get hurt."

Leaning in, I rested my chin on her shoulder. She was the best. They both were. "I know." And I did. Just... "I can't walk away from him. I don't have it in me. I know it's a mistake. I know I'll get hurt. It'll be one more fuck-up from Kellan, the weird, gay Caine boy who can't keep it together, but…I want him," I admitted. "I've always wanted him, and the way he talks to me, the way he looks at me…he wants me too. He was never supposed to want me. It was never supposed to be a possibility, not for me, but he does, and I can't walk away from that."

I wasn't fooling myself. I knew Chase wasn't in love with me. This would never go anywhere, but there was something in the way he'd spoken to me in the truck, something in the way he'd looked at me and touched me, that made me feel cared for on a level deeper than simply desire.

Maybe I was imagining it. Or maybe the close bond was because of Griff, but there *was* something there.

"You know I hate this guy, right? And when this shit ends between the two of you, I'm going to hate him even more," Josh said.

"It's not his fault. He doesn't know I'm in love with him. Most of the time, it's been me making the first move. He's not doing anything wrong." I was the one who kept pushing.

"He's hiding you. *That's* wrong," Josh gritted out.

Again, I wondered why I couldn't love Josh and why he couldn't love me. Life would be so much easier that way. "He left it up to me. I could have walked away. I told him it was what I wanted. And hell, when have you ever seen me flaunting someone I was sleeping with around Havenwood? That shit has never and will never happen. It's not like I've had all these relationships and Chase is asking something from me that isn't exactly what I always do."

"Yeah, but again, you're in love with him." Nat pulled back, grabbed my hand, and squeezed.

"And he puts Griff before you." Josh wouldn't give in. I knew him. Natalie would be easier about it all.

"You don't get it. You didn't grow up here. Chase had a horrible childhood, and Griff...Griff was the first person in Chase's life who he ever felt loved him. Griff gave him a family and friendship. He cared about Chase when no one else could be bothered."

Hearing myself speak those words hurt. I ached for Chase as a boy. That added to the shame of being part of something that would build a wall between him and Griffin. God, what was wrong with me? I was such an asshole for doing this.

"I'm sorry for what he went through, I really am, but it doesn't change how I feel. I'll support whatever you decide to do, Kell, you know that. But I'll also break his fucking face if he hurts you, and I don't give a shit if he's the law or not."

I swallowed the weight in my throat. Oh, my friends were the best. I really wasn't sure I deserved them. "It'll be fine. He won't hurt me. I know what I'm getting into." Maybe if I said it enough, I'd start to believe it myself. Chase would never hurt me on purpose. I knew that to the marrow of my bones, but that didn't mean I wouldn't end up a casualty of this.

"Okay, that's enough talk about Chase Hawthorne. What do you guys want to do tonight?" Natalie asked.

"Watch porn?" I teased.

"I'm down!" Natalie replied, and both Josh and I laughed.

"I need food," Josh added.

So we ordered dinner and ate together. We didn't bring up Chase again, but I knew Josh was still thinking about him. What was it with me and all the loyal, protective men in my life? Josh had never been like this with me before, but then, I'd never been at risk of getting my heart broken before either.

After dinner we played board games and teased each other and laughed, and as I watched them—Natalie, the sweet girl with the glasses, who'd been my best friend all my life, the one who'd been willing to hang out with me when no one else wanted to; and Josh, my beefed-up dude-bro buddy, who had no problem sitting around and getting silly with us like we were all sixteen and having a sleepover—again, I felt lucky.

If somehow I could ever call Chase Hawthorne mine, without either of us losing Griffin in the process, or not fitting in, and if all my stupid mistakes and dealing with shitty people like Buck wouldn't matter…my life would be perfect.

# CHAPTER SIXTEEN

## *Chase*

I T HAD BEEN over a week since Kellan and I decided we were going to do the whole friends-with-benefits thing, and I hadn't seen him yet.

We both had our jobs and responsibilities, and things had been even crazier for me. We'd had an armed robbery at one of the local gas stations, something that never happened in Havenwood—with the exception of Kellan and Griff's parents' murder. Those were the only two major crimes that had happened in town since I was born, and it was a scary thought.

I'd been the first officer on-scene, but the perp was already long gone. He hadn't been found yet, so the whole town was stressed and on high alert. The twenty-one-year-old kid working there had been a mess, scared out of his mind, poor thing. None of it had left my thoughts since it happened.

Kellan had texted me every day, though. We'd joked

and chatted about random things, and it was really good to get to know him again, to get to know the grown-up version of Kell that I'd only seen a glimpse of at eighteen years old.

The day after the robbery he'd called me, frantic. *"Jesus Christ, Chase. Are you okay?"* The panic had been evident in his voice, and it soothed something inside me. Not that I wanted Kell to worry. I didn't, but it was always a shock to my system to realize people cared about me. I'd gone without it for so long, and then really only let the Caines in, that even with them, it still surprised me sometimes.

The truth was, I'd been shaken up by the robbery. It wasn't right, something like that happening at home, and I wanted to fix it. Wanted to find a way to ease the town's fears. It was why I did what I did, and why I'd eventually come home to do it.

Tonight they'd basically forced me to take the night off. I hated to admit I needed it, but the cabin felt too empty and my skin too tight, so I picked up my phone and dialed.

"Hey, you," Kell answered.

"Do you have plans tonight? If not, I thought you might want to come over?"

"Um…yeah, I'm free," he said and then whispered,

"*Stop it,*" to someone else.

"It's okay if you can't," I told him, feeling a slight twist in my gut. It was clear he was with someone.

"It's fine. Josh is just being stupid. I'd love to come over."

At the mention of Josh, my stomach tightened even more. The bastard didn't like me, and I wasn't real fond of him myself. But it was obvious he and Kellan were incredibly close. How close, I didn't know, and damn, just thinking that made jealousy slash through me again. "Bring stuff to stay the night. I'm not waking up alone this time. I'll handcuff you to the bed if I have to."

"Oh God. I nearly came. That was hot as fuck."

I smiled. Who knew, Josh may have fucked him in the past, but Kellan was mine for now; well, not *mine*, but spending time in my bed. I liked the thought of him there much more than I probably should.

"I'll be waiting."

"I'll be there soon," he replied, and then I heard, "Josh!" before he hung up.

Trying to shove Kellan's prick of a best friend out of my head, I took a quick shower and pulled on a pair of jeans. It was muggy and warm for spring, so I went without a shirt, even though I had the AC on in the house.

I went to the fridge to find something to make for dinner, but ended up ordering a pizza instead—all veggie, just how Kellan had liked it when he was a kid. I even got the sugary dessert he'd loved, and wondered if he still liked both of those things. People changed over ten years. There was no doubt Kellan had changed too.

I sat back and tried not to feel like an asshole of a friend for having invited Kellan over. It was hard, being stuck in this middle ground where I wasn't sure if I should feel bad or not. Kellan was an adult. I was an adult. We had every right to do what we wanted, but it was the lying that clawed at my insides. I wasn't a liar. I never had been, and now I was lying to one of the most important people in my life.

The doorbell rang, and I padded over to the door, unsure if it would be dinner or Kellan, which honestly, I would have been okay with skipping the food and devouring him instead.

I was surprised to see it was Kellan with the pizza in his hands. "I met the pizza guy out front and paid."

"You shouldn't have done that." I'd invited him over. Dinner should have been on me.

"Why? Were you planning an orgy with me and the pizza guy? You're already half naked. This is how so many porn videos start. I would have thought you were more creative than that."

A laugh rumbled through my chest and out of my lips. I was pretty sure the only times I'd laughed over the past week were when I was talking with Kellan. He had this magic about him. I knew he thought he was weird and didn't fit, but I'd always thought he was a breath of fresh air.

"I have a feeling you'll keep me busy enough." I stepped aside so he could come in, then closed and locked the door behind him. "You didn't eat already, did you? I got your favorite pizza and that cinnamon thing; well, if you still like the same pizza and that cinnamon thing."

Kellan set the food on the kitchen counter, cocked his head, bit his lip, and looked at me. "You remember the pizza I used to like?"

Shrugging it off, I went for plates. "It's not a big deal."

"It is to me," Kellan replied softly, and I felt this tug toward him, this energy that made my fingers twitch with the need to touch him.

I set the plates on the counter beside him, hooked my thumb beneath his chin, and tilted his head up. "Don't ever accept less than what you deserve. Not from me or anyone else. If you're fucking the same person more than once, he damn sure better give you what you want."

Kellan trembled. He did that a lot, I noticed, and I fucking loved being the one to make him do it. Loved knowing I had that effect on him.

"I don't need anyone to give me what I want. I can do that for myself."

"Doesn't mean they shouldn't want to."

"And what about what you want?" Kellan asked.

I wanted him. Fuck, did I want him…so bad, I ached with it. It was unexpected and confusing, but it was the truth. And really, maybe it shouldn't have been confusing at all. "You're already giving me that." Leaning down, I nipped at his bottom lip. Kellan whimpered, and I smiled against his mouth before giving him my tongue. He sucked on it, and then I was kissing him. I pushed him back, squeezing him between the counter and my body, tightly enough that I knew he would be on the edge of pain. Kellan had said he liked it a little rough, and I wasn't one to complain about that.

His hands went to my back, his nails digging in as he trailed his fingers up and down. His kisses turned frantic quickly. I slid my hand in his hair, tugging it as I pushed my cock against him. I shoved my thigh between his legs, and Kellan started to rub off on me.

"Oh God," he said as I kissed his neck, then bit gently, not willing to leave a lasting mark, but wishing I could.

"That's it, Kell. Ride my thigh. We'll take the edge off for you, baby boy," tumbled out of my mouth. I had no fucking clue where it had come from—the baby-boy part, at least—but he seemed to like it. He whimpered again, humping my leg as I kissed him, fucking devoured him, the taste of mint on my tongue. I tugged his hair tighter and pressed my thighs together against him. Kell kept kissing, kept riding my leg like I was a prized horse and he an expert rider. I could tell when he got close, felt his body tense up and his nails dig into me deeper.

"Fuck...*fuck*." He dropped his head back, the cords in his neck stretching as he no doubt shot a load in his pants. Damned if I didn't want to bang on my chest for being the one to make him do it.

"Shit. That was embarrassing." His gaze darted away.

"Hey." I turned his face so he looked at me. "Don't be embarrassed. It was one of the sexiest things I've ever seen."

"One of?" He cocked a brow, back to the confident Kellan I was learning he was when it came to sex.

"It's a toss-up between what just happened, you on your knees for me, and watching you come when I fuck you."

"Oh." His cheeks turned a surprising pink, as though he hadn't expected me to say the other moments were with him. I hadn't expected it either, but it was true. "I'm going to have to put on my clothes for tomorrow already."

"Or you can not wear anything at all?" I knew that was the idea that got my vote.

"I'm not walking around your house naked. Here, let me get you off first, and then I'll change."

Kellan moved to drop to his knees, but I wrapped a hand around his arm and stopped him. "I'm okay for now. That was for you. Let's get you changed. You can wear something of mine, and I'll wash your clothes for you." I swatted his ass.

"Your clothes will be too big on me."

"So? It'll be cute."

Kellan followed me to my room and stripped as I got him a pair of sweats. They were definitely hanging off his slender hips, and he had to hold them up, but it really was adorable.

I gathered up his clothes. "Come on. Let's have some dinner."

Kellan looked up at me, confusion in his eyes, but then he nodded and went back to the other room.

# CHAPTER SEVENTEEN

## *Kellan*

THIS WASN'T GOING the way I'd expected it to.

Not that I was complaining. The orgasm had been hot, but I was definitely shocked Chase hadn't let me suck him off after. This was supposed to be a friends-with-*benefits* relationship, so I didn't know why he hadn't let me give him a benefit too, especially since he'd been hard as a post.

When you added in getting my favorite pizza and dessert, how he'd asked me to stay, washing my clothes, and the sweet *baby boy* that had slipped past his lips… And holy fuck, that got me going. No one had ever called me something like that before, but I suddenly wanted nothing more than to be Chase's baby boy.

This didn't feel like fucking. It didn't feel like we were friends with benefits. It felt like a relationship, or at least the night so far did. Yeah, it was only one day, but I'd expected us to fuck like rabbits and be done with it.

That was usually how my hookups went. Maybe it was because we were close? Because Chase knew me outside of the sex we planned to have? Or hell, maybe he was this way with everyone he fucked now. I didn't know, but I did like it.

We made our plates together, he got us beers, and I realized this was already fucking with my head, already blurring lines I'd tried to keep firmly intact, even if only in my mind. I shouldn't have told him I'd stay. I should have said I'd come over, we'd have sex, and then I'd be on my way, but I hadn't, and no matter what, I wasn't leaving.

Despite the fact that it had been clear outside not long before, rain pelted against the house now. It was like that in Havenwood. Storms came out of nowhere, and though it could get frustrating at times, I loved it. There was nothing like warm rain that felt like it washed the world clean.

"Do you want to eat on the screened porch?" Chase asked. "You used to like storms. Except that one time you were home alone and the electricity went out, remember? Griff was at work and couldn't get off, so he sent me over. You almost took my head off with a baseball bat because you thought I was an intruder."

"Oh my God! I forgot about that. It was your fault,

though. You were creeping through my house and didn't call my name. What was I supposed to think?" I couldn't believe Chase remembered it. The baseball-bat thing was likely pretty unforgettable, since I could have killed him, but the fact that I liked storms? That surprised me. I was quickly realizing Chase Hawthorne was full of surprises.

"You were supposed to not try and take my head off." He went toward the side door leading to the screened porch, and I followed him.

"Well, next time announce who it is."

"Next time I save you from being alone when the lights go out?" Chase asked playfully.

"Well, I didn't need you to save me then, and I don't now. I would have thought that was obvious by the fact that I nearly killed you. You're fast on your feet, by the way; you ducked out of the way quickly. But I also wouldn't complain about being in the dark with you." I said that last part in a flirty tone, and Chase looked over his shoulder and smiled at me. It nearly knocked me on my ass. God, he had the best smile, his eyes going a little squinty, with wrinkles around them.

"I'll remember that."

We went to the porch and sat down. The air was still muggy, but it wasn't too bad. Rain beat down on the house and the roof of the porch but didn't hit us. It was nice being there. I'd lived in the same house my whole life, in town, not in the outskirts like Chase's place was.

"So, what else do you remember about me?" I found myself asking. I was a glutton for punishment because I knew all the stories would likely be of something stupid I did, or him and Griff teasing me, but I liked thinking that Chase had filed memories of me away, that he'd kept them for so long.

"Hmm…" He took a bite of pizza, chewed and swallowed. "I remember you were always one of the smartest people I knew, and also one of the most creative. You've always been good at art, and it's incredible to see that you're doing something with it."

Oh… That hadn't been the response I'd expected. I liked this one much, much more.

"I remember you always had a big heart. One time you found an injured rabbit. Griff and I didn't think it would make it. He thought it was best to end its suffering, and I agreed, but you wouldn't even consider that possibility. You were heartbroken. You wanted to fix the little thing, and that made me want to believe she could be fixed. I wanted to make her better, so I told Griff I'd take her to the vet. We put on oven mitts to protect our hands and put her in that little cage you had from your old cat. Remember that?"

I swallowed the lump that had formed in my throat. I remembered it. I remembered everything, and Chase seemed to remember a whole lot more than I thought he would.

"So I took that wild rabbit to the vet. Griff told me I was wasting my time, and I knew I was, but I just…fuck, you wanted it better so much, and I wanted you to have that. You're spoiled if you haven't realized it." Chase chuckled, but I didn't. I could hardly breathe. My heart was thudding so hard, it was scaring me. "The vet knew it was a lost cause, but I still asked her to try. Hooked the little thing up to IVs and all. She lasted two days. Broke my heart when you lost it, when she died. You made me take her home again, and we buried her in the backyard. You remember?" he asked again as he turned to look at me.

Fuck, if I didn't want to cry then and there, but I didn't let myself. I fought to school my features. "Yeah, we were lucky Doc Johnson did that out of the kindness of her heart."

Chase turned away and took another bite of pizza, and…holy fucking shit. Noooo. "That was free, right, Chase?" He'd told me the vet was doing it to be nice. Chase hadn't had shit for money back then. "Chase?" I insisted.

"Was a long time ago, Kell. It doesn't matter."

But it did matter. It mattered to me. It mattered a lot. "Chase! You shouldn't have done that. You didn't have the money to take care of some random animal just because I got all worked up about it! I can't believe Griff let you pay for that."

"I didn't tell him either. It's not a big deal."

But it felt like that to me. I'd always known Chase cared about me, that he spoiled me in some ways, and he'd always been good to me, but this felt like... It felt like *more*. "Why'd you do that?"

"I don't know, Kell. I wanted to save that damn rabbit so you wouldn't be upset, and I knew you'd feel bad if you knew I had to pay for it."

*Oh God, oh God, oh God.* My heart was never going to survive loving Chase Hawthorne. This was the Chase that Josh didn't see, the one I wasn't sure most people besides me and Griff saw. "I—"

"Don't make a big deal out of it."

"Okay." I nodded. "Thank you—for doing that."

We went back and forth with stories about each other after that, the rest of them much lighter. As we reminisced about incidents he and Griff had gotten into and stuff that had happened to me, I laughed harder than I had in what felt like forever. I also realized I wasn't sure there was much Chase didn't remember about our childhood, and I thought maybe it was because he treasured those memories. That he hadn't had happy ones outside of our family, and that made my chest ache.

The rain stopped, and we went in to have dessert, but then found ourselves right back on the screened porch, laughing and talking.

Evening turned into night, but we still didn't move. Chase yawned a few times, as if he hadn't been getting enough sleep. Because of work? I was curious about the armed-robbery case and wanted to know how it was going, but I knew Chase couldn't give me much because of legalities and such. Plus, I was sure he didn't want to talk about that.

Surprisingly, it was Chase who brought it up first. He stretched, saying, "I'm exhausted. With my extra shifts, I didn't get much sleep this week. Even when I was home, I couldn't stop thinking about it. Shit like that doesn't happen here."

"Not since my parents," I found myself saying.

"It's all I can think about," Chase admitted. "I know it's different, but—shit. I'm sure you don't want to talk about this."

"No. I don't mind. I miss them and love them, but

it's been a long time." Despite how long it had been, Chase went into law enforcement because of them.

"I know they think it was likely someone passing through town, when it came to your parents, not a local."

"Yes. And they were robbed walking to their car at night. This was a convenience store at a gas station."

"Whoever hit the store must have known their routine. The timing was too perfect," Chase added. "I don't like it. Not here. Not in our town, ya know? I already hate that we couldn't solve your parents' murder, and now I'm back and this happens."

He was so sweet, and I didn't know if he even realized it. "There is no *we* when it comes to Mom and Dad, Chase. You weren't an officer at that time. You didn't fail them or Griff. You didn't let them down."

"Us."

I frowned. "What do you mean?"

"You said *them*, like you weren't included. You need to say *us*, Kell. You, Griff, and your mom and dad. Don't leave yourself out."

My heart swelled so big, I wasn't sure my chest would be able to contain it. "You didn't let us down," I amended softly. My eyes suddenly got teary. I hadn't cried over my parents in a lot of years, but in that moment, I missed them…and I loved Chase even more. He was nothing but a big, beating heart, even though he'd spent a lot of his life with his getting bruised.

"Sometimes I wonder if they would be proud of me. If they'd think I've done well or if they would be disappointed. Griff derailed his life for me, and then I didn't go to college, the way they wanted for both of us."

"Hey," Chase said, and when I didn't respond, added, "Look at me."

It was impossible to deny him much of anything, but especially when he spoke to me in that deep, commanding voice of his. It had the power to wrap around me, make me turn my head, and face him. "They would be proud of you. Who fucking gives a shit if you went to some fancy school or not? You're an artist, a good one. You're doing what you love. You're sharing your talent. I promise you, they'd be proud of you."

*What about the rest of it?* I wanted to ask. *The men and the mistakes and everything else?*

"Nothing, Kell. There's nothing you have done or would ever do that would cause them to not be proud of you, do you hear me?"

"Yes," I answered. He said it with such conviction that I believed him.

I was tired of talking then. I didn't want to think

about my parents or childhood memories. I wanted…Chase. To feel him, have him, pretend he was really mine. I eased to my feet, walked over, and stood in front of him. "You gonna fuck me now, Officer?"

Chase sucked in a sharp breath. "You gonna get on your knees for me first, baby boy?" he asked, and my legs nearly gave out.

"Jesus, that's hot. I like it when you call me that." The nickname had come so easily to him, I didn't want to think about how many other times he'd used it, how many other men had been Chase Hawthorne's *baby boy* while he was fucking them. I wanted to pretend it was only me, that it had only ever been me. "And yes," I added as I began to kneel.

Chase grabbed my arm, stopping me. "Not out here. Inside."

I nodded, held my hand out to Chase, and he took it. My legs were weak as I led us inside. He stopped to close and lock the door behind us, and then I took Chase to his room, the whole time telling myself I would survive this. I could let Chase have his fun with me, and I'd be okay when he walked away.

It was a lie.

# CHAPTER EIGHTEEN

## Chase

MY DICK WAS already hard as a railroad spike. I wanted Kellan so bad, I ached with it. With each step we took, the torrent of desire swelled. He did something to me, something I didn't expect and didn't know what to do with other than to try and sate my desire for him with his body. My want was so brutal, so intense, I wasn't sure I would ever be able to get enough of him.

I stopped him when we got to the edge of the bed, and pulled him to me. My mouth covered his, and Kell moaned against my tongue, the sound making a beeline for my cock and making it ache even more. He kissed me like he needed me, like I was providing something for him, his arms around me, his hands clutching with this urgent desperation, making my need flare even stronger. No one had ever kissed me the way Kellan did.

"Fuck, you taste good." I licked a trail down his

neck. "You wanna suck me? Or you want me to take that sweet ass of yours?"

"Make me," Kellan replied breathlessly. "Push me down."

My dick twitched at his request, my body vibrating like there was an earthquake beneath my skin. Kellan Caine was going to wreck me, when I'd never been wrecked in my life, not over a lover. But then, I'd never had an emotional attachment to someone I was sleeping with the way I did with him.

"Suck me." I shoved him to his knees, tugged his face against my jean-covered erection, and Kellan mouthed at it like he was so hungry for me, he would take whatever I gave him, would keep his face in my groin all night, even if I kept my pants on. "Take me out."

I kept my hand in his hair, running my fingers through the strands, gently for now, instead of pulling at it like I did earlier. He made a soft sound as he worked frantically to unbutton and unzip my jeans, that sweet noise making another jolt of need shoot through me.

"Record me," Kell said as he shoved a hand inside my jeans.

"Huh?"

"Fuck, I wanna see it, Chase. Record me."

My stomach twisted, but fuck, that sounded hot.

"Kell…"

"Please? We can delete it afterward. It gets me so hot, feeling like I have other eyes on me."

I wasn't sure there was a damn thing I would deny Kellan, so I pulled my cell phone out of my back pocket. He tugged my jeans and underwear down and off, and I stepped out of them, my cock jutting out, the tip leaking. Kellan looked up at me prettily. Pupils blown wide, pink dusting his cheeks, hair messy from where I'd had my hands in it. "Christ, you look sexy. Are you sure about this?"

"We can delete it, but it really gets me going."

"I know better than this. I'm a police officer, and I've seen what can happen—"

"Just do it, Chase."

Something about the way he said it made me concede. I wasn't going to lie, I found the idea hot as hell too. So I nodded and started to record. Kellan leaned in, but I said, "Nope. Not yet." With my other hand, I gripped the base of my cock, traced his pretty mouth with it, leaving a trail of my precome around his lips.

"Please," he asked, and something shifted in my chest. This shock to my system, like my heart stopped, then pulsed back to life again, thudding wildly.

I nodded, unable to find my words. Kellan's eyes

didn't leave me as he circled the head of my cock with his tongue. I kept the phone aimed at him but looked at him dead on, not wanting anything between us.

He bent lower and nudged my sac with his nose. Inhaled my scent, which was one of the sexiest fucking things in the world, then lapped at my balls.

"I love the way you taste." His back was arched, his ass out, and I wished I'd taken the time to get him naked.

"Fuck, it's good. So good, Kell."

He licked up my shaft. "Fuck my mouth," he pleaded, and yeah, he didn't have to ask twice. I pushed between his lips, Kellan's expert skills taking me deep as I pumped my hips. My cock was slick with his saliva when I pulled out before thrusting slowly in again. I didn't take him hard or fast, just long, slow, deep strokes that Kellan took beautifully.

He looked up at the phone as he sucked, and fuck if that didn't nearly make me come. It was so hot seeing him blow me for the camera.

I sped my thrusts slightly. Spit ran down my nuts, and Kellan kept going. Kept sucking me expertly, making my balls tingle and my pulse soar.

"So good. So fucking good, baby boy. Keep going. Just like that."

He smiled around my dick like he was proud of my praise. It made my balls tighten, and I pulled back, grabbing the base of my cock so I didn't blow my load all over his pretty face. I stopped the recording and tossed my phone to the bedside table. "I need inside you somethin' fierce."

After tugging Kellan to his feet, I pulled him close, kissed him, fed him my tongue as I shoved my hands down the back of the sweats he wore. I cupped his tight ass, trembled when I thought about how it felt around my cock. Kellan ground against me, much like he had in my kitchen earlier.

"Horny little thing, aren't you?" I teased.

"You make me crazy, Chase. I'm so fucking wild for you."

I growled and bit at his neck, shoving the sweats down. I pulled away just enough to rip his shirt over his head, and then I was kissing him again, kissing him as I laid him back on my bed, nudging his body to the center with his head on the pillows. Kneeling between his legs, I looked down at him. At his trim body and the cut of his abs. The tufts of hair under his arms, the slight stubble on his face. That was different for him; he was always clean-shaven.

His cock leaked on his flat belly, his balls high and

tight, his thigh muscles straining…and that little heart on his hip.

He was so fucking beautiful, he stole my breath. How had I not seen it before? I'd wanted him that night we shared when he was eighteen, and I was attracted to him now, but damn, he was beautiful. There was no other word for him.

"Why a heart?" I asked, placing my finger over it.

"I can't tell you that."

I nodded, even though I wanted to know. Kellan had no obligation to tell me anything.

"Do you want to use your cuffs on me?"

I did, but not right then. Not only did I not want to take the time to go get them, but I wanted Kellan's touch, craved his hands all over my body. "Not this time."

"What if we don't do it again?"

I frowned. "Oh, baby boy. Unless you decide you don't want me, we're definitely doing this again."

He looked up at me, a whole world of emotion in his green eyes. It hit me right in the chest, made me both ache and feel like I was coming alive in a way I didn't understand. "What is it? You wanna stop?"

"No." He shook his head. "I want… Fuck me, Chase."

He didn't have to ask me twice. I leaned over and pressed a quick kiss to his lips, then grabbed the lube and a condom out of the bedside table. I slicked my fingers, rubbed his rim, and pushed a digit into his tight hole.

"Oh God, yes. I love the feel of something inside me." He closed his eyes while I finger-fucked him, first with one finger, then two. I watched him take his pleasure, move against my hand, and then he opened his eyes, and they locked on me, and suddenly I fucking *ached*. What was it in his stare? I didn't know, but I felt it to the marrow of my bones.

I pulled back and suited up, knowing I would die if I didn't get inside him soon. I squirted lube on my erection, then nudged him. "I want you to ride me, Kell. Will you do that for me?"

"Fuck yessss," he hissed, and we changed places, me on my back and Kellan kneeling. He straddled me as I held the base of my dick. It took a minute, and then I was pushing my cock past the first ring of muscle. My bones melted, like I evaporated into the bed, he felt so good. So hot and tight as I sank deeper and deeper inside him.

When Kellan was finally sitting on me, my dick buried to the hilt, we both exhaled a heavy breath, then looked at each other and smiled.

"That's a big nightstick you got there, Officer," he said cheekily.

"You like it, though, like it stuffed inside you. Ride me, Kell. Show me what that ass can do."

And fuck, he did just that. His sexy body bounced on my cock, and he rolled his hips the right way, leaning at the right angle, taking me deep and then pulling off. My whole body was tight with the need to take over, to slam into him, to stake my claim on his body, but I held off as long as I could, letting Kellan work me.

Soon my hands found their way to his hips, and one of my thumbs covered the heart tattoo as I held him and thrust up into his body.

"Fuck, fuck, fuck." Kellan dropped his head back.

Christ, he was beautiful. Long sinewy muscles, his Adam's apple moving as he swallowed, giving his body to me, taking his pleasure from me, and giving me so much satisfaction, I could burst.

I slammed up into him. His cock jerked, spilling precome as I fucked into him again and again.

"Yes, Chase. Right there. Fuck me," he called out, wrapping a hand around his cock. He stroked twice before his body tightened, come spurting from his cock, all over his hand and my stomach. It was the sexiest thing I'd ever seen, and I lost it, my body tumbling into orgasm as I somehow felt both weightless and heavy at the same time.

Kellan fell on top of me, and I stroked his sweaty back. Neither of us spoke. The moment felt heavy, thick and full in a way I hadn't expected.

My cock began to soften, and I pulled out before I leaked inside him, but still we didn't move. I petted his head and rubbed his back and closed my eyes when I felt his lips press against my chest.

It was as if that one kiss broke whatever was happening, and Kellan pulled away briskly. He grabbed the condom and tossed it, then went to the bathroom. "I have to take a leak. I'll be right back." He closed the door behind him, making me frown.

That had been intense. I knew I'd never had sex like that in my life, had never felt so connected to someone. It made sense. Kellan was so twined with my past, and part of my life, so yeah, emotions would be there when usually it was just two bodies coming together to sate their desire.

The minutes ticked by, and Kellan didn't come out. My nerves began wrapping around me, making my gut ache. Had I done something wrong? Hurt him somehow? I got up, walked over, and stood outside the door. "Kell? You okay?"

"Yeah," he said after a moment, and pulled open the door. "I'm fine. That was fucking hot, Chase." His gaze wouldn't meet mine.

"What's wrong?" It was evident he was trying to hide something.

"Nothing."

"Kellan—"

"Nothing's wrong, Chase. I said I was fine. Now come on. I wanna watch the video. I bet it gets me hard again."

I nodded, still not feeling right, but trying to trust him. We went back to bed, watched the video, then deleted it. We were both hard again, so I blew him, and the second he came in my mouth, I swallowed it down, and then he was kissing me as I jerked off on his abs.

Kellan stayed all night.

The next morning I made him breakfast, and then we were standing at the door and I kissed him again. Fuck, I didn't want him to go. What was wrong with me? Why didn't I want him to go? "Am I going to see you again?" I held his waist and imagined my finger over that tattoo again.

"We live in the same small town, and you're best friends with my brother. Of course we'll see each other again."

"You know what I mean, smartass." I kissed the tip of his nose, of all things. Why the fuck I couldn't keep my hands or mouth off him, I didn't know.

"Yes," he answered. "I'd totally like more benefits again."

Kellan smiled, backed away, then turned and walked to his car. I stood there watching, even after his vehicle disappeared.

# CHAPTER NINETEEN

## *Kellan*

SEVERAL WEEKS WENT by in what felt like the blink of an eye. I spent a few nights a week at Chase's place, and sometimes I still found myself there but didn't sleep over. We fucked—a lot. What was the point of benefits if you didn't take advantage of them?

But sometimes we didn't have sex at all. I'd go over, and he'd be tired after work, or my ass would be too sore from the night before, and we'd do things like cuddle on the couch and watch horror movies or grill dinner together, and one time I even taught him how to make my mom's secret recipe for oatmeal-raisin cookies.

It was in those moments that all my warning bells started to go off. Sex was one thing. People fucked each other all the time. Hell, I'd had sex with people when I didn't even know their last name, but movies and cooking made my heart ache for him even more. Made me wish for things I wouldn't even put into words because I knew they would never happen. Caused me to worry that I wouldn't survive this, wouldn't survive having Chase and losing him.

But I also didn't have it in me to walk away. That much was obvious.

They still hadn't arrested anyone for the armed robbery. It was all the folks of Havenwood could talk about. I knew it was stressing Chase out. He'd space off when we were spending time together but would try to brush it off when I asked if he was okay. Last night, though, he'd told me he couldn't get it out of his head. Somehow he'd decided it was his fault or his responsibility to figure it out. Don't ask me how he came to that fool conclusion when it made absolutely no sense, but that was Chase Hawthorne, and things like that were probably part of the reason I loved him.

Griff, of course, was being all Griff-y about it, worried someone was going to rob my shop or something because I had *so* much money lying around? That wasn't the case, but it might be nice if it were. The first time Chase had been by, he asked about the security of the place too. I did all that I could. And it was amazing showing Chase what I'd built, seeing him impressed by me.

It was Friday night, and Chase was off. He'd invited

me over, and I'd wanted to spend time with him, but I'd also promised Josh I would go to Richmond with him. We hadn't spent much time together lately, he'd said, which I knew was an excuse for him to worry that I was spending too much time with Chase.

We were going to one of our favorite gay bars in the city, which yes, I fucking loved. I didn't make enough time to go party in Richmond, and I loved to dance, but a tiny part of me wanted to stay and soak up all the time with Chase I could have.

I might have been a little obsessed with him, but he was fucking gorgeous and sweet and had a great cock, so who could blame me?

I was startled by the sound of the door to my studio opening. We were closed, but I hadn't locked it because this was Havenwood and you didn't have to do that shit here.

When I saw Buck striding toward me, I automatically frowned. "I'm afraid we're closed for the day."

"I don't want you to teach my son."

Fuck, I should have expected this. "He was signed up by his mother, Buck. I'm not going to turn him away." It had taken me a while to be able to chat with Bridget. I hadn't told her what her daughter said—that Buck mentioned him being soft like me—but I did tell her I was running a special on siblings. They got a month free and then half price. I also told her I could work with her if that was too much. Of course, there was no special, but if Buck Jr. wanted to learn art, I would make sure I could teach him, even if it was for free. I knew his mom would never accept it if she thought it was a handout, though. We hadn't had our first class together yet, but it was scheduled for next week.

"I don't want you to teach my son," he said again, his voice tight.

"We're closed. I'm going to have to ask you to leave." I'd be lying if I didn't admit my hands shook. Buck was an asshole—an asshole who was about a foot taller than me and had at least fifty pounds on me. But I wasn't going to back down. That wasn't me.

So I stood, went to walk past him to open the door, but he reached out and grabbed my arm, his fingers tight on my biceps. "I teach my son to be a man. He'll take a class with you over my dead body. Cancel with Bridget. I'm not fucking around, Kellan. I don't give a shit who your brother is either." Without another word, he let go of me roughly, pushing me slightly as he did so, and walked out.

My lungs hurt, I was breathing so hard. I rushed over and flipped the lock on the door, and saw his dad,

Jimmy, sitting in their truck. I lowered the blinds, slid down the wall, sat on the floor. I gasped, trying to get air into my lungs. I couldn't breathe. Why the fuck couldn't I breathe?

I kept seeing Buck grab me, which morphed into me being back in that apartment in Richmond all those years ago.

Closing my eyes, I counted backward, focusing on trying to calm myself, to center myself. I'd been taught that in therapy, which I'd attended for a couple of years after the Richmond incident.

It took me a few minutes to catch my breath. I wiped the stray tears that had managed to leak from my eyes, then shoved to my feet. All that over a fucking art class? I didn't understand it, couldn't make sense of what was wrong with people. Why the hell did they care so much about art or being feminine or whatever bullshit excuse Buck had? Or maybe it was me. Because I was *soft* and *gay* and he didn't want me near his son.

Fuck him.

All I knew was that I wasn't going to back down. There was no way Buck would talk me out of teaching his son. As long as I could do it with Buck Jr. staying safe, I sure as shit wasn't walking away.

"HOW DOES MY ass look in these jeans?" I asked Josh as I stepped out of the bathroom of one of the hotel rooms we'd gotten for the night. When we came to Richmond, we always got two connecting rooms because that was how we rolled.

"Your ass looks good in whatever you wear, and don't pretend you don't know it. Stop fishing for compliments," Josh replied from where he lounged on the hotel bed, looking through his phone.

"Are you on Grindr?"

He grinned. "Maybe."

"You don't plan to spend any time with me at all tonight, do you? You made me come with you, and you're going to ditch me the second a pretty boy pays you any attention." Not that I could blame him. I was typically the same when we came here. I mean, why else go to Richmond if not to get laid—well, and to dance.

But this time felt…*different*, and I wasn't going to let myself admit why.

"You're normally doing the same. You *should* be doing the same tonight." Josh cocked a brow at me.

"Get out of my head." It felt like he always knew what I was thinking. "And who said I don't plan on hooking up tonight?" Again, I knew I should. Chase and I weren't serious or committed. We were friends with benefits, but Jesus, the thought of someone else touching me made my skin crawl.

"I'll bet you money you don't. Kell…"

I held up my hand to stop him before he went any further. "I don't want to do this with you tonight. I want to have fun. I want to dance with you and flirt with you and then maybe we'll each bring someone back to our rooms, okay?"

*Liar, liar, pants on fire.* I so wasn't taking anyone back to my room.

"Sure, fine. Whatever." Josh played it off like it was a joke, but I could tell he was frustrated with me. "Why are you wearing a long-sleeved shirt? It's hot as balls outside."

"Eh." I shrugged. "Because it looks good on me." The truth was, I'd always bruised easily. Sometimes there would be a big purple mark on my arm or leg, and I'd have no idea how I got it. This time I knew, though, and if anyone else saw, they would know it didn't come from a random bump. It was in the very distinct shape of a hand being wrapped around my arm.

Obviously, I hadn't told Josh what happened earlier that day. Or Griff, or Chase. I didn't need any of them rushing to my rescue simply because Buck was pissed his son was taking an art class in case it meant he would become queer like me. I fucking hated people.

Josh and I finished getting ready. On our way out, I checked my phone, wondering if there would be a text from Chase. I wanted that, but really, there no reason for him to text. To tell me to have fun? To say he missed me?

*We're not a couple, we're not a couple, we're not a couple.* I figured it wouldn't hurt to keep reminding myself of that fact.

The club was already packed when Josh and I arrived. I shoved my phone into my pocket, determined I would *not* look for another text from Chase.

Tonight I was going to drink, have fun with Josh…and maybe find a guy to remind me that Chase wasn't the only man with a great cock and that there were other guys interested in me.

The drinking part went well. Even the having-fun part. Josh and I danced close, touching and rubbing and laughing together, but I knew I wouldn't hook up with anyone. I only wanted Chase Hawthorne.

# CHAPTER TWENTY

## *Chase*

I CHECKED MY phone for what had to be the twentieth time, wondering if Kellan was having a good time in Richmond.

Obviously, I wanted him to have fun. He deserved it, but all I could do was think about him and Josh, or him and other guys, and this wave of jealously pulled me under each and every time.

I wanted to be out with Kellan…and I wanted Kellan to be with me.

Or hell, I wasn't that much of a possessive asshole. He could go out with his friend as much as he wanted. I just didn't want him to hook up with anyone.

Stupid as it sounded, I wanted Kellan Caine all to myself. Even stupider? I was pretty sure I missed him. It was one night apart, and it wasn't even like we'd spent every day together, but I had at least *seen* him nearly every day for the past few weeks.

"You want another beer?" Griff asked. Law was there too, but Knox hadn't made it in. I wasn't sure what he was doing.

"Sure, buddy. Thanks."

The bar wasn't too busy for a Friday night, which meant Griff had a bit more time to chat. "Still nothing on the robbery?" he asked.

"Nope." My teeth ground together. It was the last thing I wanted to think about. I hated the idea of something violent happening in Havenwood. I sure as shit hated that it had happened on my watch.

"That's some crazy-ass shit," Law said. "Things like that don't happen here. Not since..." His words trailed off, but we all knew exactly what he was talking about. Not since Kellan and Griff's parents.

I put the bottle of beer to my lips and took a long swallow.

"Kellan worked late at his studio the other night, and that shit stresses me out. I have this fear of someone breaking in while he's there."

My eyes snapped to Griffin's. "Did something happen? Did he tell you he noticed anything strange?"

"No, no." Griff shook his head. "You know how I get. Just worry too much. After losing Mom and Dad."

He did worry a lot, and I got that. Plus, he loved his

brother…the guy I was sneaking around with. Fuck, I really needed to figure this shit out. "Nothing is going to happen to Kellan. I promise you."

"You and I both know you can't make promises like that," Griff replied.

But I was serious. I'd move heaven and earth if I thought Kellan was in trouble.

"I'm pretty sure the little shit is seeing someone," Griff added just as I took a drink of my beer. I nearly choked on it, coughing wildly as Lawson reached over and swatted my back like I was a kid.

"What makes you think that?" I asked, hoping my guilt didn't show. I glanced at Law, and he cocked a brow at me, curious, but I ignored him. All I needed was for people to start finding out about me and Kellan.

"He hasn't come home quite a few nights. When he does, he still comes home late. He says he's at the studio, and yeah, sometimes I'm sure he is, but I don't know. Something's up. He's smiley and acting weird and shit."

Well, that made a grin tug at my lips too. I liked the idea of making Kellan smile.

"Whoever the motherfucker is, I hope I won't have to kick his ass."

And now I was frowning.

"Why would you have to do that?" Law said. "He's a

grown-ass man, Griff. And hell, one of you needs to move out or something. Give the kid some space." Law pushed his blond curls from his face. I couldn't say I didn't agree with him. Griff was too protective of Kellan, but Kellan didn't help matters either.

"You called him a grown-ass man and a kid in the same sentence," Griff replied just as I said, "He's not a kid."

No one answered me as Griffin continued, "I think if he's spending as much time with him as he has been the past few weeks, then whoever this fucker is should make an appearance. He's obviously in Havenwood. Why are they hiding out? Why haven't I met him? It's like he's hiding Kellan away."

Guilt suffused my body and landed in my gut. Was that how Kellan felt? Hell, maybe he'd said something to Griff. Maybe he thought I was embarrassed of him. That couldn't be further from the truth. I was proud to be with Kellan. Well, if I were really with him, which I wasn't.

"Give him some credit, man," Law said. "It's only been a few weeks. I'm sure there's a good reason for it. You're a little out of control where your brother is concerned. I probably wouldn't want to tell you if I were dating him either." I was pretty sure Law had figured us out and said that for my benefit.

Griff shot him a murderous stare. "Thank God you're straight, and don't even joke around like that. I couldn't handle the idea of one of my friends screwing around with my little brother. I'm too protective, and it would cause all sorts of shit."

The guilt began spreading out, shooting through my veins until it took me over. Christ, what were we doing? This was going to end all sorts of bad. I was stuck between this intense desire for Kellan and my loyalty to Griffin, who had always been the best kind of friend to me.

"I think that's part of the point," Lawson replied. "You're too protective of him. If he's keeping something from you, it's because of *you*. Trust him. I'm sure he knows what he's doing. He's twenty-eight years old. And how do you know I'm straight?"

Both Griff and I whipped toward Lawson. Shit. Was Lawson bi? I'd wondered, but from the look on Griff's face, I was pretty sure he hadn't.

"You're not straight?" I asked, and he shrugged.

"Maybe. Maybe not. Unless we're fucking, it's no business of yours. And no offense, but you're not my type, Hawthorne." Law winked playfully.

"I don't care who you sleep with as long as it's not

Kellan," Griff added. "Fuck Chase, or maybe Josh. Chase is sort of ugly."

"Suck my dick, Caine." I grabbed my cock.

"Now, boys. What are you doing having all this fun without me?"

I turned at the sound of Becca's voice. She squeezed in beside me and wrapped her arm around my shoulders. "Plus, I'd be much better at blowing you. I remember what you like."

Everyone laughed but me. I managed a smile, but discomfort swam around in my veins. I felt like I was doing something wrong. And as much as I cared about Becca, and as beautiful as she was, hers weren't the arms I wanted around me or the mouth I wanted to sink my dick into. No, that belonged to Kellan, which was really fucking dangerous and stupid.

"You want a drink? I'll buy you a drink," I told her, wanting to be polite.

The man beside her got up, and Becca took the stool. "Nah, that's okay. I'm driving. Just thought I'd pop in and say hi. How y'all doing?"

The Kellan conversation was dropped, thankfully, as they started to chat with Becca. Every so often Griff would sneak away to take care of customers or whatever he had to do, but there were other bartenders on shift, and he was giving them all the tips so he could take it easy.

I tried to join the conversation when I could, but I found myself thinking about what Griff had said, and checking my phone, and wondering what Kellan was doing. Fucking Kellan Caine was screwing with my head, and I wasn't quite sure how to deal with it.

Griff got me another beer, which I gladly took, forcing myself to leave my phone alone and stop acting like a lovesick pup.

I couldn't get my head in the game no matter how hard I tried. Bec kept touching me, innocent touches that shouldn't have bothered me, but then I thought of Josh with Kellan. How it made me feel when they touched. They were so close, and having Becca do the same to me felt wrong.

About an hour or so after Becca got there, I pulled some cash out of my wallet and told Griff to close my tab. "I'm gonna head out." I pushed to my feet.

"You're not driving, right?" Griff asked, and I shook my head.

"You know better than to have to ask me that shit." I didn't drink and drive. Never had and never would.

"I think I'll get going too," Becca added. "I can take you home so you don't have to pay for a ride."

Griffin smiled at me, and I knew exactly where his mind was going. He cocked a brow as if to say *I told you so*. He was convinced Becca and I were going to pick up where we'd left off years ago. Of course, he didn't know I was sleeping with his brother, so I couldn't blame him for thinking that.

A customer needed Griff, so he walked away just as I told her, "You don't have to do that. Don't want you to have to go out of your way."

"I don't mind, silly." She smiled, and my stomach sank.

I said my goodbyes to Law and waved at Griff as Becca and I left the bar. I followed her over to a—"Holy shit. She's pretty." Damned if she didn't drive an older red Corvette.

"She was my daddy's, remember?" Becca said, and memories began floating to the surface. The first time I'd kissed Becca had been up against this car, but she sure hadn't looked as good as she did now. "We put a lot of work into her."

"You guys did a great job."

Becca opened the door and slid inside. I did the same. I still felt that twist of my insides. The one telling me this was wrong, and I was pretty sure she expected something. Logically, Kellan and I were only friends with benefits, and for all I knew, he'd gone home with someone tonight, but I couldn't do it. I didn't want anyone else. Just him.

The truth of how much I wanted him, how much I liked spending time with him, slammed into my chest with such intensity, I could hardly breathe.

"Bec, listen." I reached over and put a hand on her wrist as she was about to start the car. "I might be making an ass of myself with assumptions right now, but I don't feel right not telling you—I'm seeing someone." The words came out easily and felt true. I *was* seeing someone. I was seeing Kellan.

"Oh. Well, I don't know why I didn't expect that. I'm sorry for making assumptions myself. It's serious?"

My pulse sped up, and I saw Kellan drop his head back and laugh. Damned if I didn't smile. "I, um...probably not. There are a million reasons why it wouldn't work, and my own feelings are all jumbled up. Not quite sure what's going on, but I don't feel right being with anyone else."

She smiled, leaned over, and kissed my cheek. "You're a good man, Chase Hawthorne. I hope you know that."

I couldn't help but wonder if she'd think that if she knew I was going behind Griff's back with Kellan. Still, I smiled. "Thank you. I'd appreciate it if we could keep this between us."

"No problem." She started the car. "Put your seat belt on. I'll take you home even if you don't put out." Becca winked, and I laughed.

It felt good to have her as a friend again.

# CHAPTER TWENTY-ONE

## *Kellan*

JOSH SLEPT THE whole ride home the next day, the fucker. We'd had a blast together, but eventually the night was over. I'd turned down the guy who wanted to hook up with me, but Josh hadn't.

Fucking Chase Hawthorne. It was all his fault. I went to sleep with blue balls while listening to Josh having sex in the next room, and all I wanted was to be with Chase.

It was ridiculous.

Josh apparently hadn't gotten much sleep last night because he couldn't keep his eyes open, and now I was not only stabby with Chase, but with Josh too.

I pulled up in front of my house and shook my friend roughly.

Josh jerked awake. "What the fuck."

"I'm home." We'd taken Josh's car, and I was the one stuck driving it.

"You didn't want to go to my place?"

"No, I wanted to come home. I'm mad at you."

He rolled his eyes. "You're mad because I got laid and you didn't. That was your fault. If you're only friends with benefits, you should be able to fuck other people if you wanted. If you can't, then you sure as shit should be calling it more than friends with bennies."

He had a point there, but one I didn't want to think about. Ignoring him, I got out of the car and tried to walk into the house, but Josh was out too, hugging me before I could walk away. "Tell him how you feel," he whispered.

God, I wished I could, but that wasn't even a possibility. "I can't."

"Why not?"

"Because it's not what we agreed on? Because he won't feel the same? And even if he did, he wouldn't risk his friendship with Griff, and I wouldn't expect him to."

"Then he's not worthy of you, Kell. You've never seen yourself through honest eyes. You're worth more than loving someone who is just getting sex from you. And if Griff is more important than you, then Chase can fuck right off. Tell him. How you. *Feel.* And if he's not on the same page, walk away."

It wasn't the first time I'd heard something like that from Josh, and each time I did, it wormed its way deeper inside me. Because I knew he was right. Because I knew I wouldn't survive it if I kept doing this.

But I didn't want to lose Chase either. Not when I'd just gotten him after a lifetime of want.

"I'll think about it."

"That's all I ask." He kissed my forehead, and I handed him his keys. "Were you planning on getting your bag out of my car or just running away from me?"

I rolled my eyes at him. "Asshole."

"What did I do?"

We went back to his car, and Josh handed me my bag.

When I got inside, Griffin was sitting at the kitchen table with his laptop and a cup of coffee. He looked up at me and smiled. "You have fun with Josh?"

"Yes, Dad."

Griff shook his head as I walked over and began making a cup of coffee. "All I did was ask if you had a good night. I wasn't acting like your dad."

"It's the way you say things sometimes. Like you're checking up on me. I can't explain it."

Once I had my coffee doctored, I sat at the table with him. "But yes, I had fun with Josh."

Griff chuckled. "It seems like you guys have been spending even more time together lately. Either that, or you've been with someone else a whole lot. Are you and Josh seeing each other? Or you and someone else?"

I didn't look him in the eyes because Griff was pretty good at knowing when I was lying. Still, this was hard. It wasn't that I didn't want to be truthful with him. But this whole thing was messy already, and it had only been a few weeks. "No."

"Liar. If he's asking you to hide your relationship, then—"

"Maybe it's me. Did you ever think of that? Why is it always that someone has to be using poor Kellan? Maybe Kellan is using them. Or asking them to keep the relationship quiet." Griff always assumed I needed help or was being taken advantage of.

"Are you using someone? Asking them to keep quiet about your relationship?"

My eyes darted away.

"That's what I thought."

"Screw you, Griff. Stay out of my business."

He held up his hands in defeat. "I wasn't trying to be an asshole here, I swear. Honestly, I was just making conversation and making sure you had a good night. I'm starting to feel a bit left out, though. Everyone is getting some except me."

My stomach swooped and tumbled. *Don't ask, don't*

*ask, don't ask.*

Obviously, that wasn't going to happen. Somehow I knew exactly who he was talking about. Had he noticed Chase had been spending a lot of time with someone? He and I were together more than I thought we would be. "Knox or Law?" I asked casually.

"No, Chase. He went home with Becca last night. If there's ever anyone he could be serious about, I think it would be her."

Oh God. I felt like I was going to be sick. My gut tightened, and my vision swam. Chase went home with Becca? I didn't know why I was surprised. I had no reason or right to be, but then, I guess I wasn't surprised.

I was crushed.

Even though he didn't owe me anything. Even though we were friends with benefits, it hurt.

"Good for him. They make a good couple." I stood up and went to the sink, setting my full coffee mug by it.

"I didn't say they were a couple. I said he went home with her. Hell, for all I know they went and played Scrabble. Or they were having a little fun. Chase isn't the type to settle down, really."

Luckily, I had my back to Griff. There was a window in front of the sink, so it would seem as though I was looking out it. I squeezed my eyes closed tightly, and when I opened them, a tear leaked free.

Fuck. I should have known this would happen. I *did* know it would happen, but I thought... I'd *hoped* for more. That eventually Chase would see something different in me. But that wasn't going to happen, and all I was doing was hurting myself.

Josh was right.

"I'm not really feeling so hot. Josh and I had breakfast at some hole-in-the-wall place, and I don't think it agreed with my stomach. I'm going to take a nap."

"Do you need me to run to the store and get you anything?"

"Nah, I think I'm fine. Nothing a little sleep won't help."

"Okay. I have a few errands to run, and then I'm heading to the bar. I'm working two-to-ten tonight and have someone else closing, so let me know if you need something."

"Thanks, Griff," I replied, then walked away. I went straight to my room, closed and locked the door behind me, and fell onto my bed.

I hadn't expected it to be over so soon. And the least Chase could have done was have the decency to tell me if he was fucking someone else. I could have enjoyed myself more the night before, if nothing else.

My phone buzzed with a text. Without looking, I knew it was him.

**Hey, Kell. Just checking to make sure you got home okay this morning. Call or text me.**

But I didn't. I tossed my phone to the floor and went to sleep. I woke up a few hours later to see he'd texted again, but I didn't answer that one either. When he called me later that afternoon, I turned my phone off.

Fuck Chase Hawthorne. I didn't need to hear him tell me about Becca or to say this was over, or hell, even to give some lame-ass excuse to check on me.

I didn't need him, and I was going to find a way to stop loving him.

# CHAPTER TWENTY-TWO

## Chase

I WENT TO Griff's to casually bring up Kellan, and discovered he'd gotten home early that morning. Considering I'd texted him a couple of times and then called him, it was obvious the younger Caine brother was avoiding me.

It was after four by the time I decided to make the trip over to their place. It wasn't that he *had* to call or text me, but if something was wrong, I wanted to know. It was curious that this all happened after he'd gone to Richmond for a night, and all I could think was that he'd hooked up with someone and decided he was done with whatever it was we were doing.

The thought sent a jolt of disappointment through me. I should be done with Kellan, but I wasn't ready for this to be over. That truth worried me and excited me in equal measures. I was always ready for something to be over, and realizing I didn't feel that way with Kell settled right in my bones. It felt natural. Thinking about having those feelings for someone had never felt that way before.

Thinking he likely hooked up with someone, though…that was white-hot, searing pain in my veins. Jealousy and possessiveness, this relentless and foreign feeling inside me, even though he had every right to do that. Kellan wasn't mine. We'd made no commitments to each other.

His car was out front when I pulled up. I knocked, and it only took him a moment to answer.

"I should have known you would come over." He walked away, leaving the door open.

O-kay.

"Well, you've been ignoring my calls all day, so I thought I'd make sure you were still alive." I closed the door behind me and looked over in time to see him roll his eyes. It was such a Kellan thing to do that I snickered. He acted like a big kid sometimes and always had.

"Of course you had to make sure I'm okay. I mean, I went to a club! Think of all the things that could have happened to me! What would I have done if you hadn't come over today to make sure I was okay?"

It was my turn to roll my eyes. "You're acting like a child, Kell."

"Screw you, Chase."

He tried to shove his way around me, but I grabbed his arm. Not tightly, just to try and stop him, but Kellan winced, making me let go. Christ, he didn't even want me to touch him anymore? That left a cold ache deep in my chest, one that I wanted gone immediately.

"It's okay if you hooked up with someone last night. Is that what this is about? We said we were only friends with benefits, so I'm not going to fault you for having some fun." The words were bitter on my tongue. I wanted them back, because the idea of Kellan being with anyone else made me nauseous. I wanted him with me and only me, and holy fuck, what was I thinking? It was all too much hitting me at once—wanting him that much, the possessiveness I felt.

The way he grimaced made it clear I'd said the wrong thing. "Why is it okay, Chase? Because you don't give a shit about me? Because you won't ever see me *that way*? I'm just a warm hole to you right now? Fuck you!" He poked his finger into my chest. "Are you feeling guilty because you hooked up with Becca last night, so you want to make sure I got some too? I could have fucked Josh, you know? At least if I was going to fuck someone, I made sure it was someone who wasn't in Havenwood!"

A low growl started in my gut. The thought of Kellan with Josh made me want to tear the whole world apart. I could maybe deal with a random guy in Richmond I'd never see again, but thinking about his best friend with him made me... Well, shit. It hurt. "Don't fuck Josh," I said with a little more vulnerability than I'd have wanted. "And I don't even know what in the hell you're talking about. I didn't sleep with Becca. I told her I couldn't, that I was seeing someone else, which makes me fucking crazy, I guess. I know what we are, and I knew you were likely with Josh or someone else last night, but I—"

"You told Becca no?" Kellan asked softly, cutting me off.

The air in the room changed with that. It wasn't heavy and thick anymore, though I couldn't say exactly what it felt like. "Yes."

"You told her you were seeing someone else?" he confirmed, and he looked so...almost sad. Like he wasn't sure what it meant, and the truth was, I didn't fully know either.

"Yeah." I ran a hand through my hair and began pacing the living room, then stopped to look at him and shrugged my shoulders. There was nothing I could do, really, other than share the truth. This was Kellan, and I couldn't lie or hold things back from him. "I can't seem to get you outta my damn head, Kell. I don't want anyone else but you."

"I don't want anyone else but you either. Josh was giving me shit to hook up, and my brain kept telling me he was right, but I just...couldn't do it."

My whole body relaxed in that moment. I hadn't even realized how tight I was, how on edge, but knowing that Kellan hadn't been with anyone else, knowing he only wanted me, was a balm to my soul I hadn't known I needed. Like all these things that had been mismatched and lost before clicked into place.

"What are we going to do?" he asked. "Griff and..."

"Shh." My body was against his then, pressing Kellan against the wall. When in the hell had I moved? I couldn't even recall getting closer to him. "I want you. Fuck, I want you so bad, it's eating me alive, baby boy."

Our mouths clashed, an uncontrollable force connecting us. I pushed my leg between his because I knew how much Kellan liked riding my thigh. His arms went around me, his hands in my hair as we kissed messily and rubbed against each other.

I didn't know what it was about him, what it had always been about him, but this felt right. And the thought of walking away made every instinct inside me rebel against it. I'd always felt like I belonged in this family, like they were my home, but that feeling multiplied when I was with him, like this was where I should have been all along.

"Chase…" He said my name as I trailed kisses down his neck.

"You make me fucking crazy for you." I couldn't believe I was doing this here, but I couldn't have stopped if I'd wanted to. I grabbed the bottom of Kellan's shirt and tugged it over his head. I reached for him, and that's when I noticed the finger marks on his biceps. My whole world rocked, my eyes going hazy. "What the fuck. Did I somehow do this to you?"

"What? No, it's nothing. You know how easily I bruise." Kellan went to pull away, and I let him. I sure as shit wasn't going to put my hands on him and hold him there. Whoever did that to him, I wasn't the same as that person.

"Who did that? Who grabbed you?" Fire burned through me, exploding into an anger I couldn't even put into words. My hands were shaking, because if this had been some accident, if it wasn't what I thought it was, he would have told me what happened already.

"I can take care of myself. It wasn't a big deal."

"Was it Josh?"

"What? No! Why in the hell would Josh grab me? It was Buck. He's pissed because he thinks it'll make Buck

Jr. gay if I teach him. I told him I wasn't going to stop. He grabbed my arm and told me he wanted me to and then left. He didn't hold on to me hard. You know how my skin is."

I saw nothing but red. My heart sped up, slammed against my chest, and I worried I was going to stroke out. I was going to kill the motherfucker for putting his hands on Kellan that way. Without another word, I went straight for the door.

"Chase, what are you doing?"

"Going to make sure he knows to keep his fucking hands to himself."

I pulled the door open and rushed out. By the time Kellan got outside, I was already in my truck, pulling away.

My hands fisted on the steering wheel as I drove to Buck's place. It wasn't too far from my own, on the outskirts of town. When I pulled up, he was sitting on the front porch with a beer in his hand. I jumped out of the truck and slammed the door.

"Chase Hawthorne, what can I do for you?"

"Are your kids here?" I spit out.

"What?" He shoved to his feet. "No, they're with their mother. Is everything okay?"

Without thinking, I pushed him against the house,

my forearm against this throat—not hard enough to hurt him, but enough for him to know I was serious. "You want to pick on someone, pick on me. You keep your fucking hands off Kellan Caine."

Buck's eyes widened as if he hadn't expected that. "What did the little fag tell you? I hardly fucking touched him."

"You call him that again, and I won't be able to keep my anger in check. I'm holding on by a thread right now," I gritted out. Jesus Christ, I couldn't handle people like this. He reminded me of my father—judgmental, ignorant bigots.

"Is an officer of the law threatening me?" he asked, and my heart stumbled slightly. I hadn't even thought of my position, about who I was. All I'd thought about was Kellan and the hand mark on his arm. "Thinking twice, huh?"

Buck pushed me off him, and I let him.

"He sent his boyfriend to fight his fights for him? What a pussy. That's exactly what I don't want for my boy—to be soft like him."

Kellan wasn't weak. Kellan was one of the strongest people I'd ever known. *Do you treat him like you know that?* tumbled through my head. *Do you show him you know he's strong, or do you try and fight his battles for him like you're doing now?*

"Don't touch him again. Don't speak to him again. Don't even look wrong at him again." Without another word, I turned and started to walk back to my truck.

"The new patrol officer is a fag too? I wonder what the God-fearing residents of Havenwood will think about that!" he called after me. "Or is it that Griffin Caine has his dick so far up your ass that you protect his baby brother too? There was always somethin' weird about the two of you!"

I nearly stumbled at his words, not because I cared what he or anyone else thought, but because I knew there would be people who agreed with him. It was shitty that there were people in this world who would care. That they would think assholes like Buck were better than people like Kellan…people like me…because of who we were attracted to or who we loved. It was bullshit, but that's the way it was. I sure as shit didn't care, and I wouldn't hide who I was. Fuck them if they had a problem with it. Fuck Buck or anyone else. I didn't give a shit. I only cared about Kellan.

I got in my truck and drove away.

# CHAPTER TWENTY-THREE

## *Kellan*

I DIDN'T LOOK up from my seat on Chase's porch stairs when I heard his truck pull down the driveway.

I didn't want him to get home, because if he got home, we would have to talk. And when we talked, I was going to have to tell him that this wasn't going to work between us. It didn't matter that he'd said he didn't want anyone but me. I couldn't keep this going if he didn't trust me enough to take care of myself, to know that I didn't need him, but that when I did, I would go to him. He sure as shit didn't have the right to run off to fight my battles when I'd asked him not to.

It had taken him a while to get here. He went back to my place first, and called when he realized I wasn't home, and I texted back that I was here.

The truck turned off, then the door opened and closed. I heard his feet along the gravel before I saw his sneakers stop on the bottom step.

"Did you defend my honor?" Finally, I looked up at him.

"What are you talking about, Kell? I went over there and told him to keep his fucking hands off you, that he doesn't have a right to touch you. That's all I did."

"You're exactly like Griff! You don't think I can take care of myself!" I shoved to my feet, my body flushing with anger as my pulse throbbed in my ears.

"No! I care about you, and that's what people do when they care about someone!" he yelled back, and I sucked in a sharp breath. My whole life I'd wanted to hear Chase say he cared about me. Yes, earlier he said he couldn't get me out of his head and that he didn't want anyone but me, but that could be about sex and nothing more. Saying he cared felt heavier, like there was more meat to his words, more emotions, and part of me wanted to forget I was angry and drop to my knees or climb in his arms, but I couldn't. If I did, I'd regret it. I'd be angry with myself for not being stronger and sticking up for myself.

Caring wasn't enough. Not if Chase was going to keep appointing himself my savior. Not if he thought I couldn't take care of myself.

Chase sighed. "Let's go inside."

I shook my head. If I went in there, I wouldn't want

to leave. It was easier to be strong out here, and I was determined to do what I needed to do, no matter how much it hurt. "This isn't going to work. I think we need to put the brakes on what we're doing."

Chase frowned. "Because I told Buck not to touch you?" It sounded so small when he said it, but it wasn't small to me.

"Because you didn't listen when I asked you not to do it. Because you don't think I can handle shit on my own."

"That's not true at all," he said, then ran a hand through his hair and cursed.

"I already have a brother. If you're going to be my lover, that's all I need you to be. Someone I'm dating or fucking or whatever it is we're doing. I need you to be that, not another Griff."

"Fuck." He locked his hands behind his head and paced in front of the porch. I could see the wheels turning in his brain, see him working it all out in his head. What I didn't know was if he would be able to accept it.

"You know what kids used to say? That they had to be careful how much they teased me, or what they did to me, in case Griffin or Chase found out. No one gave a shit about me. They didn't mind picking on me. They *liked* picking on me, and they had no worries about what I would do or say. They didn't feel I could protect myself. They worried about what Griffin or Chase would do."

Chase stopped moving and looked at me, heavy emotion in his eyes, but I couldn't stop. I had too much to say, and it had been locked inside me for too long. "And when I got older, it didn't get any better. In high school I was Griffin Caine's little brother. I was the kid Griff came back to take care of, the kid he stayed in Havenwood for. They gave me shit for needing my big brother or Chase to fight my battles for me. I'd go to the grocery store or the post office after Mom and Dad died, and all I heard was, *What about poor little Kellan Caine? What's going to happen to Griff's future because he has to take care of his little brother?* And when I graduated and you left, I told Griff he could leave too. He didn't have to stay here anymore, but he said, *What if you need me?* And I get it. I know I'm impulsive. I know I get myself into stupid situations, but I'm not dumb or helpless, and I don't need you, Griffin, or anyone else to fight my battles for me."

"I'm sorry," Chase replied, his voice raspy with emotion, eyes downcast, his pain evident in the way his shoulders curled in.

There wasn't a part of me that thought Chase meant to treat me the way he did or meant to hurt me, but the fact of the matter was he did.

"Fuck, Kell. I never wanted you to think I don't trust you or that I don't feel like you can take care of yourself. I know how strong you are. You're the one who had the guts to kiss me when you were only eighteen. And you've dealt with all this shit in town for years and you're still unapologetically you, no matter what. Do you know how fucking brave that is? I just…I wanted to bear some of the weight. I don't know how to do this. I've never cared about someone this way. I mean, yeah, like a brother the way I care about Griff, or even the way it used to be with us, but this…this is different. I don't know how else to show what you mean to me."

My poor, sweet Chase. God, I loved him. He had such a big heart, and he was afraid he didn't know how to love. That was why he never got serious with anyone—I knew it. Chase didn't think he knew how to love, but he did.

"I know it comes from the heart. I get that, but I don't want to be your responsibility. I don't want to be your little brother, Chase. I want…" My heart was pounding. Blood rushed through my ears, and I felt dizzy, but I had to do this. In that moment, I knew I had to. If not then, I never would, and I'd regret it for the rest of my life if I didn't get the words out. "I'm in love with you. I've been in love with you since I was fourteen years old. I don't remember what it's like not to love you, and I don't know how to stop."

Chase's eyes went wide. His pupils expanded, and fuck, he was shaking. I could see him shaking from where he stood. I didn't know what the look I saw was—shock, yeah, but outside of that, I was lost. All I could think was that he wanted to run, that he was going to tell me he didn't feel the same, which I knew. I'd always known.

"I don't expect you to feel the same or say it back," I added quickly. "Please, don't even try, because if you say those words to me, I need to know they're real. It would kill me to hear them, only to realize they're not true."

"Kell... I..."

"Don't." I held my hand up. "Even if by some miracle you think you might, don't tell me unless you know. I'm asking you not to do that to me."

He nodded, and I knew he understood. He hadn't obeyed my wishes when it came to Buck, but he would now.

I didn't believe Chase loved me. I wanted him to, but I didn't think he did. I believed he cared about me.

He liked sleeping with me. And likely for the first time in his life, or at least since he was very young, he heard someone say they loved him. That had to fuck with his head. It had to be confusing, and the last thing I wanted was for him to say something in that moment that he would regret.

"I don't want to lose you," he replied softly. "I'm sorry I went to Buck, and I swear I won't do anything like that again. I trust you, and I believe in you, and the thought of stopping this, of walking away from you, is like someone is gnawing through my bones. Like they're taking out my heart or my lungs. I don't know what that is. I don't know if that's what you feel, but I don't want to stop. Is it okay that I said that?"

He was so sweet. How could I not love him?

"Yes. That's okay. So what do we do now?" We were in a strange place, Chase and I, and it wasn't as easy as deciding to date and doing it. We had Griff to worry about, and this was Havenwood. I had no idea if Chase even wanted to be out here.

"We figure out a way to tell Griff about us. That we're...hell, dating, I guess? That word feels wrong, but I don't know how else to say it."

Jesus, I thought my stupid heart was going to jump out of my chest. "Really? You want to be with me and to tell Griff?"

I hated the vulnerability in my voice, but again, I didn't know how to not be vulnerable with Chase. It was something that had always been there, my feelings for him a truth I'd always known.

"Is that okay with you? Is that what you want? I don't want to assume."

"Yes."

Any other possible words were cut off by Chase's mouth coming down hard on mine. My arms went around his shoulders, my hands in his hair, and Chase lifted me as he kissed me. My legs wrapped around his waist, and we kept kissing as he walked toward the porch stairs. His foot caught and he tripped, making us almost fall, and then we were laughing while kissing, and there was nothing in the world that tasted better than Chase Hawthorne's laugh.

I slid out of his arms and onto my feet. "I think I better walk."

"You don't want to try and carry me?" Chase teased, waggling his eyebrows.

"Um…no."

He unlocked the door and kicked it closed behind us. He reached for me, but I jerked away. He cocked his head as if he was surprised at first, but then I ran toward his room and he started chasing me.

I kicked out of my shoes and jumped onto his bed, and then his body was covering mine. My legs were hanging off the side of the mattress, and Chase was leaning over me, kissing me and thrusting his groin against mine. "God, you feel so good, baby boy. Why do you feel so goddamned good?" He lifted my right leg, and I wrapped it around him as Chase's hand slid down to palm my ass.

"You feel good too, and I still really like it when you call me that."

"You like being my baby boy?" He kissed down my neck, then knelt and shoved my shirt up to kiss my stomach.

"Oh God, yes." There was nothing in the world like it.

Chase unbuttoned and unzipped my jeans, then tugged them off along with my underwear. I pulled my shirt over my head, and he growled when his eyes latched on to the finger marks on my arm.

"Be good. My cock is right here, and you're worried about my arm?" I turned his head so he was facing my dick.

That seemed to snap him out of it, and he leaned forward. Instead of putting his mouth on my erection, he kissed the tattoo on my hip. "I don't know what it is about this thing."

Okay…well, I'd already told him I loved him, so I figured there was no use in holding anything back now. "It's because it's for you."

His brown gaze caught mine.

"I got it afterward. When you grabbed me and pulled me to your lap? Well, you know I bruise easily, and there was a fingerprint there. I got the heart tattooed over it." That was embarrassing to admit, how much that one moment had meant to me, how much Chase had always meant to me, but I couldn't take it back and didn't want to. My body flushed with heat as his eyes held mine as though they had some magical power over me and I couldn't turn away.

"Kell… I… What did I do to deserve you loving me that way?" He really sounded at a loss, like he couldn't understand why he was so special.

I shrugged. "You're you."

He rubbed his fingers over the tattoo as if he couldn't turn away, then leaned in and kissed it again. "You got me all tied up. Not sure I'll ever be untangled from you." Chase's breath ghosted over my sac, making me tremble.

His eyes didn't leave mine as he licked my balls, sucked one, then the other into his mouth. He still watched me as his tongue made a journey along my shaft, until he got to my crown, which he sucked into his mouth.

"Oh God, Chase. You feel so good."

He jerked me as he blew me, our eyes never disconnecting. I felt his stare like a touch, the gentlest of caresses all over my body. Chase worked my rod, stroking it and sucking it, my body writhing beneath him. There was nothing like the sight of Chase on his knees for me, my dick in his mouth as he looked at me in a way he never had—hell, in a way no one ever had before.

"I think you're melting my brain. You're making me crazy. I need inside you."

I thrust up into his mouth. "I need that too."

Chase pulled off, slowly fondling my cock as he reached over to the nightstand and pulled out the lube and a condom. He tossed the rubber onto the bed and let go of me long enough to squirt some lube onto his fingers, then traced my hole.

A shiver rocked through me. I pulled my legs back, and he growled again, pushing a slick finger inside me.

"More," I begged, and Chase obliged, pulling out, then working two fingers in.

"So sexy. Christ, you don't know what you do to

me."

Chase worked me open, and fuck, it felt good, but it wasn't enough. I didn't need all the prep. I needed him. "Fuck me." I pushed against him, riding his fingers. "Fuck me, Chase."

He ran his hand down my chest, my stomach, and I arched up into his touch. "Holy fuck, you're beautiful," he said, then pulled his fingers free.

He ripped open the condom and rolled it down, squirted more lube onto his shaft, and then he was leaning over me again, our eyes locked as his cock stretched my hole, past the first ring of muscle. I melted against him, savored the growing feeling of being full as he continued to work his way in deep.

Chase.

Chase, who knew I loved him and was still here.

Chase, who wanted to be with me, who wanted to tell Griff about us.

Chase, who said he didn't want to lose me.

The Chase I'd loved my whole life and didn't think I would ever have.

The truth swelled inside me, radiated through every inch of my body as Chase fucked into me. He called me his baby boy and told me how good my hole was for him, how much he loved being inside me, and it was almost like an out-of-body experience. Like my mind was fuzzy and all I was made up of was *feeling*.

Of Chase inside me, and on me, and God, I loved him so much.

"Hey…you okay?" he asked, his cock lodged in deep.

"Yes. Unless you're going to stop fucking me. Then I won't be okay at all."

Chase smiled and kissed me. He lifted me, his dick still in my hole. My legs wrapped around him as he maneuvered his way onto the bed. It wasn't smooth, and eventually he fell out, but then he knelt in the center of the mattress, arms around me, the backs of my thighs on the tops of his, and pushed back in.

"Best hole I ever had," he said, and then he was fucking into me hard. Our breathing picked up, and my whole body shook. We were sweaty and holding each other, our eyes locked as Chase took me. My balls were full and tight, and each time he thrust into me, precome spilled from my slit.

"You gonna come for me, baby boy? Think I can make you spill your load without a hand on your cock?"

"Fuck yes," I replied because damn it, I was already there.

He slid one hand to my hip and pressed against the tattoo there, rubbed it as he kept thrusting into me, and then he smiled, and Jesus, he looked so happy, so fucking gorgeous, that when he pumped his hips again, fucking me just right, my eyes fell closed and color exploded behind my lids. My body shook and broke apart as I shot all over my stomach.

Chase's hold on me tightened, his teeth went into my neck as he thrust up and trembled, and I knew he was coming too, wished he was spilling in my body instead of the condom.

Later, after we got rid of the condom, we lay naked in bed together, Chase's fingers traveling up and down my spine. "I need to be the one to do it…to tell Griff."

I turned so I could look at him. "We can do it together."

"If you want to, but I really think it should be me alone. I know Griff. He needs to hear it from me."

"Okay." I nodded, trusting him.

"I'll ask him to go fishing with me next weekend and tell him then."

I kissed Chase, not wanting to talk about my brother, just wanting to savor this moment between the two of us.

# CHAPTER TWENTY-FOUR

## *Chase*

K ELLAN WAS IN love with me.

The thought hadn't left my brain since he'd told me the night before. He was in love with me, said he had been, well, since he was a kid. I couldn't stop thinking about how it must have felt when I'd left him all those years ago. When I'd run away, because that was exactly what I had done.

Yes, I'd had plans to go into the Marines already. I'd wanted to do something with my life and knew I never would if I didn't leave Havenwood, but there was no sense in trying to fool myself into believing I hadn't run from Kellan. If that night hadn't happened, I would have kept in touch with him too and I would have come home to visit.

The truth was, I'd been scared, because being with him, kissing him and feeling him, had unlocked something inside me. I'd wanted him, wanted *more* from him, even then, and he'd been so young, and there had been Griff to worry about and the fact that I was nothing back then. What did I have to offer Kellan or anyone else?

So I'd run, and now I was back, and I realized that so much of what I did was about him. That I'd cared for Kellan more than I'd been willing to admit, since he kissed me all those years ago.

*"I'm in love with you. I've been in love with you since I was fourteen years old. I don't remember what it's like not to love you, and I don't know how to stop."*

Christ, how could he love me that much? It didn't make sense, not to me, but fuck was I glad he did, because I'd never felt for anyone else the way I did for Kellan.

I kept telling myself that would make all the difference with Griffin. That being with Kellan wouldn't come between us because I was serious about him. I cared about him. I wanted to be with him in a way I'd never been with anyone else. But I wasn't sure it would matter. Not with Griff.

As I drove out to Bridget Johnson's house, I tried to get my mind on the situation with Buck. I'd spoken with Kellan that morning before I went in to work and he'd gone home. The truth was, I was worried about Buck and his reaction to Buck Jr. taking the class. If he was willing to manhandle Kellan that way, would he lay a hand on his son? I'd been so one-minded, only thinking about Kellan when I saw the mark on his arm, that I hadn't let myself think about the rest of it. Kellan agreed, and I thought the best place to start was with Bridget.

When I pulled my cruiser up in front of her old A-frame house, she was taking groceries out of her car.

"Let me help you with those," I said as I got out of the vehicle.

"Is everything okay? Is there something wrong?" she asked, concern making her voice tremble.

"No one is hurt or anything."

When Bridget nodded, I plucked the rest of the bags from her trunk, and the two of us went inside. "Are the kids home?"

"No, they're with my mom. What's going on, Chase? You're worrying me."

I set the bags on her kitchen counter. "I wanted to ask you a few questions about Buck."

She frowned. "Okay."

"Buck Jr. is starting a class at Safe Haven, right?"

"Yes." Her brows pulled together.

"Buck paid a visit to Kellan. He's not happy about his son taking classes from him."

"Oh God." Her hand went to her mouth. "He didn't hurt him, did he?"

It concerned me that that was her first thought, that she obviously believed her husband capable of hurting Kellan. "He's fine, but it's important that I know if Buck has a history of violence."

"He never laid a hand on me or the kids, if that's what you're asking. I wouldn't let my kids visit with him if he did. He's...he's been a lot angrier lately, I can tell you that. It's like he's mad at the whole world. I figured it was because of the separation, my filing for divorce, and then the fact that he lost his job. And, well, Buck and his daddy have never been real accepting, if you know what I mean...with Kellan...and people like him."

My jaw clenched, and my hands fisted. I could tell she was trying not to be offensive and wasn't sure how to say it, but I was fucking irate that people like Buck gave a shit who someone else loved or slept with.

"I never would have expected him to go and say something to Kellan, though. If so, I wouldn't have let Buck Jr. take the class, or I would have kept it from Buck or something. I'm sure you know Buck's been staying with his daddy and, well, the two of them kind of feed off each other. He gives Buck a hard time about everything, and any prejudices or homophobia Buck has, he got from his father. For that reason alone, I don't like letting my kids stay with him, but the judge ordered shared custody, so I talk to them before and after each visit. Try to counter anything they might say about others. I'm close with my kids, Chase. Buck doesn't hurt them. I'd know if he did."

I nodded, feeling grateful for that piece of it, at least.

"I take it Buck didn't want the separation?"

"No, not at all. He was really angry that I was leaving him. Jimmy didn't help with that either. You know Buck's mama left them when he was a kid. Jimmy tried to tell him I was doing the same thing. He had all sorts of stuff to say about Buck's mama and, well, women in general. He is old-fashioned in his beliefs, as I'm sure you know. He held a tight grip on his wife and tried to get Buck to do the same with me. It was different in the beginning, ya know? Buck didn't want to be like his father, but the older he got, the more like him he became…started accusing me of being like his mom. I had to get out of there, Chase."

I put a hand on her shoulder in support. "I understand." It was something I'd forgotten about—Buck's mom leaving like mine did.

A few more questions followed, all of which Bridget answered. Satisfied for now, I said, "Thank you, ma'am.

I appreciate you talking to me."

"Oh God. I'm only a couple of years older than you. Don't call me ma'am. It makes me feel old."

We both chuckled, and Bridget walked me to the door. "Do you think I should stop taking my kids to Kellan's classes for a little while? The last thing I want to do is cause trouble for him."

Part of me really fucking wanted to say yes, but Kellan and I had had this conversation when he knew I was going to see Bridget. I knew what he wanted, and I wouldn't push his feelings aside again. "As long as you're sure your kids are safe from Buck while they're going, you can keep bringing them. Kell would hate the thought of them not being able to learn art because of hatred." Kellan said art had saved him. He wanted to share that with others.

"Thanks, Chase. You've always been real good to Kellan, like a brother to him. I'm sure you'll take care of him." She smiled.

"I appreciate the compliment, but Kellan knows how to take care of himself. And I care about him a lot, but not like a brother."

Her eyes widened, so I thought she caught my meaning. It was a risk, because I didn't want it to get back to Griffin before I could talk to him, but I also didn't want to deny Kellan.

"I hope you're happy," she said, and I could hear the sincerity in her voice.

"Thank you."

My mind was spinning when I got back to the car and drove to town. I hadn't realized Buck had lost his job. That, on top of the recent separation, would be enough to make him angry. Was it enough to make him rob the gas station? He would be familiar with the schedule and who was on shift and when. Buck had always been an asshole, but I didn't remember him being the kind of asshole who would grab someone the way he had Kellan. That could mean he was the same kind of asshole who would hold up a store for some cash.

But I also knew his daddy. Buck's dad, Jimmy, was friends—and I used the word loosely—with my father. When I was a kid, Jimmy used to come over and drink with my dad. They'd rave on about my mom and Jimmy's wife, especially after they both left. He was the definition of asshole, like my dad was, only Jimmy hid it better. He didn't get drunk and make a fool of himself in town, and I'd never heard rumors of him abusing his kids.

I was driving down Main Street when I got a call from dispatch. "Chase, we're gonna need you to head over to Wyman's. It's your daddy."

Ah, hell. That was exactly what I didn't want to deal with on top of everything else. "I'm on my way there now," I replied.

It didn't take long to get to the bar. It had always been one of my dad's favorite places to drink. More his crowd than the patrons at Griff's ever would be.

I got out of the cruiser and headed toward the old brick building that had been around longer than I'd been alive. It was only five in the afternoon, but I had no doubt my dad would be falling-down drunk.

He was over by the pool tables when I got inside the dimly lit building. "Don't be such a pussy," my dad said, shoving a man I didn't recognize.

The other guy held his hands up. "You're drunk. I'm not kickin' your ass 'cuz of it. But you lay a hand on me again, and I'll change my mind."

My father went for him, but the guy stepped out of his way, and he stumbled against the pool table.

"Hey!" I called out.

"Who invited the pig?" my dad taunted. "Ladies and gentlemen, I'd like you to meet my son. What a fucking disgrace. Little bastard chased his mama away when he was just a boy. Was too weak to be a man, so he always had the precious Caine family fight his battles for him, and now he's a pig."

"George, man, that's enough. Don't talk to your son that way—or the law," Mr. Richards said. He owned a feed supply.

"I don't care what he says about me," I told Mr. Richards. "He's not worth my time, but thank you." I grabbed my dad's arm. "Let's go."

"Who called the cops on me? Who was it?" Dad yelled.

Mr. Wyman, Richards, and the guy my dad pushed followed us out.

"Calm down, George," Wyman said. "I don't know who called, but you need to have some respect. Go home, sleep it off, and don't act like that in my bar again."

I put cuffs on my dad and took him to the cruiser. "Calm down. You're not under arrest. I just need to see what happened," I said as he fought me.

"Fuck you," he spit out, and I pushed him into the back seat and closed the door.

"Sorry about that, kid," Mr. Richards said. "I'm the one who called."

"As you should have, and like I said, I don't give a shit what he says about me."

"He don't need to be arrested. Just got a little out of

hand. You know how he can get sometimes," Wyman added.

I got the name and information of the man my father had been arguing with, but he didn't want to press charges, nor did anyone else. As always, they let it go, let him get away with being a drunk who treated people like shit.

I didn't have much choice except to take him home.

He didn't spend the whole drive cursing at me that time. When I pulled up to the house, my stomach twisted. Just the sight of it made me feel like that helpless kid again.

I cursed as I killed the engine and got out of the car. I pulled my dad out, and as I unlocked the cuffs, I said, "You should get some help. I'll take you. Get you sober." He didn't deserve that, but I'd do it. Hell, I'd even help pay for it if I could. It wasn't like I had a lot.

"Fuck you," he slurred and pulled away. "It's your fault, you know that? It's all your fault. We were fine until you came along. Then you made us miserable, chased her away, and I got stuck with you."

His words punctured my already damaged heart. "I was your son!" I shouted, surprising myself. "I didn't *come along*. You two had me. If you didn't want me, you should have been more responsible. And I didn't chase shit away. You did that all on your own." I went for the cruiser door. "Get your shit together."

"You think you're so much better than me?" he shouted. "You're not! You're not Robert Caine's son, you're mine. You're part of *me*, Chase. You're no better than I am. I don't care what job you have or if those perfect do-gooder motherfuckers took you in. You're not a Caine, you're a Hawthorne, no matter what you want, no matter if you think you're better than me like he always did. One of these days your smug ass is going to get what's coming to you like he did too."

My blood went cold, and I saw nothing but red. "What did you say?" None of what he said about me mattered. Hell, most of what he said about Mr. Caine hadn't either, but that last part, about getting what's coming to him like they did—that mattered.

"You heard me. I wish I knew who did it. Would have thanked them," he said. It took everything inside me not to hit him, not to take a lifetime of anger out on him, but he wasn't worth it. Not worth my career. "Get the hell off my property."

He turned and walked away, and I let him go. My hands were shaking when I got back to the cruiser. I'd always known my dad didn't like Kellan and Griff's family. They all grew up together in Havenwood, and like everyone here, they'd known each other their whole lives. But that anger right there? Saying they deserved to die? That sent a chill through me.

Vomit crawled up my throat and landed all over the gravel.

I never hated anyone as much as I hated him in that moment, and all I could think was, what if the answer to the murder of Kell and Griff's parents had been staring me in the face the whole time? What if it was my father?

How could Kellan or Griff ever forgive me if that was true? How could I ever forgive myself?

# CHAPTER TWENTY-FIVE

## Kellan

THE FOLLOWING DAYS were perfect. I'd planned on staying home the night after I told Chase I loved him. I figured we needed the space to come to terms with everything. Poor Chase had called me, though, told me he'd had a run-in with his dad, and asked if I could come over.

My heart ached for him. He was too good a man to have to deal with his daddy, but it meant the world to me that he'd called me when he needed someone there. That he knew he could not only trust me, but that I would somehow help make it better. Most of the time, it seemed people thought I needed to be soothed or fixed or supported, but Chase saw something in me that few others did—that I could be there for someone too. Chase could have gone to Griff or Becca, yet he'd chosen me.

I ended up spending the next few days at his house. I went to work and went home, but every evening I was in

Chase Hawthorne's bed, and there was nowhere else I'd rather be.

I planned to be there later tonight too, but right then, I was sprawled across Josh's couch, with Nat's feet on my lap while Josh sat across from us.

"So…someone seems like he's been super happy. I don't think that smile has left your face all afternoon, and I haven't seen you in days."

"Who? Moi?" I pointed to myself.

"Yes, you, dumbass," Josh teased, throwing a pillow at me. I swatted it toward Natalie.

"Hey! I was nice," she said, and we chuckled. "Seriously, though. Are you going to hold out on us, or do we get the deets?"

I couldn't stop my smile from spreading even more. "I told Chase I'm in love with him."

"Holy shit." Natalie's feet slid off my lap, and she sat up straight.

"Good man," Josh added.

"I assume it went well?" Nat asked.

"He didn't tell me he loved me, but I told him not to. He said he cared about me. That he didn't want to lose me, and we're dating. He's going fishing with Griff this weekend, and he's going to tell him."

"Holy shit," Nat said for the second time.

"You already said that."

"Well, it bears repeating. This is like when someone is a little kid and they dream about growing up and getting their Prince Charming. Chase Hawthorne is your Prince Charming!" Nat exclaimed.

Josh huffed out a laugh. "Chase is anything but Prince Charming. He's a regular guy like the rest of us."

"Why are you throwing shade at my fairy tale? Can't a guy pretend he gets his Prince Charming?" I teased. I mean, I wasn't really thinking Chase was going to take me to the ball and we'd live happily ever after like Nat seemed to think, but I wasn't Mr. Negativity like Josh either.

"You know that no one wants you happier than me. But you also know that he hasn't won me over yet, because I hate the fact that you've loved this guy all your life and somehow, you think you're not good enough for him. Maybe that's not his fault, but by keeping you a secret from Griff, he sure as shit didn't help the situation."

"Okay, why can't you guys be in love?" Nat asked. "That was really sweet, Josh."

I smiled at him. "He's the best." And he really was.

"I'm his best friend. I'm supposed to always have his best interests at heart. And I wouldn't risk that by catching feelings for him."

Natalie sighed. "Catching? It's not a cold."

"Yeah, it's worse," Josh replied, and I went over and sat on his lap, wrapping my arms around him.

"Aw, don't pretend you don't love me, Joshy-poo. But I'm saving myself for Prince Charming."

He rolled his eyes and smiled. "I really am happy for you. No matter what, you did good, and I hope it works out. I might have to start liking him, though…"

"You'd like him if you gave him a chance." I went to sit with Natalie again.

"He a good fuck?" Josh asked. *Now* we were talking.

"A gentleman never tells."

"I don't see any gentlemen here," Nat replied, and we all laughed. God, I loved my friends. In that moment, everything in my life felt perfect.

IT WAS AFTER eight when I got to Chase's. Josh had fed us, and I took a plate of lasagna home for Chase. I knocked, then slid his front door open. He was sitting on the couch, watching sports highlights.

"Hey, you. I brought you dinner. It was just a frozen lasagna, but it's not too bad."

"Hey. Thanks." He smiled and tugged me down to the couch with him. He set the plate on the coffee table. "How was your day?" Chase pushed my bangs off my forehead sweetly. I loved when he did little things like that or asked about my day. It made what we had feel even more real, like it wasn't just about sex even though the sex was fucking awesome.

"It was good. I had Annabella today. She's one of my favorites. She's the sweetest little thing. Her passion and hard work are really a thing of beauty. This one time..." I went into one of my favorite stories about her and then told him a story about another one of my kids, which prompted me to think of yet another story to tell him.

Chase listened quietly and let me ramble on, even though I knew it couldn't be something he was super interested in. When I was finished, he said, "You really love what you do."

"Yes. I can't imagine doing anything else. I'm not rolling in the big bucks, but that doesn't matter."

"And you're good at it. I can tell. You're giving these kids an amazing gift, Kell. You should be proud."

I couldn't help but grin. It wasn't that hearing Chase say it made me more proud of what I did. Truly, I always had been, but it was nice to hear. "I am."

"You'll have to teach me to make something sometime."

"Really?" I never imagined Chase would be interested.

"Of course. Why not? I mean, I doubt I'll be the next great artist, but I'd love to see you in your element…and have you show me how to do something that's important to you."

I loved seeing this sweet side of Chase, the one he only showed to certain people. It was why I'd always loved him. "You should eat your dinner before it gets too cold. Do you want me to warm it up for you?"

"Nope. I'm sure it's fine how it is."

Chase ate and was sort of quiet after that. He'd been that way off and on the past few days. I wasn't sure if it was because this was all so new for him and he'd be telling Griffin soon or what. Or hell, maybe it had to do with seeing his dad lose it the other day. He hadn't told me exactly what went down, but it couldn't have been easy. Or maybe it was because of work, or Buck. There was a whole hell of a lot weighing down his mind at the moment.

"Wanna play around tonight?" I asked, waggling my eyebrows at him.

"I like where this is going." Chase set his empty plate on the coffee table. "What did you have in mind?"

"Your handcuffs. Me on my knees and your dick in my throat?"

"Oh God." Chase grabbed me, pulled me to his lap, and nuzzled my throat. "Best. Boyfriend. Ever."

I was pretty sure I would never get tired of hearing him say things like that to me. We'd said we were dating, but the *B* word hadn't been used. It might have been my new favorite word.

He kissed me until I was dizzy, until I forgot my name, then looked at me. "Thank you."

I frowned. "For what?"

"Loving me. I'm gonna do everything in my power to deserve it."

Oh, he was going to wreck me. "Chase…you already do. Don't you know that?"

He gave me a sad smile, which I didn't return. Something was definitely on his mind. "What's wrong?"

"Nothing." He shook his head. "Why don't you go get ready for me? I'll be in there with the cuffs in a couple of minutes."

"Okay." I nodded.

I went into Chase's room. The blinds were pulled open on the floor-to-ceiling windows, the moonlight shining through. It was so beautiful that I was stuck watching it for a moment, taking it all in. Then I remembered Chase was going to handcuff me while I blew him, so I ripped my clothes off and knelt there waiting for him.

He came in a moment later, with his shirt off and his jeans unbuttoned. "Fuck, look at you, baby boy. Gorgeous," Chase said, and I trembled. He walked over to where I knelt in front of the window, the cuffs clanking together. "You sure about this?"

"Very."

He stepped behind me, knelt, and hooked them around my wrists. "You're shaking," Chase said when he stood in front of me again.

"Just because I'm excited...and I can't believe I'm here with you."

"I can't believe I'm here with you either."

He took his time with me after that. I nuzzled him through his pants, letting the jeans rub against me. Chase removed his pants, and I rubbed my face against him again. It felt like an eternity before he was naked, his cock hard and leaking. He painted my lips with his precome, then pushed his dick into my mouth. He went slow, worked his way in, then pulled back.

"More. I want more," I begged, and Chase gave it to me, fucking into me, while he looked down at me lovingly, petting my hair, telling me I was beautiful, making me feel like the most special person in the world.

And then he came down my throat, saying, "Kell…oh fuck, Kellan, that's it, baby boy…Kell…Kell…Kell…" over and over again.

My brain felt fuzzy after that. Chase dropped to his knees and jerked me off. Then he uncuffed me and carried me to the bed, held me, and I fell asleep in his arms.

# CHAPTER TWENTY-SIX

## *Chase*

THERE WAS NOTHING like waking up with Kellan in my arms. We were able to sleep in a bit. He didn't have any classes until that afternoon, and I was working a swing shift.

Christ, I didn't know what he was doing to me. The past few days had been difficult for me in a lot of ways. I couldn't stop thinking about my dad and the things he said. It felt like I was keeping something from Kellan and Griff, and that sat like a heavy weight in my chest. But then, what did I tell them? That my dad was an asshole who hated their family, me, and anyone who cared about me? That was common knowledge. My dad had even been questioned when the Caines were killed, but he had been cleared.

Thoughts of my dad were twined with thoughts of Buck, and with worries about telling Griff and Kellan, but also the urgency to hurry up and do so. I was ready to have it out there, to stop hiding. Griff deserved to know. Kellan and I owed him that—*I* owed him that. And I wanted to make sure he understood there had never been a damn thing in my life that felt as good as calling Kellan mine. Being with him somehow helped everything, like it had last night.

His stomach growled, and I chuckled as he rolled over and said sleepily, "Feed me, Chase."

"Someone's getting a little bossy," I teased.

Kellan kissed my neck, my chest. "Please feed me, Chase."

"Like I could ever say no to you." I swatted his ass and rolled out of bed.

I made pancakes, which we ate together, and then we jumped in the shower.

Afterward, with a towel firmly wrapped around my hips, I grabbed my razor and shaving cream.

"Can I do it?" Kellan asked, and I cocked a brow at him. "Please?"

I nodded, and Kellan hopped up on the bathroom counter. I stood between his legs, my hands on his hips. He was still naked, and it was hard not to play with his cock, but I was good as he lathered my face with shaving cream and began to clean up my scruff.

"I've never shaved someone else before," Kellan admitted.

"I've never let anyone shave me before, so I guess we're having a first together."

"Aw, who knew Chase Hawthorne was so sweet?" he teased as he finished up, then set the razor down. I leaned in, rubbing the extra shaving cream all over his face. Kellan laughed and playfully tried to fight me off, and we ended up kissing.

"Ew. I'm eating this stuff, and it's not very good," he said when I pulled away.

"Sorry, baby boy." I pressed a quick kiss to his lips again, and he jumped down from the counter. I rinsed my face off, and had just tugged on a pair of jeans—Kellan was already in his—when a banging sound came from the front door.

Our eyes caught, held on, and I think we knew, we somehow both fucking knew it was Griff and he'd found out about us.

"Shit," I cursed and headed out of my room, Kellan right behind me.

"Chase... I..."

"It's fine, okay?" I cupped his cheek. "We'll figure it out. I'm not going anywhere, no matter what." I didn't want him to think this would end. That even if Griff didn't understand, even if I lost him, I wouldn't walk away from Kellan. Not now.

He nodded and stepped aside as I opened the door. The second I did, Griff's angry face was there, and then a fist was flying through the air, connecting with my jaw and making pain explode there. I stumbled backward. Christ, that hurt.

"Griffin! What the hell?" Kellan shouted as I wiped the blood off my mouth with my hand.

"You feel better now?" I asked.

"Fuck you, Chase."

"We were going to tell you. I was going to tell you when we went fishing."

"Tell me what? That you're taking advantage of my brother? What the hell is this, Hawthorne? What the fuck are you doing to him, and who in the hell did you piss off to drag Kellan into it?"

Huh? None of his words were making sense. Not really.

Griff shoved something against my chest. A piece of paper fell from his hand and landed face up on the floor. My heart stopped. My vision went blurry as rage coursed through me.

My eyes snagged on Kellan, stared at him as he looked at the photograph on the floor. It was of us—last night in my room, Kellan naked and in cuffs on his knees. He was partly in shadow, so you couldn't see his whole body, but it was obvious he was naked, his face buried in my underwear-covered groin.

"Oh God," Kellan said. "Oh God, oh God, oh God."

My hands tightened into fists as I began to tremble with fury. "Where did you get this?"

I ripped the photo off the floor. There was no denying who it was, but I didn't give a shit about myself. It was Kellan I worried about.

"This one? It was on my doorstep, my fucking *doorstep*, Chase, but that's not the worst of it. They're all over town, taped onto doors and windows and buildings. I spent all morning tearing them down. I can't fucking believe you did this to him. Not you. Goddamn it, Chase! Not you."

"Do you think I'm not pissed too? I fucking hate that anyone has seen Kellan like this. That they've taken an intimate moment, in my *home*, with my boyfriend, and used it against us like this."

"Your boyfriend?" Griff seethed. His fists were tight, and I thought he was going to hit me again. "He's your fucking boyfriend now? You don't do relationships, and now you're in one with my little brother? You went home with Bec not too long ago!" Griff turned to look at Kellan. "Come on, Kell. Let's go home. We'll figure this shit out."

"Hey." I grabbed Griff's arm as he tried to walk away. "He's a grown-ass man who can make decisions for himself." I looked at Kellan. "If you want to go, I'll understand, but know I want you here. I'm so sorry this happened, but where we go from here is up to you."

Griff jerked out of my grasp. "Do you not understand what's happening here? Christ, Chase! You know how it's always been for him! He's always been seen as an outsider, and now there are photos of him naked and handcuffed, obviously about to blow you. You know how Havenwood works! You'll come out of this shit unscathed, and Kellan will take the wrath of it."

His words slammed into me, made me dizzy, and nausea rolled through my gut. He was right. I fucking hated that he was, but eventually I'd be okay. I wasn't sure if Kellan would be. He'd be the laughingstock of town. "I'll tell them it was my fault. I'll fix it. Fuck, I'll find a way to fix it, okay?" I wanted to. I'd do anything to fix it, but I wasn't sure I could. Not really.

"You never should have done it!" Griff yelled. "I trusted you. You were my best friend. My *brother*—which means you're a brother to him! You went behind my back for God knows how long. Lying to me, keeping this shit from me. Listening to me when I said I thought

Kell was dating someone and wondered where he'd been spending his nights, and it was with you the whole fucking time! Oh, except the night you were with Becca."

"I didn't sleep with Becca," I shouted back. "I told her I couldn't. That I was seeing someone else."

"Oh, that changes everything. Give the man a fucking medal. Fuck you, Chase. You lied to me and put the most important person in my life at risk."

"I—"

"Stop fighting!" Kellan yelled, cutting me off. He began pacing, his hands in his hair, tugging at the messy strands. "Stop fighting. Please stop fighting. I can't take this. I can't handle the two of you arguing like this." He stopped and looked up at Griff. "The photos were everywhere?" His voice broke when he spoke.

Griffin nodded.

I moved forward, wrapped my arms around Kellan, and held him tight. "I'm so sorry, so sorry, baby boy. We'll figure it out, okay?" I was angry at myself, at the town, at the world. Who in the hell could have done this?

Kellan's nails dug into my back. He held me, buried his face in my chest. Over his head, my eyes found Griff, who was watching us. His jaw was tight as he took in the sight, but there was confusion in his stare too. Like maybe he was seeing something he hadn't expected in Kellan and me. "I'm not using him. I don't want to hurt him. I'm sorry I lied to you, Griff. You're my brother, my best friend, but I...I'm in love with him," I admitted. The second the words passed my lips, I knew they were true. I was in love with Kellan Caine. With his laugh and his confidence and his resilience. With his heart and love of art and teaching kids. I was in love with every part of him.

Kellan's whole body was rigid against mine. It was shitty that the first time I said it was under these circumstances. If I was honest with myself, I'd probably admit I'd known it for a while. Whether or not I did, I knew to the marrow of my bones that it was true.

Kellan pulled back slightly and looked up at me. "Chase?"

I shrugged. "I'm in love with you. I know you didn't want me to say it."

"You can say it," he said quickly. "I wanted it to come naturally."

Christ, he was adorable. "I love you."

"I love you too," Kellan replied.

"Fuck," Griff cursed, dropping down to my couch, elbows on his knees and face in his hands.

"I'm sorry I lied to you, Griff. You gotta know that, man, but I can't be sorry this happened with Kellan. I never..." Never thought this would happen for me. Never knew I could care so much. Never thought someone would care about me this much.

"We're both adults," Kell said, pulling away from me to walk over to his brother. "I apologize too, but this has nothing to do with you. Whatever happens between Chase and me is between us."

Griff looked up at Kellan. "You know I want you to be happy, kid. That's all I've ever wanted, but the lying from Chase...that's gonna take me some time to work through."

I closed my eyes, hating to hear the words, but understanding where he was coming from. It never should have been that way. I should have told him from the start. Griff had always been there for me, and I'd betrayed him by keeping this from him. "I understand," I told him. "I'll be right here waiting for you, Griff. I'm not going anywhere. You're my best friend whether you see that right now or not."

Griff ignored what I'd said. "That's all fine and dandy, but what about the photos? I'm real glad you two seem happy and all, but I think we're forgetting a really fucking big piece of it."

"I have some ideas," I said through gritted teeth. I also realized my lip hurt and it was likely a little swollen. "I need to head to the station and check on some things—hell, talk to the chief, about the photos too."

"Yeah," Kellan added. "I should probably make some phone calls as well, try and do damage control." It would be a mess for Kellan. I knew that. It didn't matter that it was a moment between consenting adults; people would make a big deal of it.

"I'll go with you," Griff told Kellan.

"I don't need you to babysit me," Kellan countered.

I wanted Griff to go with him so bad, it hurt, but I also knew if Kell and I were going to have a chance, I had to trust him. "He's right, Griff. He can take care of himself." My eyes found Kellan. "I know you don't need me or him or anyone else, but please keep in mind that we don't know who did this. Someone was *watching* us together last night, Kell. We don't know what they want or if they have something else planned. I need you to be safe. You...you mean too much to me."

He gave me a sad smile, then looked at Griff. "Sure, I wouldn't mind some company." I knew why he was doing it. Yeah, part of it was to make us feel better, but I also knew Kellan well enough to know he was trying to build a bridge between us and Griffin. There was no doubt this had to feel like the biggest betrayal to Griff, and Kell wasn't going to leave him out to dry. "Let me go get my stuff," Kellan added, then disappeared down the hall toward my room.

"I really am sorry, Griff. You gotta know that. There's just…something about him. I think there always has been, but the timing wasn't right or he was too young. He makes me feel good in a way nothing else does. Makes me feel happy, complete." Like maybe I deserved a little more than I always thought I did.

"Maybe next time you cuff him, you can take the time to close the blinds first," he said with a finality to his voice that reminded me he truly would need time. He would stick by us and do anything to help, because that was who Griffin was. He was loyal to the bone, but he was hurt, and he had a right to be.

Kellan came out with his shirt on and his cell in his hand. His skin was pale, almost like he was going to pass out. "I have about a hundred missed calls. Some from Josh and Nat, but there are a lot from the parents of my students too."

Fuck. It was starting already. "I'll fix it, okay? I'll do my best to fix it." I pressed a quick kiss to his lips, and yep, mine was definitely swollen.

"It's not your job to fix it, but thank you."

Actually, it was my job to fix it, literally, but I didn't tell him that.

Griff walked out without a word, leaving the door open.

"He'll come around," Kellan said. "He loves you."

I sure as shit hoped so because being friends with Griffin was the first time I'd ever felt loved. The second was from Kellan.

"I love you," he said.

"I love you too."

Kellan gave me another sad smile, and then he was gone as well.

It took every ounce of self-control not to lose it. Not to try and tear the whole motherfucking world down. Someone had been *watching* us, taking photos of us, trying to hurt us. Trying to hurt Kellan.

The first two people who popped into my head were Buck and my dad. But I also knew I had to get my ass to the station before I did anything else.

It felt strange driving through Havenwood, seeing people and wondering if they knew; if they had seen the photograph of Kellan and me. What were they thinking? My jaw tightened as I gripped the steering wheel.

The second I walked into the station, all eyes were on me—some in support, some in disapproval, and some in shock. Officer Winthorp squeezed my shoulder in support. "Sorry 'bout what happened, kid. Chief Potter wants to see you."

"Thanks." I wanted to see him too. I sure as shit wasn't letting this go. We needed to figure out who had been watching us.

I knocked, even though the door was open. "Chief…"

"Close the door, Hawthorne," he said, and I did.

"Do you know who did it?" he asked as I sat in the chair on the other side of the desk.

"No, but I have some ideas."

He nodded. "I want to hear about those. We need to write up a report and talk to Kellan, but we have to take care of a few other things first."

My muscles tightened. "What things?" I asked, my lips tight, even though I knew exactly what he was talking about.

"We're in a sticky situation here. The folks of Havenwood are concerned. With the nature of the photos…"

"You mean me being with another man? With all due respect, Chief, that sounds a whole lot like discrimination to me. You knew I was bisexual when I was hired, but even if you didn't, my sexuality has nothing to do with how well I can do my job."

"It has nothing to do with Kellan being a man, at least not for me. I don't give a shit who you fuck, kid. But you had him in handcuffs, a pair that whether they were or not, people will assume are your police-issued set, and you were in a very…intimate position. Evidence of that is now all over town, for everyone to see. It's complicated and a sensitive matter. You know I hate to tell you this, but I need you to take some time—paid, of course. We need to let things blow over, and we also need to figure out what's going on here."

I shoved to my feet. "What's going on is our rights have been violated! Someone was fucking *watching* us, Chief. They were at my house, looking through my windows. I don't know who it was or how dangerous they are, and you're worried about a bit of publicity?"

He sighed. "That's not how it is. And you're right, we do need to get to the bottom of this, and I sure as shit plan to do it. I promise you, this is a priority, and it's not personal. If the situation happened to anyone else, they'd be told the same thing."

Rage surged inside me again. There wasn't a part of me that wanted to accept this, but I also knew I had no choice. But with his help, and legal or not, I planned on figuring out who did this.

"Yeah, fine, whatever."

"It's just a little while."

I didn't reply to that because I wasn't sure how I should. Whatever way you looked at it, the situation was fucked. Private, intimate photos of Kellan and me were out there, we were being watched, it could be my own dad, and now I was being put on leave.

"I'm gonna call Davies in here. He came down from DC. I want you to tell me everything you know."

Which wasn't a whole lot. After I finished telling them about the conversation with my dad, along with Kell's and my run-ins with Buck, Davies left us alone again.

"I'm going to need you to trust me on this, Chase. Don't try and take matters into your own hands. Don't go to your dad's. We'll take care of it."

With that, I was dismissed, and I had to force myself to do as told. The last thing I wanted was to screw up this investigation.

# CHAPTER TWENTY-SEVEN

## *Kellan*

"**Y**OU GOING TO talk to me, or what?" I asked Griffin. We were at my studio, and I'd finished fielding calls from the parents of my students, all of which had canceled other than Bridget and Annabella's mom, Tracey. Not gonna lie, I was pretty devastated by it all, but I also wasn't sure it had truly hit me yet. I was trying to prolong that process as much as I could.

"I don't really know what to say. I just found out that my brother and my best friend have been lying to me for God knows how long. I found out from intimate photos being dropped on my doorstep, which are also all over town. It's a lot to take in, Kell. I feel like it's always something."

"With me, you mean. It's always something with *me*." Somehow, it always came down to that. "And Chase and I didn't lie to you."

"You went behind my back, which is the same

thing." He sighed. "I didn't say it's always something with you."

"But Jesus, Griff, it's true. We both know that's what you meant. It's our fault that some psycho was watching Chase and me together? Am I not supposed to have sex with my boyfriend?" Griffin winced. "That's what this is about? I'm not a fucking child—"

"Chase!" Griff interrupted angrily. "You're not supposed to have sex with Chase. I didn't think that was too much to ask."

This strange twisting sensation attacked my chest. "I love him," I said, looking away. "I've always loved him."

"I know," Griff replied softly. "You think I never knew how you felt about Chase? I did. I just never saw *this* coming. I'm working through it in my head. I'll come around, but you can't expect miracles. We got hit with a lot today. I can't process it all that quickly."

"Okay. And thank you for trying. It means more than I could ever say. You really are the best brother in the world."

Griffin looked over at me and winked. "I know."

We steered clear of dangerous conversations after that. I prepared for Annabella, Ava, and Buck Jr. to come in. I'd combined their class today, considering there wasn't really a class and it was only them. It burned a hole through my chest thinking about it. What would happen if I didn't recover from this? If I lost my business?

I shook those thoughts from my head, unwilling to let myself think about them right then.

Buck Jr. wasn't there with Bridget, and I didn't have it in me to ask her about it.

It surprised me that Griff left when my class started. I worked with Ava and Annabella. They were sweet as ever, and while teaching them, I could almost forget everything that had gone down. But the moment class ended, it all came roaring back to me, this loud, painful scream in my head.

Tracey picked Annabella up first. She hugged me and thanked me and said she was sorry I was going through what I was. It reminded me that she knew about intimate moments between Chase and me. That like everyone else in town, she'd seen photos of us together, that our moment had been taken from us. White-hot anger spiked inside me again.

"Can I go to the bathroom before we go?" Ava asked Bridget when she arrived.

"Of course, sweetheart," Bridget replied. As soon as she walked away, Bridget was hugging me. "I'm sorry, Kellan. No one deserves this. Is there anything I can do?"

"Thanks, and no. It'll blow over." God, please let it blow over. What would I do if it didn't blow over?

"I... You don't think...Buck?"

"I don't know," I answered honestly.

"I would feel terrible. I mean, I already do, but—"

"Hey, even if it was him, it wouldn't be your fault."

"He's been so different, so angry since the separation, and then with his feelings on the class..."

"Still wouldn't be your fault. We'll get it figured out."

Ava came out of the bathroom then, and I said a silent thank-you. It was getting harder and harder to hold my feelings back.

The second they left, Josh was there, locking the door behind him, and then I was hugging him. He held me tight, and I let the tears flow. "It's so fucked up, Josh. Everything is so fucked up."

"I know. I'm so sorry, babe." He ran his hand up and down my back, hugging me and letting me get my emotions out. I'd been trying to hold it in for hours.

"Griff knows, of course. He's the one who told us. He brought the photos over. He's angry and hurt, and Chase has to take on all the responsibility for it, because that's how he is. Everyone canceled their classes except for two people, and I just... What if I finally have Chase and lose everything else?"

"Hey, you're not going to lose everything else, okay? I promise."

"You can't make promises like that."

"I just did. We'll figure it out. How is Chase dealing with all this?"

"He told Griffin he's in love with me. He's not running or backing off, if that's what you think. I don't know if his friendship with Griff will ever be the same." That was the hardest part of all this. I didn't want to come between Chase and Griff, but I already had, hadn't I?

"None of that is your fault or your responsibility. You love Chase. You hooked up with Chase, which you had every right to do. Maybe you wouldn't have kept it from Griff if he weren't so uptight when it comes to you, and now Chase is in love with you too. Griff wants you happy. He'll find a way to come around, and if he doesn't, that's on him."

"Whether it's on him or not doesn't change the fact that it'll hurt Chase and it'll hurt Griff too."

"Then I guess Griff better pull his head out of his ass, huh?"

Josh was always so logical about shit like that, but it wasn't that easy for everyone. "Thanks for coming."

"Where else would I be?" We hugged again, and I saw Chase at the door. He looked...fuck, he looked like it had been a really long day for him too. Those intense brown eyes of his were dimmed, and his body almost sagged.

"Chase is here," I told Josh as I pulled away, then went to the door to unlock it. Chase slipped inside. "Hey, how did it go? Did you hear anything?"

He shook his head. "They put me on a paid leave until things get figured out."

Bile rose in my throat. "Shit, Chase. I'm so sorry."

"Homophobic, much?" Josh asked. "They can't do that."

"They can, and they did. Apparently, it has nothing to do with my sexual orientation and Kellan being a man. And I mean, I get it. I'm a police officer, and sexual photos of me are all over town, but I just...fuck, it makes me so angry." Chase sighed, and then his eyes snagged on mine. "But enough about me. I'm more concerned about you. How did it go today?"

I shook my head, unable to make words come out.

"Shit. I'm so sorry, baby boy. I'll fix it, okay?" Chase pulled me close and kissed the top of my head. "I'll find a way to fix it."

"You can't fix it any easier than I can."

"I know, but I gotta try. *We* gotta try."

"I like the we," I replied.

"Me too." He kissed me again, and then I pulled away.

Josh cleared his throat. "Listen…I know I haven't always been fair to you, and I'm sorry about that. Kellan is important to me, and I didn't want him to get hurt."

"I understand," Chase replied. "I'm glad he has someone like you. We all, um…we all need that." Chase ran a hand through his hair, and I knew he was thinking about Griff.

"If there's anything I can do, for either of you, let me know." Josh and Chase shook hands. "I should get going. Call me later, okay, babe?" Josh hugged me, I kissed his cheek, and he walked out.

"I'm so sorry you're on leave," I told Chase again.

"It's fine. It's only temporary. I spent the whole damn day driving around, trying to work through my shit, so it's a little easier to handle right now."

"Do they have any leads? Anything else to go on?"

Chase looked away, and I could tell it was a sore subject for him. "They're talking to a couple of people today, Buck being one of them. He's going to be pissed, Kellan, so you keep an eye out, okay? I'm trying not to make you feel like I don't trust you to take care of yourself, because I do. We both need to be careful. We don't know how dangerous whoever did this is."

A shiver raced down my spine. How did this happen? I couldn't imagine anything like this happening in Havenwood, and two out of the three times it had, my family was involved. "Can we go home? I don't…I don't want to risk seeing anyone."

"Yeah, yeah, of course we can. Should we stay at your place? Will you feel more comfortable there? They were out at my house investigating today."

I hadn't thought of that, that the police would have to go to Chase's. That someone had been watching us, at Chase's. But then, Chase's house had become *our place*; at least, that was how it felt to me. It was like we were in our own little world there, and now someone had tried to take that away from us.

"I want to go home…to your house, I mean. I don't want to lose that. It's us."

"Okay." Chase nodded. "I agree."

I grabbed my things, locked up, and then the two of us went outside. I didn't have my car since I'd left with Griff that morning, so I hopped into Chase's truck with him.

"Maybe we should get a dog," he said, his eyes on the road.

My heart felt like it jumped through my chest and floated away. "Together?"

He shrugged. "Yeah, sure, if you want. We can pick it together. I've never had my own dog before, but I loved Ranger."

I smiled at the memory of our old Rottweiler. He had been the best dog growing up. He was protective but also had the sweetest disposition. "I haven't thought about Ranger in a long time. Remember when he used to try to squeeze between us if you sat by me?"

Chase laughed, a rich, happy laugh that wrapped around me. "I do. He was protective of his Twerp." He winked.

We spent the rest of the ride home telling stories about Ranger and trying to figure out which breed of dog we wanted for our own.

# CHAPTER TWENTY-EIGHT

## Chase

I T FELT STRANGE being in my own house, and I hated that. I'd taken a walk around the property to be safe. There was an area marked off where they thought whoever had been watching us had stood. A chill raced through me at the thought.

When I got back inside, I locked the doors and made sure all the blinds were closed.

The dog conversation earlier had been spur-of-the-moment, but now that I'd mentioned it, I liked the idea. It would be nice to have an animal around the house. It made things feel more homey, more settled, in a way I'd never wanted before but suddenly found myself thinking about. And there was the added benefit of someone watching out for people who didn't belong.

Kellan called Griffin to tell him he wouldn't be home that night. His brother wasn't happy, and I hadn't expected him to be. He'd wanted us to stay at their place, and hell, maybe he was right. Maybe it was stupid and selfish to bring Kellan back here, but when he'd said my place was *us*, I'd felt a warmth spread through me. I felt that way too. Our whole adult relationship had been in there, and I didn't want some asshole to take that away from us.

An asshole who could be my father.

We made dinner together and then watched a movie. I kept my gun—not my police-issue firearm, but the one I was licensed for—in the lockbox on the table beside us. I was likely overreacting, but I wasn't taking any chances. My fellow officers were also planning on doing some drive-bys throughout the night, even though my place was out of the way.

When the movie was over, Kellan was playing texting games with Josh back and forth, so I went to take a shower. I appreciated how much Josh cared about Kell, and it had been nice to be on the same page with him earlier, especially now that he seemed to realize what Kellan meant to me, as well.

Once I was clean, I dried off and wrapped a towel around my waist. When I stepped out of the bathroom, I saw Kellan was lying on my bed in a pair of sleep pants and a shirt. He'd turned off the lights other than the lamp on the bedside table, and Christ, did he look right in my bed. It was where he belonged, where he'd always belonged.

"You're looking at me like you want to devour me, but there's something else too. You're sad," Kellan said, and he was right, so fucking right.

"It's been a long day." I couldn't believe it was only that morning that he'd been shaving me and things had seemed so fucking perfect.

"Come here," Kellan told me. I tossed my towel into the laundry basket and crawled into bed with him.

"How are you? Are you okay, being here?"

He cuddled in beside me, his head in the crook of my arm. "I feel a little weird, if I'm being honest. But I don't want to leave. I don't want to let them win."

Fuck, I loved him. He was so strong. I kissed the top of his head. "Yeah, that's how I feel too."

"Why are you so sad? I mean, there's the obvious, of course, but it feels like more than that."

Maybe it should have shocked me that Kellan saw me, *really* saw me and what I was feeling in ways I didn't think anyone could, but it didn't. There was a part of me that wondered how I didn't always know that this was where I belonged, with him. Hell, maybe I did. Maybe that was why I ran.

"I hate that this happened to you…that it happened

to us. That they took our moment and made it public. I want to know who did it. It's eating me alive. I've got this sick feeling in my gut that I can't get rid of. What if we don't like the answer we find?"

"I think that no matter who it is, we're not going to like the answer we find."

The pause stretched out between us as I tried to push the question free. "What if it's my father?" I made myself ask.

"Do you really think that's a possibility?" His brows pulled together.

Honestly, there wasn't much of anything I would put past him. "We'd fought. He hates me, Kell. He said some awful things."

"Oh, Chase. I'm sorry." He kissed my chest, my collarbone. "I'm so fucking sorry."

"Yeah," I replied softly. "I'm sorry too." Because it felt like my fault, all of it somehow did, and if my father had anything to do with any of this, I didn't see how we got past that. And even more importantly, I hated how it would hurt Kellan and Griff. I could deal with my own pain, but the thought of theirs was tearing me up inside.

"No matter what we find, you know none of this is your fault, right?"

I danced my fingers along the smooth skin of his shoulder. Goose bumps followed my touch, and I watched them.

"Chase, you know that, right?" Kellan asked again.

"Yeah, sure. Of course."

His hold on me tightened, and damn, did he feel good there. I had no doubts that it was exactly where he belonged. "I thought about you a lot...after that night. The one on the couch. I thought about you over the years, wondered why I couldn't shake it, ya know? I didn't really let myself think about what it meant, that I couldn't forget one messy blowjob."

I said that last part in a teasing voice, and Kellan caught on and playfully pinched my side. "Hey! Be nice. It was my first one, and I was freaking out because it was with the boy I was secretly in love with."

Christ, it felt good to hear that. I didn't think I'd ever get tired of hearing Kellan say he loved me.

"Plus, I'm a whole lot better at it now."

I chuckled. "Yeah, you are. And it may have been messy, but it was memorable. Like I said, I'd think about it...think about you. I'd ask Griff how you were doing and wondered if you ever thought about it too." Kellan had always been beneath my skin, had a piece of my heart. It had just taken me too long to fit the puzzle together myself.

"Are you kidding? I thought about it all the time, Chase. Every guy I was with, I wanted them to be you."

And maybe it would have been if I hadn't been a coward. "I'm here now."

"I finally wore you down," he joked. "Got tired of me giving chase and had to give in, huh? And that was cute as hell—giving chase, you know, your name."

A deep laugh vibrated through my chest. He could always do that to me—make me laugh. "You're a dork. I'm glad you didn't give up, but know that I'd be the one to chase you now if I had to."

"I know," Kellan replied and kissed my chest. "I don't think I'm going to be able to sleep tonight. I thought I'd be able to, but I can't help but wonder if someone is out there."

"Yeah, I know. Me too. We can head to your place if you want."

"No." Kellan shook his head. "I want to stay right here."

"Then we will. I'll talk to you until you fall asleep."

But he didn't fall asleep. Neither of us did. We lay there and talked all night, about our childhood and funny memories. About Griff, and Kellan's art, and my time in the Marines. We talked and held each other until the sun came up, then made love before getting up for coffee.

And as I sat there with him, I knew there wasn't anything I wouldn't do to keep Kellan Caine in my life.

# CHAPTER TWENTY-NINE

## *Kellan*

THE MORNING WAS a long one. Both Chase and I were tired from not sleeping. We'd already decided we'd stay at my place for a bit, which I hated giving in about. It felt like we were letting whoever had taken the photographs of us win, but I also knew I couldn't go without sleep. I wasn't sure I was ready to stay at Chase's house, even though I wanted to.

"Are you sure it's a good idea that I go with you?" Chase asked after our third cup of coffee. "It's Griffin's home. I don't want to make him uncomfortable."

"It's my home too, and I want you there." The thing was, I knew my brother well enough to know he would too. Yes, he was angry that we hadn't told him about us, and yeah, he wasn't comfortable with the idea of Chase and me as a couple yet—which *eek!* Was totally fun to think of us that way—but he also loved Chase. Griff would want Chase safe. It was the way Griffin was. I didn't think there was a man with a bigger heart than my brother, a man who was such a caretaker as he was, except for the man I'd fallen in love with, who was the same.

"I'd still feel better talking to Griff about it first. And I can always get a room somewhere if you don't want me to stay home."

Oh, was that not the sweetest thing ever? Chase wasn't afraid to stay home, but he'd still stay at my place. If that didn't work out, he was willing to get a room if I didn't want him to stay alone. "If you go get a room, I do too. And if Griff isn't comfortable with it, we'll stay with Josh."

He nodded just as the doorbell rang. We both tensed up. Chase shoved away from the table, stalked over, and looked out the window. "It's Chief Potter." He tugged the door open.

"Chase," the gray-haired chief said. "Kellan." He nodded at both of us.

"Do you have any news?" Chase asked.

"Come in," I added, walking over. "Have a seat. Do you want some coffee?"

"Sorry. One-track mind," Chase said.

"No worries, Hawthorne." Chief Potter came in and sat on the couch. "And that's okay, Kellan. I appreciate the offer, but I won't be here long. I wanted to let you both know that Buck has an alibi for the night the photos were taken."

"Who is it?" Chase asked.

"You know I can't tell you that, son."

"Fuck," Chase gritted out. "This is such bullshit. I shouldn't be on leave right now, and you know it."

"Yes, you should. Any officer would be. My hands are tied here."

I put a hand on Chase's arm in support. Jesus, I hated that all this was happening and that Chase felt helpless.

"My dad?" Chase asked. His voice was clipped, like there was no emotion to it, when I knew there had to be.

"That's the thing...we can't seem to find your daddy. He's not home and hasn't been there. He's not in any of his regular hangout spots, and all his friends say they haven't seen him."

My heart dropped to my gut, my whole body feeling too heavy and my heart aching. Not for me, but for Chase. His dad being gone wasn't a good sign. It would kill Chase if his father was somehow involved in this.

"Shit." Chase pulled away from me, walked to the window, and looked out. His back was to us, and he stood there, tense and silent.

"What does this mean for now?" I asked. "It's not concrete proof of anything."

"No. Absolutely not. We need to talk to George, is all, and hell, it's not like he hasn't gone on benders for a few days or more and disappeared. This isn't exactly out of character, so there's no need to jump to conclusions. I wanted the two of you to be aware. I have a feeling whoever did this is harmless—"

"What he did wasn't harmless!" Chase shouted. "All Kellan's clients have canceled with him except for two. There are photos of him out there that no one has any business seeing. That's not fucking harmless."

It didn't escape my attention that he hadn't mentioned what this did to him—only to me. "I'm fine, Chase. We're okay." Did I hate that people had seen our moment? Hell yes. Did I worry about my career? Definitely. But we would figure it out as long as we did it together.

"You're right. That was a bad choice of words. It's not what I meant," Chief Potter apologized. "Do you have any idea where your dad might have gone?"

Chase shook his head. "None that you wouldn't already know. It's not like we're close."

The chief didn't stay long after that. He had a few more questions for us, which we answered to the best of our abilities. Chase was tense the whole time, and it was me who walked Chief Potter to the door and thanked him for filling us in.

"Will you continue to stay here? If I need to get ahold of you?" he asked at the door.

"No. We're going to head back to my place. We'll both be there if you need us."

He nodded. "I'm, um…real proud of you, Kellan. You're a good man. Your parents would be proud too. You take care of Chase, ya hear?"

I couldn't help the warmth that spread through my chest at hearing that. It wasn't as if I knew the chief well or anything, and it wasn't often that random people in Havenwood said things like that to me. "Thank you. I appreciate that, and I will."

He nodded again before turning and walking away. I stood there for a minute, letting his words soak in, and…they helped. Sometimes it felt like I was so different from everyone there, like I was on the outside looking in, even with Griff, Nat, Josh, and Chase, but maybe, just maybe, it wasn't as bad as I thought. Sure, there were assholes, but there had to be as many people who weren't.

And he was right. I knew my parents would be proud, that they would have loved the idea of me and

Chase.

I closed the door and went to Chase, who was sitting on the couch. I straddled his lap and held his face. "Mom and Dad would have loved us together."

He closed his eyes, like it was too much for him to take in. A few moments later, he asked, "Do you really think so?" his voice gentle and vulnerable. "Even with all this?"

"I know so. They loved you. And I love you. You were a son to them, Chase. I know it's not the same as your own blood, but you're so much better than George Hawthorne could ever be. You had a mom and dad who loved you."

He wrapped his arms around me and pulled me tight against him. He held me, breathed me in, then whispered, "Thank you."

"There's nothing to thank me for."

He looked at me like he didn't believe me. "I love you."

"I love you too...and since you love me, you'll take me puppy shopping today! Oh my God, I'm so stoked to get a dog!"

Chase laughed. "Sounds to me like a good way to spend the day."

We got dressed, and Chase packed a bag to take

home with us. I shot Griff a text, letting him know Chase and I were going to be coming home or would be staying with Josh, and asking him which he preferred. Like I knew he would, Griff replied: **This is your home, Kell, no matter what.**

We drove out to Richmond, to one of the shelters there. They'd gotten a litter of German shepherd puppies in, the owners having abandoned them. I hated people who treated animals that way.

Chase and I sat in a room surrounded by playful pups. One of them was climbing all over Chase's lap and licking his face like crazy.

"Oh, you're a cuddly boy, aren't you?" Chase asked as he petted the pup. He grinned at the dog like he was already in love, and I knew he was the one.

"I think we should pick him."

"Yeah?" He looked over at me, his smile growing.

"Yep."

"I agree."

We let them know which one we wanted, filled out paperwork, then grabbed some dinner and headed back to Havenwood. It would be a week or so until we could bring him home. There was a whole process involved to make sure we would be good daddies for him. I told them we wouldn't be good, we'd be *the best*, because obviously we would.

The house was dark when we got back home. Griff would be at the bar. Chase checked the place out first because he was a worrier like that, and then we showered, changed, and ended up on the couch, watching a movie.

"Remember that BJ I gave you ten years ago in this living room?" I fluttered my lashes playfully.

Chase nodded. "I do."

"I think I need to give you another one, right here, for old times' sake, you know?"

Chase grabbed me, pulled me to him, and kissed me. I laughed against his mouth, and he was doing the same. Even with all the shit going on in our lives, I'd never been happier.

# CHAPTER THIRTY

## *Chase*

I WAS LOSING my fucking mind.

It had been a few days since we'd been staying at Griff and Kellan's. It was...awkward, to say the least. Griff and I hardly spoke. I was giving him space, and he was obviously still angry about everything, not that I could blame him. Kellan was trying hard to pretend everything was normal, when it so clearly wasn't.

I missed my home. I wanted to be there, but I also wanted Kellan with me, and I wanted him safe and comfortable, which meant being at his place for now.

From the first day I'd met Griff, he had always been there for me. If I was struggling or dealing with something, I always knew I had him by my side. I loved having Kellan with me, loved knowing he was mine, that no matter what happened I had him, but I missed my best friend. I missed Griffin.

My dad still hadn't come back to town, so that was

weighing on us. I wasn't working, and Kellan only had the one class, even though there were a couple more kids who had come back to the studio now. Every moment of every day the question in the back of my mind was, what if my father had done this? And even worse, what if he had something to do with the death of Kellan's parents? I was sick to my stomach all the time, knowing it was a possibility. It felt like everything was unraveling, like my life was falling apart, but then, then it felt more full than it ever had too—because of Kellan. Because I had him.

How everything could feel like it was both a disaster yet the most complete I'd ever been, I didn't know, but that was how it was.

It didn't help that we stayed at the house most of the time, not getting out much because of the photos everyone had seen. It was hard looking people in the eyes when they'd seen our private moment.

It was a Friday night. Griff was at the bar, like he always was. Kellan and I had made dinner together, had eaten, and now we were doing what we did every night, pretending everything was normal, when Kellan shoved off the couch. "Let's go!"

I frowned. "Where are we going?"

"To Griff's. We're doing something. We're not going to waste away in this house. We're not going to let them *win.*"

His words were exactly what I needed, were one of the things I loved about him so much—his strength, his determination to be himself and live his life his way, no matter what.

"Come on, Chase. I'm serious! Fuck them. I don't give a shit if they know I like to get a little kinky with my boyfriend. Most of them are probably jealous. I mean, you're hot, and I give the best blowjobs, so—"

I stood and pressed my mouth to his before he could continue. It wasn't that I was so excited about going out. Hell, I wasn't sure I wanted to, but it was hard not to feel his enthusiasm and impossible not to bask in Kellan's light when he felt strongly about something. "Oh, baby boy. You're going to kill me, I think. You got me all wrapped up."

"Just where I like you." Kellan grinned. "Now can we go out? I need a drink, and I miss the three musketeers. I need Nat and Josh time—with you, of course."

I couldn't pretend I wasn't a little nervous about going out. If someone said something to us, I wasn't sure I'd be able to keep my temper in check, but still I said, "Yeah, let's do this. Let's go have a little fun."

We showered, got ready, and Kellan messaged Natalie and Josh, telling them we were going out.

Nerves licked up my spine as we parked the truck alongside Griff's. After turning the key, I reached over and put my hand on Kellan's leg. "You sure this is a good idea?"

"Absolutely not." He grinned. "But I've been impulsive all my life. I don't plan on stopping now, and at least this time, you're by my side."

"You and me," I replied. We got out, and I reached for his hand, threading our fingers together.

We walked in, and half the eyes in the bar turned our way and stared…then the other half. Some shrugged and went about their business, other people watched us, a few whispered and laughed.

Kellan's hand tightened on mine. "It's fine. Don't do anything. Don't say anything. Don't let them know it bothers us."

It was the hardest fucking thing I'd ever done, but I did it for him. Because he asked. Because he had never needed anyone's approval to be himself, even if people looked at him and didn't understand him, so I could do the same.

There was the sound of wood scraping against the floor, like someone pushed a stool back. I automatically went on alert, expecting someone to say something to us or, hell, to take a swing, but it was Lawson who'd stood.

"Is there a problem?" he asked, looking around the room at everyone.

Then Josh was on his feet beside him…then Knox…and Natalie, followed by Becca, who gave me a supportive, shy smile.

Then…then Griffin walked around the counter and stood with them…our friends…our family. No matter how upset Griff was, he would be there. It's how he was built. It reminded me that I wasn't alone—that we weren't alone. Before Griff, I'd spent my childhood feeling that way. Then I had the Caines…and now I had these people in front of us too.

"Would any of you be brave enough to walk in here if someone had violated your intimate moment like that?" Law added.

The whispers stopped. The laughter. A few people got up and left, but I didn't give a shit about them. There were a few mumbled noes to Law's question.

The attention turned away from us, everyone going back to their drinks and their conversations. When I glanced over at Kellan, his eyes were watery. Damned if mine didn't feel that way too. "Come on, baby boy. Let's go sit with our friends."

A few people looked our way and nodded, or offered small smiles of support as we joined our group.

"Thanks, man," I said to Law.

"Not a problem. I'm sorry all this happened. Let me know if there's anything I can do."

"Will do," I answered.

"We got your back, brother," Knox added.

Kellan let go of my hand and hugged Josh.

"Hey, babe. You holding up?" Josh asked him, and the endearment didn't bother me. They were best friends, and I knew Kellan loved me.

"Yeah, we're doing okay." Kellan pulled away to hug Natalie next. Josh reached over and squeezed my shoulder in support.

Then Kellan hugged Griffin, who looked over Kell's shoulder at me and gave me a simple nod before finding his way around the counter again to get back to work.

"Margaritas for the three musketeers?" Griff asked.

"Obviously," Kellan replied playfully.

Griff nodded and handed me a bottle of beer before making their drinks. Kellan lost himself in conversation with Natalie and Josh, laughing and talking. When a new song played overhead, he said, "Ooh. This is Remington. I love this song!" He was so much better at dealing with shit like this than me, though I had other things on my mind as well.

"I hate this song," Law grumbled.

"How you doing, Chase?" Becca asked, standing beside me.

"I'll survive. Just hate that this happened to him." My gaze found Kellan as he told some story to Josh, his arms moving around and his voice animated. A smile stretched across my face. No matter how shitty I felt, he could always make me do that. He was so incredibly alive that it was impossible not to feed off his energy.

"You love him. I can see it in your eyes," Becca said.

"Yeah, I do."

"I didn't know you, um, swung that way." Her cheeks flushed pink, and I chuckled.

"I like women and men equally. Like him more than anyone, though."

"Good for you. I'm happy for you, Chase Hawthorne. And I respect you even more for coming home. Havenwood could use a little shaking up. Most people are too stuck in backward thinking and stereotypes. It'll be good for them to see you and Kellan together."

"Thanks, Bec. That means a lot to me."

She winked, then grinned playfully. "All the good ones go for other boys."

We chatted for a few minutes more before Becca went to talk with some other people. Griff was pretty busy, but I could also tell he was avoiding us on purpose, or at least avoiding me. I couldn't help but wonder what would happen if my fears came true…if my father had anything to do with the Caines' murder or even if he knew who it was. I didn't see how Griff and I could be the same after that.

"Want another beer? My treat?" Law asked, and I shook my head.

"No, thanks. I appreciate it, but I have to drive." Plus, I didn't really feel like drinking anyway. Had too much shit on my mind.

He paused for a moment, like there was something he'd been mulling over, then said, "It's good to see you and Kellan happy. The kid deserves it."

I cocked a brow at him. "He's not a kid."

"Yeah, I know. Spending too much time with Griff, I think. And listen, I just want to say, I know things are rough right now—the photos and Griff."

Which meant he knew Griffin was upset with me. Maybe they'd spoken, or maybe it was simply that obvious.

"Can't help who you love, ya know?" Law took a swallow of his beer. I couldn't tell if he was speaking from experience or being polite.

"No, you can't." My eyes scanned the bar and landed on Kellan. As if he knew I was looking at him, he paused in his conversation with Josh and smiled at me. "And I don't want to."

"Good man," Law replied, then went back to speaking with Knox, while I went back to worrying about all the shit on my mind and what would happen from there.

# CHAPTER THIRTY-ONE

## Kellan

IT HAD BEEN a few days since our night out at the bar, and with each one that passed, I knew more was going on with Chase than he was letting on.

We had a lot to deal with—I understood that. Between his being off work, the photos, his dad being gone, not staying at home, and the wall between him and Griffin, yeah, it was more than anyone should have to deal with. I hated that I couldn't do anything about it. Sure, he laughed at all the right times, and it wasn't like he was pulling away from me or anything. We spent our time together and cooked together and watched movies.

He hung out at Safe Haven with me, and I'd even tried to teach him how to make a vase with pottery. We had this *Ghost* moment and, you know, that's obviously hot. But Chase was struggling, and that weighed heavily on me. I wanted him happy. I wanted to fix it, because Chase always tried to fix things for others. He deserved someone to mend something for him.

So I tackled the only part of this equation I had some control over—my brother.

Chase was off doing something. Hell, I didn't even know what. So I asked Griff to go out to lunch with me. We went to Mr. Tom's, this little hole-in-the-wall café in Havenwood, where chances were we wouldn't run into someone we knew. There was Law's place, Sunrise, but I thought we needed privacy for this.

Griff and I found a seat in the corner and ordered cheeseburgers, fries, and chocolate milkshakes.

"We gotta talk about Chase," I said to him when we were alone.

Griffin rubbed a hand over his face and groaned. "How did I know that was why you wanted to go to lunch?"

"Whatever." I rolled my eyes.

"No, I'm serious, Kell. If we're going to talk, let's be real. When was the last time we spent time together? When was the last time you said, *Hey, brother. Let's go to lunch?*"

His words sank into my chest in an uncomfortable way. He was right. Of course he was right. I wasn't sure Griffin was ever wrong about anything, but it wasn't something I'd really thought about. "You haven't said that to me either. Plus, we live together. We see each other all the time."

"And if I had asked you to hang out? You always seem to think there's an ulterior motive."

"Because there always is," I countered. Fighting was the last thing I wanted to do with him, but I also wasn't going to take all the blame for…whatever it was that was happening here. "You act like you're my dad. You make me feel like a kid, Griff. You always make me feel like I'm doing something wrong, or like I'm a screw-up who can't take care of himself. It's like you're always scolding me and I'm never…like I'm never good enough."

The moment the words left my mouth, I knew they were true. It wasn't something he meant, but Griff made me feel like I wasn't good enough.

"And I get it. We're different," I continued. "You're much more responsible than I am, and I haven't always made the smartest choices, but it's hard, knowing you don't ever trust me."

He frowned, his stare pinning me intensely. I could see the thoughts twisting around in his brain, but I didn't know what they were.

"I never meant to make you feel that way."

"I know. You don't think I know? There isn't a mean bone in your body, but that almost makes it worse, like

I'm...fuck, I don't know. Like your life revolves around me, because you love me so much and you're such a good person and I'm...not."

"You're a good person, Kell. What are you talking about?"

"Yeah, I mean, I know that, but it's hard to feel it sometimes. Or hell, I don't know, maybe I'm not explaining it right, but like I'm such a mess, you can't have a life of your own. It has to all be about me, which makes me feel like shit."

Griff sighed, his finger tracing the edge of his water glass. "I don't know how to be any other way."

"I know." I reached over and put a hand on his arm. "I know. You're the best brother there is." And he was. Griff loved me with his whole heart. He loved Chase that way too. "But you have to let me fuck up. You have to let me go, in some ways, and know that I'm not going anywhere. You never would have walked away from me, and I'll never walk away from you. We're brothers."

And maybe that's what it was. Griff held on to me so tightly because he didn't want to be alone, because he didn't really let himself have a life outside of me. But he needed to. He deserved that.

He nodded. Margaret brought us our food, and we were quiet for a moment.

"Feels like somehow I'm gonna lose both of you," Griff finally admitted. You could have knocked me over with a feather, I was so surprised. "You and Chase have both always been so different from me. You think I don't trust you, and that's not true. I worry about you, yes, but hell, I envy you in a lot of ways. It's easier to focus on you than my own shit. You let everything roll off your shoulders, while my brain obsesses about it all."

"That's because you're a whole lot less selfish than me."

He rolled his eyes. "That's not true."

"I don't mean I'm selfish in a bad way. You just, you care about everyone else so much, you don't leave room to care for yourself. You have nothing to envy me for. There's not a better person than you."

"I mean…I know," Griff tried to joke, but I didn't take the bait.

"I'm serious. Do you think I'm not thankful every day that you're my brother? I am. I know that I can be who I am, that I can stand proud and just live my life because of you. Because I know I'll always have you." As I said the words, it struck me that as much as I'd always gotten upset with Griff for being overprotective, I was as much to blame. I knew Griffin was always the net I could fall back into. I knew that whatever happened, he would be there. I'd never tried to move out or do my own thing, and maybe it was time I did.

"Yeah?" Griff asked.

"Yes. We've both been a bit dependent on each other, I think, and that's not good for either of us."

"No, I guess not. You know I'm proud of you, right?"

"I do." I didn't think I acknowledged that until today, though. "I want you to be happy."

"I'm happy," he replied.

Was he? On the surface he seemed to be, but what did Griff really do or what did he have except me, his bar, and Chase? Yeah, he was buddies with Knox and Law, but that was different. Had Griff ever had anyone for himself? Anyone besides—Holy shit. Chase. He'd always had Chase. Their friendship was always the most important thing to Griffin outside of me.

My chest ached. My heart broke and tumbled down into my gut. "I don't want to take Chase away from you. That was never my intention. The fact that you guys are at odds is killing him, Griff. You gotta know that. He loves you. He'll always love you, and you'll always be his best friend."

"I know," Griff replied, but I wondered if he really did.

"Do you…are you in love with Chase?" My tongue felt swollen, like I could hardly speak. I'd asked Chase before, made sure he didn't have feelings for Griff, but I'd never asked Griffin. What would we do if Griffin was in love with Chase? I would die if I'd hurt my brother that way.

"No, no. That's not it." My eyes didn't move away from his, and he kept going, "It's not, Kell. I don't love Chase that way. He's a brother to me. I see him the same way I see you, which is one of the reasons this is a little weird for me, and I just…"

"You what?"

"I don't know that I'm really cut out to love someone that way. It's weird. I don't seem to feel it."

I frowned, my thoughts beginning to build a puzzle in my head, Griffin never really dating being a huge piece of it. "Do you mean you don't really find yourself attracted to people? Or is it that you don't think you can feel romantic love at all?" It had never even occurred to me that Griff could be demisexual, asexual, or aromantic. I suddenly felt like I had failed him in that. I assumed he was too busy focusing on me and his bar, instead of thinking that maybe he simply didn't feel things the way I did.

"Fuck." Griff rubbed a hand over his face. "This is

embarrassing."

"There's no reason to be embarrassed."

He nodded and said, "I'm not really sure. More the first one, I think. I've dated a few women and slept with them, but it's because I felt like I should do it more than actually wanting it—with them. But I don't feel myself wanting to sleep with men either. Still, I think I have sexual feelings... It's all sort of confusing."

That made a lot of sense when I thought about my brother. Again, I wondered why I had never considered it before. "It sounds like you're demisexual, Griff. Some people don't feel attraction or sexual attraction the same way as others. There has to be some kind of emotional bond there first. You're sure you don't feel that bond with Chase?"

"No." He shook his head vehemently.

"There's also something called aromantic, where you don't feel the desire for romantic relationships, or you don't feel romantic attraction toward others. And then there's asexuality—not feeling sexual attraction toward others, but it sounds like you think you might. There's nothing wrong with you or how you feel, and I hope you've never thought that."

He shrugged, which was such a typical Griffin response. "I never thought much about it, really.

Just…worried about my bar, I guess, and focused on you." He laughed, and I did too.

"Well, now you know. You can research those terms, hell, sexuality in general. I'm not an expert, and there might be other options out there. If something fits, great. If not, that's okay too. And if you ever want to talk about it, I'm around." It wasn't often that I had advice or had to give Griffin a pep talk. It was quite the role reversal.

"I need to fix shit with Chase," he said a moment later. "This helped. Talking with you."

"Good. I'm glad." It felt like a weight had been lifted off my chest, like before I couldn't breathe and now I was able to.

"It's good to see you happy, Kell. It really is. And if I'd pulled my head out of my ass sooner, I would have told you how obvious it is that you two are good for each other. Chase…he loves you. I can see that. It's nice that the two most important people in my life are happy together."

I couldn't help it. I stood up, went over, and hugged him. "God, I love you. You're the best big brother in the world."

"I love you too," Griff replied. When I sat back down, he asked, "Where is Chase, anyway?"

"I don't know." I pulled my phone out to look at it.

"I texted him, and he hasn't replied yet." Which was weird. Chase was good at answering quickly.

"I'll have to try and get ahold of him too. I miss the dumb sonofabitch."

We both laughed as I glanced at my phone again, and I shot another text to Chase.

"Well, now that our food is cold…" Griff said.

"Right? I've been known to talk a little too much, I guess."

The heavy conversation was done by then, so Griff and I ate our cold food. All the while, I couldn't help but keep looking at my phone, wondering where my boyfriend was and why he wasn't replying.

# CHAPTER THIRTY-TWO

## *Chase*

IT WASN'T HARD to get into the home I grew up in.

It was old and hadn't been taken care of, but I also knew that the window in my old bedroom didn't lock. I couldn't remember when it broke, but it had never been something that was important to fix. Plus, it was loose, so you could wiggle it open easily from the outside, and yeah, even after I left home, Dad hadn't found the need to repair it.

It was strange standing in the room that had been mine until I'd turned eighteen. It was full of junk. Dad was a collector of things—shit he'd find doing odd jobs, stuff off the side of the road; if there was a FREE sign, he took whatever was free whether he needed it or not, and if things weren't free but he wanted them, well, he took that shit too. Apparently, he'd turned my space into a storage area for all that stuff. Yard signs, a broken table, an old sewing machine, of all things. My father didn't sew. He used to fix things up and try to sell them, or trade them for things with his buddies if there was something he needed.

I remembered lying in this room at night, listening to my parents fight.

Then I listened to Dad drunk-rage that Mom took off and left him with me.

I listened to parties. To him and his friends drink and argue and put down everyone in town, especially the Caines.

And as I'd lain there, I'd dream I wasn't in my bed, but in another room, in a house on the other side of town. That the Caines were my family. That Robert and Susan Caine were my parents. That Griffin was my brother. I didn't remember ever wishing that of Kellan. It wasn't that I didn't care about him as much as Griff. Hell, I called Kell my brother when Griff and I got close, and I teased him like he was, but I'd never lain there and wished he was my blood the way I had Griffin. Maybe that meant something. Even back then, Kellan had always been different for me.

I went over to where my dresser still stood in the corner, the top drawer missing and the front of another one broken off. Scooting it aside, I fumbled with the third slat of wood flooring, which lifted easily, then pulled the gloves on my hands up tighter.

The metal tin was still inside. I didn't know why I never took it when I moved out. Partly, I thought, because I wanted to leave old memories and wishes behind. I'd wanted to stand on my own without hoping for things that wouldn't be. When I moved out, even though I was still in Havenwood at first, it was my goodbye to my old life, and I'd been determined to become a new Chase Hawthorne.

I sat down and opened it. Spiderman was on the front. Inside there was a photo of me, Mom, and Dad…and we were all smiling. It was the only photo I had of all of us, and it sure as shit was the only one where we were happy. We'd taken it at the lake cabin in North Carolina the one time we went. Mom had asked the neighbor at the nearest cabin to take it for us. It was right before she left. Now I knew that she'd likely already decided to go, that she'd already made the decision to walk away and leave me with him. There was a chance I was wrong, of course, but I didn't believe that.

At the time I'd been…happy.

Setting the photo down, I looked at the other items. There was a small journal inside. I hadn't written in it much. That had never been my thing, but there were about ten entries—one the day I met Griff, another when he called me his best friend for the first time, one when his parents threw me a small birthday party at their house and Susan made me a cake. One about Kellan, how I'd gone to their house after a bad day and Griff hadn't been home. I'd written about him being an annoying kid, but then about how he made me laugh...and how when I left, I'd felt better. I'd called it his Twerp Superpower, and said it had worked its magic on me. He was still working his magic on me.

And at the bottom of the box was a sketch...one Kellan had drawn. It was of me. Griffin and I had gotten home, and he'd been at the table. His eyes had gone wide when we came in, and he'd crumpled up whatever he'd been working on and tossed it into the trash.

Later that day I'd seen it there, on the floor behind the can. He'd obviously missed when he'd thrown it. I didn't know what made me grab it, smooth it out, and look, but I had, and it made me feel...good. Like I meant something. Like I was important enough that he would choose to sketch me.

Fucking Kellan Caine. It was always meant to be me and him. There wasn't a doubt in my mind about that, even though it had taken me too long to see it.

Closing the tin box, I tucked it under my arm and stood up, then put the board back and pushed the dresser into place.

I had no business being in this house. Except for the box, I couldn't say exactly why I'd come, what I hoped to find. I knew the sitting around and waiting was killing me. The not knowing was gnawing through my thoughts, into my muscles, making its way to my bones. If there was anything here, any proof of anything, I knew it wouldn't be admissible in court, but still I hadn't been able to stop myself from coming.

Trying not to disturb things too much, I looked around, riffled through boxes, and just...hoped to get lucky. I didn't know if that meant finding proof of a list of crimes that could belong to my father, or hoping that I didn't find anything.

When nothing jumped at me in that room, I went to the living room, then the dining room. They were all similar to my old bedroom—full of old crap and projects and boxes.

My stomach was heavy as I made my way to my father's room. I didn't know why I had saved that one for last. The idea of being in his space didn't sit well with me, but I was losing my damned mind.

It was crazy how fast I found it. All it took was opening the drawer on my dad's messy nightstand to see the ring sitting there like...like nothing. Like it hadn't meant the world to Susan Caine. Like it hadn't represented her marriage to Robert. Like it hadn't been on her finger when she was killed yet missing when she'd been found.

The room began to spin. Nausea ate at me, and my eyes blurred. I stumbled, knocking things down, running into others. I almost didn't make it to the toilet before I lost everything in my gut, vomited and cried, screamed and wailed. My whole body was shaking. My chest hurt, and my heart crumbled.

When my stomach was empty, I slid down to the floor, huddled along the dirt and grime as tears trailed down my face.

Oh God. What was I going to do? It was my father, my flesh and blood. He'd killed Robert and Susan Caine—the people who had been like parents to me, the people who had loved me, the parents of my best friend in the world and the man I loved.

Nothing would ever be the same again.

# CHAPTER THIRTY-THREE

## *Kellan*

"**S**TILL NOTHING ELSE?" Josh squeezed my shoulder as I looked at my phone for the thousandth time.

"No," I replied softly. We were all crowded around the living room of my house—me, Griffin, Josh, Natalie, Lawson, and Knox. It was late, almost midnight, and I'd received one text from Chase all day.

**I'm okay. Gotta figure some shit out. I love you.**

When I hadn't heard from him earlier, I'd gotten ahold of everyone to see if they'd seen him. When no one had, we ended up looking for him until finally the text came. I was scared and angry and a million other feelings I couldn't work through.

"At least we know he's safe," Griff said.

"No, we don't know that at all. Anyone can send a text. Someone was *watching* us together. They took photos of us, and then his dad went missing, and now

Chase is gone too." I rubbed my hands over my face in frustration and shoved off the couch. "Fuck!"

My chest got tight. Each second that went by, the fist around it squeezed with more and more strength.

"What if something happens to him? What if he's not okay? I can't…" I couldn't lose Chase like I'd lost my parents.

"Hey…it's okay, babe. He's okay." Josh's arms went around me. I buried my face in his neck and cried, sobbed really, my tears running down my best friend's skin. I was so scared Chase was hurt, that something bad had or would happen to him. The text could have easily been faked. We'd notified his police chief, but there wasn't much they could do at this point. I didn't know how I'd survive if something bad happened to him.

Then there was the part of me that also feared he was okay, but that he just didn't know if he wanted me anymore.

"God, if he's okay, I'm going to kill him!" I pulled away from Josh and wiped my face, trying to compose myself. Now wasn't the time to lose it. That wouldn't help anything.

"Mind if I help you?" Griff asked.

"Yeah, me too," Law added.

"And me," Knox agreed.

"One more?" Natalie raised her hand.

We were trying to lighten the mood, trying to pretend we weren't all worried sick, but it wasn't working.

"Thanks, you guys," I told them. "I appreciate you all being here, but really, there's not much we can do. You can all go home if you want. I'll let you know as soon as I hear anything."

"Pfft," Josh huffed. I'd never thought for a second he or Natalie would leave. Griff lived here, obviously, but I was surprised when Law and Knox both said no as well.

"If you hear from him or the police contact you, we want to be here in case you need us," Law said, and damn, it felt good. It seemed wrong to feel that way when Chase was missing, but I never had this—a room full of people who were my friends, who would be there for me. It wasn't about being Griffin's brother or Chase's boyfriend. They were there for me too.

"Thanks. That means a lot to me."

We settled in for a long night. There wasn't much talking after that; everyone sat on couches, chairs, or on the floor, and Knox was the first to fall asleep, followed by Natalie, then Josh, then Griffin.

Unable to sit still, I sneaked out from beneath Josh, who had his head on my shoulder, and pointed to the back door so Lawson knew where I was going. I didn't think he would follow, but he surprised me by doing the same.

"You okay?" he asked as we sat on the back porch, phone tightly clutched in my hand.

"Not really."

"Yeah, I guess that was a stupid question."

"No, it's okay. I get it. We all want to say something in a situation like this, but what is there to say?"

He nodded, pushing his blond curls behind his ear.

"Have you ever been in love?" I found myself asking him.

Law was quiet for a moment, then said, "Yeah…once. Didn't end well."

"I'm sorry."

He shook off my apology. "No worries. It is what it is."

I couldn't help but wonder who the woman was that Law had been in love with. I hadn't seen him date anyone seriously since he'd returned to Havenwood. He grew up here but moved away after high school, then found his way back about five years ago.

There was a noise behind us, and I wasn't surprised to see Josh standing there.

Law cleared his throat. "I'll leave you guys to it." He stood and walked into the house as Josh came out. He sat beside me on the porch swing, and I dropped my head to his shoulder.

"Chase is worried that it's his dad who took the photos of us," I admitted. It wasn't something I'd shared with anyone, especially not Griff. He would lose his mind.

"Oh shit."

"I know. It'll kill him if he figures out it was."

"That's not his fault."

I chuckled humorlessly. "You don't know Chase. It doesn't matter if it's his fault or not, he'll feel like it is."

"Yeah, I can see that."

"I keep thinking that maybe he found out it was his dad and he did something? Not that Chase would hurt him, but maybe he feels guilty and took off, or maybe his dad hurt him. I just…I don't know. Why would he leave, Josh?" Why would he leave me? Again…

"He didn't leave *you*, Kell," Josh answered my silent question. "See, I know you too, and I know that's part of your worry. Of course you want Chase to be okay, he's your primary concern, and I know I gave you shit about this guy… I know I thought I hated him, but I don't. I see the way he looks at you. He loves you. He didn't leave you, and he'll come back."

God, I hoped he was right. "What if his dad hurt

him?"

"Chase can take care of himself, I don't doubt that. And I think you know it was him who texted you. You'd feel it if it wasn't. I think maybe Chase did find out something he didn't want to be true, and he's figuring out how to deal with it. I can't fault him for that. I'd do the same thing."

I nodded.

We swung together the whole night. Part of me believed Josh was right. The thing was, I could tell there had been more than Chase was telling me where his father was concerned. He'd been worried about more, and it had been eating him alive.

I should have fought harder for him to tell me.

I should have made sure he knew that whatever it was, I wasn't going anywhere.

And there was another part of me, one I was scared to acknowledge, that wondered what Chase's dad could have done to upset him so much.

I was afraid to know the truth.

The next day my phone finally rang. I looked at it, hoping, praying to see Chase's name, but it wasn't. It was the Havenwood Police Department, and my heart sank.

# CHAPTER THIRTY-FOUR

## *Chase*

THE LAKE CABIN looked the same as I remembered it. The front porch was a bit newer; it had obviously been rebuilt. But from the outside, the rest of it was the same.

You could see a few more cabins in the distance. None too close. The man who'd taken our photograph had been staying at the nearest one. The lake was out front, with a small dock that also looked as if it had been rebuilt. The whole area was surrounded by thick green trees for as far as the eye could see.

The closest cabins looked empty, and I had my fingers crossed they were. I also hoped my father was staying here now.

I didn't know how likely that was. It wasn't something I had even thought to mention to the chief. My dad didn't have a sentimental bone in his body, but I hadn't known where else to go. I'd just...driven. I wished I could forget what I found, but I knew I couldn't. That wasn't something I could ever do to Kellan and Griff. Plus, it was why I did what I did, wasn't it? I'd told Kellan that I'd gone into law enforcement because of his parents, and that had been true. I'd always wanted to figure out who had killed Robert and Susan, and now...now that I knew, I couldn't pretend I didn't.

My gun was on my hip. I wasn't that guy who typically carried his personal firearm around, but I also didn't trust my father.

I'd taken the first step onto the porch when I heard the faint sound of wood creaking from the back, and I took off running around the house. Sure enough, my old man was there, looking like shit, with bloodshot eyes and in bad need of a shave.

"Fuck," he cursed.

With a quick scan, I saw he wasn't holding anything, but that didn't mean he didn't have a weapon anywhere else on his person. "Is anyone here with you?"

"Fuck you," he replied.

"Get back in the goddamned house." He was alone. There wasn't a doubt in my mind about that. The last thing I wanted was to do this outside. Plus, I had to be careful how I went about this and what I said. I'd illegally searched his home. I was on leave from the department. Yeah, I definitely shouldn't have been there, but I was.

To my surprise, my dad went back for the cabin. When we hit the back porch, I ordered, "Stop," and searched him. He didn't have a weapon on him.

"Bet that's your favorite part of the job, huh?" he asked with a sneer.

"Christ, what's wrong with you?" What kind of person thought that—what kind of person said that to their own son?

"What's wrong with me is I have a queer for a son and had a bitch for a wife. All this shit is your fault—both of you."

I felt like I was going to be sick again, but I bit it down, held it back. "Go," I said as he stumbled into the cabin, obviously not sober, but not as drunk as usual.

I hadn't come here to talk about him or about my mother; neither of them was worth my time. He was an abusive asshole, and she'd left her only son with him.

When we got inside, I closed the door, did a quick sweep of the cabin, then directed him to sit on the faded brown couch, while I went to the chair across from him. I fell down into it...exhausted, physically and mentally. Tired. Sad. Drained. Scared.

"The best time I remember us having was when we came here. I felt like we were a real family, ya know?"

He sneered. "It was her idea, the bitch. She took us here, then left us. Left me with you."

"Yeah," I agreed. "She did. I used to pretend she had a reason, that she would come back for me. But no matter what, she chose to walk away from me, so excuses didn't matter. I understand her wanting to get away from you. She deserved that, but…" But leaving me, I couldn't forgive that.

"It was her fault!" Dad yelled. "She was always startin' the fights, and she was the one who wanted you. Made a mess'a everything, the two of you. Should have taken you with her."

There was a time when his words would have hurt, but not anymore. I hated him. Because he was vile and evil. Because he'd hurt Susan and Robert. Because he'd hurt Kellan and Griffin. "I found it, Dad. I know the truth."

His pupils went wide, and he shifted, trying to mask his fear. "Yet you're here by yourself, and I know you were put on leave because they didn't want a cocksucker to work for them. You suck Kellan's cock too, don'cha?"

I wasn't going to play into his ribbing, even though his words made me sick. "I know what you did."

"Yet you have no proof, or it wouldn't be you here," he jeered.

There was no sense in denying it, so I didn't. "Why?" I asked with more emotion in my words than I'd wanted to show. "Why did you do that? Why did you hurt them? Was it so I would suffer? Did you hate me so much that you had to murder the only real family I had?" My voice broke as pain pierced my chest. I still couldn't believe it, didn't want it to be true.

"What the hell are you talking about?" Dad's voice rang out, filled with…holy fuck, with shock. It was plain as day in the rise of his tone and the panicked expression on his face. "I didn't kill nobody."

"The Caines," I said, trying to figure it all out in my head. "Susan Caine's wedding ring. It was stolen when they were murdered. You have it, and they know you have it. The department knows." The second part was a lie, of course.

At that Dad shot to his feet, ran a hand through his shaggy hair. "That dirty motherfucker," he gritted out. "I didn't kill them. Wish to God I could have and not cryin' a tear that they're gone. I stole that ring from Jimmy!"

Jimmy…Buck's dad? Could he be telling the truth? It sounded like he was. There was fear and surprise in his voice, not guilt. My pulse was pounding, but I tried to ignore it, tried to figure out what to do, what to say. "Lying isn't going to help. You have the ring, Dad. One anonymous call was all it took to send them to your place." Another lie, but as he paced frantically, I could see the growing agitation and fear. He wasn't thinking clearly. He would believe anything I said.

"I didn't kill nobody! Goddamned Jimmy! I shoulda known it was him. Robert Caine couldn't keep outta anyone's business—the bastard helped Jimmy's wife leave! Stepped in where he didn't belong. Probably helped your mama too!"

My brain was spinning with all this information. Had Buck's mom been Robert's client? Had he been her therapist and known she was going to leave Jimmy? Or was this all something Jimmy and my dad cooked up in their hateful brains? "Is that why you helped Jimmy kill them?" The more I scared him, the more he would want to protect himself and spill the truth.

"I told you I didn't kill them! Are you stupid? I admit I took those pictures of you and your little cocksucker."

My hands tightened, and it took everything in me not to launch myself at him. He could talk about me but, "Don't mention him. Keep Kellan out of whatever the fuck you have to say."

He ignored me, his panic rising as he tugged at his hair and words continued to spill from his mouth. The alcohol probably helped loosen his lips. "I'm not going down for that shit. I'm not going down for killing those bastards. I took those photos because Jimmy was blackmailin' me. He wanted to get you and your little boy back for him screwin' with Jimmy's family."

I gritted my teeth. All Kellan had done was teach his grandson. That was why the photos were taken? "What did he have against you? What was he blackmailing you with—Susan and Robert's murder?"

"How many times do I gotta say I didn't kill them!"

And…I believed him. Not because I wanted to, but because I knew it was true. All the pieces were fitting into place. Robert had likely been Jimmy's wife's therapist, so when she left, he blamed Robert. There was no doubt he had been abusive. That was why Jimmy and Buck hated Kellan, hated the Caines…and maybe he'd helped my mom leave too…leave me. Was that why they'd taken me in? Did he feel guilty?

I shoved those thoughts from my brain. That wasn't what was important. But Jimmy's hostility toward Kellan made more sense…and the robbery… "It was you. You're the one who held up the gas station. And Jimmy knew, so he blackmailed you with that to take photos of me and Kellan." The ring...I could see my father stealing it. He pocketed whatever the hell he could, and this time it happened to be the wrong damn thing.

I didn't even remember doing it, but somehow, I was on my feet. My hand wrapped around my father's biceps. "Let's go. You're coming with me."

"The hell I am!" He tried to pull away. "I'm gettin' the hell out of here! I'm not admittin' shit! If you had a case against me, you wouldn't be here right now."

Before I could say anything else, before I could fight him on it, the cabin door burst open. "Police! Put your hands in the air!"

North Carolina officers stormed into the room, we were handcuffed, read our rights, and both of us were arrested.

# CHAPTER THIRTY-FIVE

## *Kellan*

M Y LEG WAS bouncing up and down like crazy. No matter how hard I tried, I couldn't keep it still. The first call that day from Chief Potter had been to ask if I knew where Chase was. Apparently, they had something on his father, were searching his place, and needed to find Chase.

Then later, the other call had come in. The one that had us at the police station now.

"You're sure?" Griffin asked Chief Potter.

"George Hawthorne was picked up in North Carolina. They took Chase in with him, because no one knew what the hell was going on or who he was. I've been on the phone with them all day. It took a while to get things sorted out, but they're releasing Chase. He went up looking for his daddy. I called the two of you this morning because we'd gotten a tip on another case. While searching the Hawthorne place, we found evidence to suggest—"

Griffin held up his hand. We didn't need Chief Potter to say it again—they found evidence to suggest that George Hawthorne had killed our parents.

"I'm going to be sick." I fell to the floor and heaved into the trash can. There was nothing in my gut to come up, but I kept dry heaving. Chase's dad... God, Chase's dad had killed our parents? I didn't know what to say, what to think, what to feel. It was all too much, and I just... "How's Chase?" This would be killing him. It was wrecking me too, but I thought I was a bit in shock. It hadn't sunk in yet. I'd never expected their murder to be solved, and now it likely was, and it was... Oh God. I closed my eyes. Chase would hate himself for this. He would blame himself.

"I didn't speak with him yet," Chief Potter replied.

"But you're sure? You're really sure?" The whole thing wouldn't sink in. It was too unbelievable.

"If you get hold of him before we do, can you tell him we love him and we want him home?" Griffin asked the chief, and my eyes shot over to him. This didn't change anything for me. It wouldn't. I loved Chase too much. But I'd been scared about Griff.

"Yeah, Griffin. I'll tell him," he replied just as his phone rang. "If you'll both excuse me, I have to take this.

It's from North Carolina."

"Okay," I replied as we both got up and walked out of his office.

Griffin closed the door behind us, and I wrapped my arms around my brother. "God, Griff. What do we do? How do we work through this? Mom…Dad…Chase…" The words wouldn't come out. I couldn't say them. It hurt enough just thinking them.

"I know." Griff hugged me back.

There was a loud crash behind me. I jerked away from Griffin and turned around to see the door to the station had been shoved open and hit the wall. Chase stood there, his clothes wrinkled, his eyes intense and…so broken and pinned directly on us.

He had that little pinch in his forehead that he got sometimes when he didn't know what to do. Neither of us moved. We just stared. It was as if my feet had grown roots. I knew what I wanted, which was him, but I couldn't seem to move, couldn't seem to go to him.

There was a nudge against my back—Griffin—and that little push unstuck whatever had been frozen inside me. I went for Chase, ran to him, and he did the same. The second we were together, his arms around me and mine around him, our bodies touching, so familiar and right, I knew that no matter what, it would be okay. It had to be okay. Being with him made things better. Not perfect, not even good, I didn't think, because there was so much to work through, so much to figure out, but it was better.

"I'm sorry." Chase cupped my face, kissed my forehead as he apologized over and over. "I shouldn't have left without telling you what was going on, and then when I found out everything...Christ, I needed to get home to you. I don't know if I'm too late, but I didn't want you to hear it without me being here."

"They said your dad..." My words trailed off. I still didn't think I could say them, not out loud and not to Chase.

"Wait. Come on. Let's go find a place we can talk." Chase glanced up then, and from the way he looked, I could tell his gaze had snagged on Griffin. "I, um...I think you should come too."

Griff cleared his throat. "Yeah, okay. Thanks."

Chase held on to my hand as he led us into what looked like a conference room. "We're going to be in here for a few minutes," he said to one of the officers sitting at a desk in the next room.

"Sure thing, Chase. We hope to have you back soon."

Chase nodded and closed the door. When he turned

around, I was struck again by how tired he looked. There were dark circles under his eyes and a curve to his spine that wasn't typical for him.

"I—" Chase began, but Griff cut him off.

"Before you go on, I'd like to say something." Chase nodded. "I know I've been walking around with my head up my ass since I found out about you and Kell. It was a shock, and I wish you'd trusted me enough to tell me, but I understand why you didn't. And I want you to know, Chase, that I love you. Being with Kellan isn't going to change that. What your fath—" Griff's voice cracked, but then he continued. "What your father did, that won't change it either."

There was more they would have to say. How couldn't there be, but I was glad Griffin had said that. He'd let Chase know that regardless of what his father had done, Griff wouldn't hold it against him.

Chase stood there for a moment, and then…then he closed his eyes, and I could practically see the relief wash through him. "You think my dad was involved in your parents' murder and you still feel that way? Both of you?" He looked back and forth between me and Griff.

I couldn't help but notice his use of the word *think*, which confused the hell out of me, but still I said, "Yes," because I wanted Chase to know that no matter what, I wasn't walking away.

"Yeah, man. Always," Griffin added.

"I don't know what I did to deserve both of you, but I'll spend every day of my life thankful I have you," Chase replied.

Griffin stepped forward and clapped Chase on the shoulder. "You've always deserved better than the hand you were dealt."

They looked at each other in this macho dude-bro way where I knew they were saying all sorts of things to each other without words.

"Thank you." Chase cleared his throat, then reached for my hand and pulled me closer. "Come on. Let's sit down." The three of us took chairs around the long, rectangular table. "I can't give you all the details since it's an open investigation, but it wasn't my dad—with your parents. It wasn't my dad."

"What?" I asked. "But Chief Potter said—"

"We thought it was at first—I thought it was. It's a clusterfuck how it all went down, but I was with my dad when I shouldn't have been, when I went looking for things I shouldn't have."

The way he said it, I could tell it was something we weren't supposed to know. "Chase!"

"I know, baby boy. It was stupid, but there's no

going back now. At the same time, Timmy, the kid who works at the gas station that was robbed, had been blabbing. They found out he'd worked with my dad. He pretended to get robbed, passed all the information my dad needed to him, and then they split the money." Chase glanced back at the door, which was still closed. "We have to make this quick. When Timmy got caught, he folded and told them everything. When they searched my dad's house to find evidence on the robbery, they found…they found your mom's ring."

My stomach dropped out. Griff cursed.

"Yeah, that was my thought too because I found it before that. They hadn't had enough evidence to run his plates or credit cards when it came to the photos, but they had it then. They found Dad in North Carolina, and I was…I was with him. When they came in, I had just found out what really happened. It was a mess after that, took me a while to get it all sorted out, but it's not what we thought."

"What happened, Chase? Please tell us," I asked, my heart in my throat.

He paused for a moment, took a breath, and said, "Dad took the photos of us. He admitted that. He did it because he was blackmailed by Jimmy, who knew about the robbery."

"What about Mom and Dad?" Griffin asked, and Chase's eyes moved to him.

"It's all a little murky from here. I don't have all the answers, the why of it. Once there are more answers, Chief Potter will be made aware."

I wondered if that was the phone call Chief Potter had gotten.

"They're heading to search Jimmy's place," Chase added. "According to my father, he stole the ring from Jimmy. He didn't know what it was. His eyes damn near fell out of his head when I told him it belonged to your mama."

"Jimmy?" Griff asked, his voice tight. I couldn't find mine. This whole time it had been Jimmy. "You believe him?"

"I do," Chase said. "Maybe it's because I want to believe him. Maybe I'm lying to myself because the alternative is too fucked up to consider, but I believe him."

"But why would Jimmy..." Really, why would Chase's father have done it either? Why would any of them?

Chase knelt on the floor in front of me. "I don't know for sure, Kell. I shouldn't have even told you guys this much. And it could all be wrong. I don't know, but I just…I wanted you to know, and I needed to be here with you. I never should have left. I should have told you my fears from the beginning. I was scared and thought my father had done it, and I didn't know how to deal with that."

I didn't have the chance to answer. There was a sharp rapping on the door before it was pulled open and Chief Potter came in. "Chase, I hope you're not doin' anything you shouldn't."

"No, sir." Chase stood up.

"Just got a phone call that made shit go to hell around here even more than it was a little while ago. I'm gonna need the three of you to stay here. We're gonna have some questions for you all. Griffin, Kellan, the two of you are going to have to look at some evidence and tell us if it belonged to your parents."

The nausea hit me again. My whole world was spinning. I had no idea which way was up, what was happening. Chase's dad had taken the photos of us, and he'd maybe robbed the gas station, and had my mom's ring and maybe other things of my parents'? Either George or Jimmy had been responsible for their deaths. "I think I'm going to be sick again."

Then Chase was there, by my side, and again, things weren't good, hell, they didn't even make sense right now, but they were better.

# CHAPTER THIRTY-SIX

## *Chase*

W E WERE AT the station for hours. There were more questions to be answered, the ring to identify, and eventually Jimmy had been arrested. They had to have had more evidence than my dad's word to make an arrest, but I wasn't currently in a position to know what it was. By the time we were able to leave, we were all more exhausted than any of us knew how to deal with.

"Do you feel comfortable coming home with me?" I asked Kellan as we stood outside the department. I brushed his chocolate-brown hair off his forehead.

"I think I want to go back to my house today...to feel close to my parents."

Shit. I hadn't even thought of that, but it made sense. "Okay." Leaning forward, I kissed the tip of his nose. We were at a weird place at the moment. I'd taken off, and then all the stuff with my dad. It was like we were in a field of landmines, and I wasn't sure where to step or what was expected of me.

"Will you come home with me?" Kellan finally asked, and some of the pressure leaked from my chest.

"Yeah, baby boy. Of course."

Kellan smiled before looking over at Griff, who was ten or so feet away from us, likely hanging around to see what would happen. "I'm going to ride home with Chase."

"Our place?" Griff asked, and Kellan nodded.

We were quiet on the drive to their house. Quiet as we went inside. We needed to talk, but I was letting him lead the way.

"I feel gross. I need a shower. You're welcome to join me."

"I'd love to."

We stripped bare and hopped into the shower in Kellan's en suite. He was the first to slip under the spray, water sluicing down his slender body, his hair plastered to his forehead as he closed his eyes.

My chest swelled as I stood there looking at him, at this man I had known most of my life and had loved maybe longer than I'd let myself see. "Christ, you're beautiful." I brushed my finger along his collarbone.

Kellan's eyes opened, and he stood there looking at

me. "I don't think I'll ever get used to hearing you say things like that to me, Chase Hawthorne."

"It's true. You are. I'll never stop saying it, but I also love that after everything, I still affect you that way."

"You always will, silly man," he said with a playful smile, but one that told me he wasn't ready to talk about everything yet. I nodded that I understood.

We washed up, got out, and dried off. With the towels wrapped around our waists, we brushed our teeth, still quiet and almost unsure around each other.

"I know we need to talk, but I'm so tired, Chase. It's been a lot to take in, the past few days. Hell, the past few weeks."

It had been like a roller coaster. We were so high that morning in my bathroom, Kellan shaving me after the night we'd had. From there it felt like one thing after another: Griff finding out, the photographs, the consequences for our jobs and personal lives, me pulling away, running, my father, his parents. We were due some downtime after all that. "I'm not going anywhere," I replied, hoping he knew I wasn't.

We took off our towels, I turned off the lights, and we climbed into bed together. Kellan was asleep the second his head hit the pillow, but he wasn't resting peacefully. I wondered where his mind had gone, what he was dreaming or thinking about.

It took me a while, but eventually I fell asleep as well. The next thing I knew, I woke with a start and looked at my cell phone to see I'd slept for about twelve hours. Kellan was still passed out beside me, his forehead creased, a small frown on his lips.

As quietly as I could, I slipped out of bed and pulled on a pair of sweats. Not wanting to wake him, I used the bathroom in the hallway, then made my way to the kitchen. It was early morning. I didn't expect to see Griffin sitting at the table with a cup of coffee in front of him, but there he was.

He looked up at me as I walked in, an awkward moment between us that had never been there until recently, then nodded toward the coffeepot. "It's fresh. You're welcome to it."

"Thanks. Did you get any sleep?" I asked as I got some much-needed caffeine.

"Some. Probably not enough. Kell still in bed?" His voice was raspy and tired.

"Yeah, he needs it. You do too."

"And you," Griffin said as I sat in the chair across from him. We were quiet, each sipping our drinks, the air heavy with tension and unsaid words.

When I couldn't take it anymore, I said, "I'm sorry,

Griff, about how things went down. That I kept something so important from you. It was wrong. I should have told you, but I was afraid to lose you. You're my brother. My best friend. The first person in this world who ever made me feel worthy of some kind of love. I know that's not an excuse, because I hurt you, and I'll never forgive myself for that, but…I can't regret him. I really do love him. Being with Kellan is…it's *right*."

Griffin took a sip of his coffee, then cleared his throat. "I know. I can see how much you care about him, and he's sure as shit always loved you. The thing is, as angry and hurt as I was, I don't think I was surprised. It just…fit. You've always had a soft spot for him. You've always cared about him in ways that weren't simply the little brother of your best friend. I didn't want to admit that because…hell, I don't even know why. And the truth is, I probably wouldn't have made it easy on you had I known from the beginning, because I'm pretty sure it didn't start out as serious as it is now."

He cocked a brow at me, and I couldn't help but chuckle. Damn, it felt good to laugh with Griffin again, but I definitely wasn't going to tell him about hooking up with Kellan. "No comment."

"Yeah, I wouldn't have let you get into it either. I'd rather not know." We both laughed again before Griff continued. "I've put a lot of pressure on Kellan, and that's something I have to work through and come to terms with. He's his own man, and I haven't treated him that way. I trust him. I trust you."

"Thank you." Christ, I'd needed to hear that. "I don't want to lose you, brother."

"You never will," Griffin replied.

It wouldn't be completely smooth sailing, how could it be? The dynamics of our relationships had changed, but sitting there with him, I somehow knew it would be okay. At least this part of it.

As if he could read my thoughts, Griffin said, "This whole thing with your dad, though, and with Jimmy. It's a clusterfuck, and I don't quite know where it'll end up."

Neither of us did. My dad could be lying. Hell, my dad could have played a part in it with Jimmy. My gut believed him, but again, that could be wishful thinking. "I don't know what I'll do, Griff. I don't know how I'll—"

"You'll keep on going like you always do. And you'll stay loyal, and you'll love my brother, and you won't let that other shit matter, because Kellan sure as hell won't let it. *I* won't let it."

I shook my head, unable to understand how I'd gotten so lucky. How these two men could be willing to stay by my side, even if it did somehow come out that my father had something to do with the murder of their parents.

"You're not him, Chase. You never have been and you never will be, and you can't hold yourself accountable for his shit. None of it will be easy, but we'll get through it, no matter what."

"Thank you." And then we were both standing, then hugging, and in that moment, all the other shit disappeared. We were Chase and Griffin, best buds. Brothers.

At the *creak* of a floorboard, we both turned to see Kellan there. He looked sleepy, his hair messy, a pair of low-slung sweats on his slender hips, that tattoo peeking out at me.

"I'll give you two some privacy." Griffin grabbed his keys off the hook on the wall, then his phone. On the way to the door, he ruffled Kellan's hair. Kell jerked back and groaned, Griff was laughing as he left.

"Hi," Kellan said softly, vulnerably.

"You want some coffee? I can make you a cup."

He shook his head, walked over to the couch, and sat down. He pulled his knees close to his chest, his feet flat on the cushion, and wrapped his arms around his legs.

There was an uncomfortable tightness in my chest as I walked over and sat beside him.

"I thought you were running away from me again," Kellan said, his words piercing my heart.

Shit. I hadn't even thought of that. "I wouldn't. I'd never do that."

"Maybe you know, but I didn't. You left when I was eighteen because you couldn't handle what happened between us, and I thought…I thought you couldn't handle everything again, and that you weren't going to come back. Maybe I shouldn't have because you texted, but that didn't matter. I can't be afraid that every time something happens that spooks you, you're going to run."

Guilt sat heavy, a weight in my chest. "You're right. I shouldn't have done that. My head was all screwed up. I was afraid my dad had something to do with your parents, and I…" I'd run. But not for good. I would never have left Kellan again. I couldn't. I loved him too much. "My reasons don't matter. You're right, and I'm so sorry for that. There's nowhere I'd rather be than by your side. I won't run, not ever, no matter what."

"I've spent my whole life wanting you, my whole life giving chase, and I can't do that anymore. I love you and want you. It would kill me to lose you, but we have to be in this together. Things might be a whole lot harder before they get easier, Chase, and I can't worry that you're going to take off because you feel guilty or don't know how to deal with it all. You have to be honest with me, all the time. You have to trust me. You have to trust *us*."

"I trust you." I reached out and cupped his cheek, brushed my thumb beneath his eye. "I trust us. I'm not going anywhere without you. As long as you want me, this is where I'll be. You're it for me. You're my home."

His chin trembled slightly, but he didn't cry. He pushed forward and straddled my lap, his hands on my face as he looked at me. "I love you, Chase Hawthorne. I'll always love you."

"I love you too, baby boy."

A smile pulled at his lips, and he gave a mock-tremble. "*God*, that's so hot. I don't think you understand how much that gets me going."

Hunger swept through me, fierce and uncontrollable. There were still so many things to say, and we'd say them, but right now... "I need you."

"I thought you'd never ask." Kellan winked playfully and climbed off my lap. He started running for his room, and I chased him. He said he'd been giving chase his whole life, and I'd spend the rest of our lives chasing him if I had to.

When we were in his room, I kicked the door closed

behind us and tackled him to the bed. Our mouths pulled together, eager, in a *clank* of teeth and rushed movements.

One second we were clothed, and then we were naked, Kellan beneath me, looking up at me in a way that made me feel so damned powerful, like there was nothing I couldn't do or would ever be unable to do, as long as he kept gazing at me like that.

I slid down to the floor, knelt between his legs, and took his cock as deep as I could. Kellan arched off the bed. "Chase!" he cried out as his hand tightened in my hair.

I sucked him and lapped at his balls, rubbed my finger over his rim until he was writhing beneath me, mumbling inaudible words.

"Please," was the first one I could understand.

I pulled off his dick and nuzzled his balls. "What is it? What do you want, baby boy?"

"I want to taste you too."

I stood, my legs feeling weak and shaky. My cock ached, my balls full with my load. Kellan went to get on the floor, but I shook my head. "Lie on the bed."

He did as I said, the pillows beneath his head. I straddled him, my erection in front of his face, and he grinned, looking up at me while I pushed my cock between his lips. "So fucking sexy, staring at your man with a mouth full of his cock."

Kellan cupped my ass, and I fucked into his throat. He took it, urged me on, pushing me closer so he could swallow me down. My orgasm was bearing down on me, burning through me like a wildfire I couldn't contain. Right before I lost it, Kellan pulled off.

"Fuck, I need to come," I gritted out as his fingers teased the crease of my ass.

"Can I?" he asked.

"You want to fuck me?" It wasn't something he'd ever shown any interest in before.

"Yeah. If you don't want to, I'll take your cock. You know I love being full of you, but…"

"You can have me, Kell. Anytime you want. I'm already yours."

I rolled off him and onto my back. Kellan plucked the bottle of lube and a condom from his nightstand.

"Do we need that?" I asked, pointing to the rubber. "I'm negative. I was checked when I moved back to Havenwood, and I haven't been with anyone but you."

"I'm negative too," Kellan replied. "I haven't been with anyone other than you since the last time I was checked, and I'm on PrEP."

"It's up to you. I want to, but only if you do."

"Are you kidding me? God, it might kill me, and I'll probably bust my nut the second I'm inside you, but yes, I want it. I've never had sex bare before—fucking or being fucked."

"Me either," I replied.

Kellan tossed the condom, lubed his fingers, and leaned over. His tongue pushed into my mouth as he teased my hole. It had been a long time since I'd been fucked, and it wasn't something I'd done a lot of, but Christ, I couldn't wait to have Kellan inside me.

He pushed a finger in, trembled. "Fuck, you're tight. Please don't hold it against me if I'm quick."

I laughed, which made me tighten and feel him more. He kissed me again, fucking me with that one finger, then two, working me open at a leisurely pace.

"So good," I said as he licked my right nipple, his finger brushing over my prostate. "Can't wait to feel your cock inside me, feel you spill your load so deep."

"God, I can't believe you're mine," he said, then lashed his tongue over my other nipple.

"I'm yours," I reassured him.

"I really need inside you, Chase. Can you take me?"

"Yeah, I think we're good."

"I'll try and go slow." He knelt between my spread legs, pumping lube onto his long rod, rubbing it down the shaft and over the head. He pushed my legs back, rubbed the head of his prick against my rim. Fuck, that simple touch felt so good, my hunger for him surged through me.

"Fuck me, Kell. Take me."

He cocked his head, so much emotion in those expressive eyes of his that I gasped. Yeah, this was it, this was where we were supposed to be.

Then Kellan was pushing inside, slow, so damned slow. The stretch made me suck in a sharp breath, but then I said, "Keep going."

Kellan did, working his way inside, pressure and fullness, and then, then he was there, his groin against my ass as he pushed my legs back with his arms. He was shaking like crazy as he looked down at me, a few beads of sweat on his temple. "I can't move. I really fucking can't move. You're so tight, Chase...so hot."

"Make me come, baby boy."

An explosion of fire lit up his eyes, and I wrapped a hand around my cock and stroked as Kellan started to thrust. It still wasn't quite comfortable yet, my body adjusting to having someone inside me after so long. I fumbled with the lube, slicking up my hand and working myself with tight, long strokes.

"Jesus, I love you. This is incredible. So sexy, so

fucking hot." The more Kellan rambled, the more he worked me up. He sped his thrusts and adjusted the angle, and then every time he moved, a zing of pleasure shot up and down my spine.

My balls started to ache and tighten as I watched the corded muscles in his neck clench. Kellan fucked into me harder, telling me how good I felt, how much he loved me. When he bent over and bit the top of my shoulder, my balls drew tight, and his cock pulsed inside me. I cried out in orgasm, shooting on my stomach and hand as I felt the rush of Kellan's release inside me.

He fell on top of me, sweaty and smiling. "The best. Oh God. So good. I can't wait to feel you fuck me bare. I can't believe I held off until you came."

With a chuckle, I kissed the top of his head. We lay there like that for a while, Kellan on top of me, sweat and come making us stick together, our chests moving in sync as we breathed.

No matter what happened, I knew this was exactly where I was always meant to be.

# EPILOGUE

## *Kellan*

***Six Months Later***

"**W**HAT THE FUCK?" I heard Josh yell from the living room, where he and Chase were watching sports.

"Yeah, motherfucker! I told you!" Chase countered.

I looked down at our dog, Bowie, who loved sleeping beside the desk in my art room. "Daddy is crazy, and so is Uncle Josh." He sat up, and I scratched behind his ears.

It had been…well, it had been a wild six months, full of highs and lows. I'd moved in with Chase, which was *every-fucking-thing*. I loved living with Chase, being with Chase, being loved by Chase. Through everything, our love had never faltered.

Before I moved in, Chase surprised me by changing the spare bedroom into an art room for me. Above my desk was a wrinkled sketch I'd drawn of him a hundred years ago, that I hadn't known he'd had. It was a little bit ridiculous and nauseatingly sweet, but that was basically us.

Chase and Josh had gotten closer, which meant a lot to me. It felt good knowing that the two men I loved most in the world besides my brother were friends. Griff and Chase were great too. It was like nothing had happened, and sometimes it was annoying because they'd tease me like they used to, but now it ended with Chase pulling me to his lap, kissing me and telling me he loved me as Griff rolled his eyes, so it really wasn't that bad.

So yeah, lots of good, but we'd dealt with a lot. There were trials for both Jimmy and George, and they were both locked up now. It had been Jimmy who had killed our parents. His wife had been a patient of my father's, and when she left Jimmy, he blamed Dad. That was why my parents were dead. Because an abusive asshole had been angry that his wife had walked away.

There was no evidence that Chase's mom had been a patient of Dad's, though really, that was something they couldn't share even if there was. Chase had found her about two months ago, but he didn't contact her. He'd wanted to know she was alive, that she truly had left his father and not something else, but because she'd left him too, he'd walked away.

Things were better for Bridget and Buck now that Jimmy was gone. They weren't together, but without his dad urging him on, Buck wasn't so hard on Bridget or Buck Jr. Though if you asked me, Buck was still an asshole. Still, he didn't harass me again, and he didn't give Buck Jr. shit about taking classes with me—classes that had slowly filled up again. People's memories were short, or hell, maybe they realized they didn't care. Why would what Chase and I did behind closed doors matter?

George Hawthorne had been convicted of armed robbery, and there had been no connection between him and what happened to my parents, but Chase didn't want to have anything to do with his father. He always said he already had his family—me, Bowie, and Griff.

Josh and Chase started yelling at each other or the TV screen or whatever again, so I pushed out of the chair and went into the living room. "Are we going to go or what?"

"Just a minute, Kell," Josh said, not tearing his eyes away from the game.

"Josh! You're my best friend. Not Chase's," I teased.

"You know I love you, but I gotta see the end of this," he replied.

Rolling my eyes, I went over and sat between them, pouting until the game was over and Josh was talking shit to Chase because his team won.

"I'm feeling very neglected right now." I crossed my arms as Chase leaned over and nuzzled my neck.

"Aw, come on, baby boy. You know I love you. I don't like Josh very much, anyway."

Josh laughed and flipped him off. "You're pissed because your team sucks."

"I don't think I want you guys to be friends anymore," I joked.

"Yes, you do." Chase poked my side. He stood up and held his hand out for me. "You ready to go or what?"

"Because it was me we were waiting for!" Ignoring his hand, I stood, and Chase laughed. God, I loved his laugh, loved everything about him. There were still times I'd look at him, simply watch him and think about how lucky I was, that I couldn't believe he was mine. But then, there were times I'd notice Chase watching me too, and somehow I knew he was thinking the same thing.

Finally, the three of us headed out for Griff's. We'd told Nat, Knox, and Law that we would meet them there. My brother was working, as always. We hadn't spoken anymore about his possibly being demi or aromantic. It didn't feel right to ask, so I let him know I was there if he needed me. He hadn't dated either, but that didn't surprise me. Blamed it on work, on the trials, and while I knew those things were true, I also knew

Griff and that there was more to it than that.

Josh took his truck, and the two of us went in Chase's. Everyone was already at Griff's when we got there, Natalie with this guy Harry she'd been seeing for about a month.

"Margaritas for you three and a beer for Chase, right?"

"Do you still need to ask?" Josh replied, and Griff rolled his eyes at him and mumbled a teasing, *fucker*.

We drank and laughed, Chase only having the one beer as he would be driving back. At one point I went to the bathroom, and when I came back out, I stood against the wall and just watched them for a moment.

As if he could feel my eyes on him, Chase looked over his shoulder, his brows tugging together. He walked over and cupped my cheek. "What are you doing over here?"

"Just watching you guys. We have a good life, don't we?" It wasn't something I'd ever envisioned for myself, not this way, not in Havenwood, and I was happy. I was complete. And I'd done it all by staying true to who I was.

"Yeah, yeah, we do." He leaned in, held my hip and rubbed his finger over my tattoo, then pressed a gentle kiss to my lips. "I love you."

"I love you too."

Join Riley's Newsletter

Find Riley:
Reader's Group: facebook.com/groups/RileysRebels2.0
Facebook: rileyhartwrites
Twitter: @RileyHart5
Goodreads:
goodreads.com/author/show/7013384.Riley_Hart

**Keep an eye out for Havenwood book two, Lawson's story. May 2020**

# Other Books by Riley Hart

**Standalone titles with Devon McCormack:**
Beautiful Chaos
Weight of the World
Up For The Challenge

**Standalone titles with Christina Lee:**
Of Starlight and Stardust
Science and Jockstraps

**Boys in Makeup Series with Christina Lee:**
Pretty Perfect

**Fever Falls**
Fired Up
#Burn by Devon McCormack
Whiskey Throttle
#Royal by Devon McCormack
Game On co-authored with Devon McCormack
Boyfriend 101

**Saint and Lucky**
Something About You
Something About Us

## Standalone
His Truth
Looking for Trouble
Endless Stretch of Blue
Love Always
Finding Finley

## Jared and Kieran
Jared's Evolution
Jared's Fulfillment

## Metropolis Series: With Devon McCormack
Faking It
Working It
Owning It
Finding It
Trying It
Hitching It

## Last Chance Series:
Depth of Field
Color Me In

## Wild Side Series:
Dare You To
Gone For You
Tied to You

**Crossroads Series:**

Crossroads

Shifting Gears

Test Drive

Jumpstart

**Rock Solid Construction Series:**

Rock Solid

**Broken Pieces Series:**

Broken Pieces

Full Circle

Losing Control

**Blackcreek Series:**

Collide

Stay

Pretend

Return to Blackcreek

**Forbidden Love Series with Christina Lee:**

Ever After: A Gay Fairy Tale

Forever Moore: A Gay Fairy Tale

# About the Author

Riley Hart has always been known as the girl who wears her heart on her sleeve. She won her first writing contest in elementary school, and although she primarily focuses on male/male romance, under her various pen names, she's written a little bit of everything. Regardless of the sub-genre, there's always one common theme and that's…romance! No surprise seeing as she's a hopeless romantic herself. Riley's a lover of character-driven plots, flawed characters, and always tries to write stories and characters people can relate to. She believes everyone deserves to see themselves in the books they read. When she's not writing, you'll find her reading or enjoying time with her awesome family in their home in North Carolina.

Riley Hart is represented by Jane Dystel at Dystel, Goderich & Bourret Literary Management. She's a 2019 Lambda Literary Award Finalist for *Of Sunlight and Stardust*. Under her pen name, her young adult novel, *The History of Us* is an ALA Rainbow Booklist Recom-

mended Read and *Turn the World Upside Down* is a
Florida Authors and Publishers President's Book Award
Winner.

Find Riley:
Reader's Group: facebook.com/groups/RileysRebels2.0
Facebook: rileyhartwrites
Twitter: @RileyHart5
Goodreads:
goodreads.com/author/show/7013384.Riley_Hart

Printed in Great Britain
by Amazon